Maxwell's Silver Hammer

****

When it goes down you'd better be ready...

Andy Rivers

Byker Books

Published by:-

Byker Books
Banbury
Oxon
OX16 0DJ

www.bykerbooks.co.uk

2010

ISBN 978-0-9560788-6-5

Typeset by Byker Books, Banbury

Printed in Great Britain by Lightning Source, Milton Keynes

Andy Rivers has been a Butlins barman, pretend chippie on a Spanish construction site, coach holiday rep, mobile sandwich salesman and outdoor traffic cone washer to name but a few of his eclectic 'career' choices. Originally from the East End of Newcastle he now lives in Oxfordshire where, as well as following Newcastle United around the country, he passes the time by indulging in his passion for 'Professional Geordie-ism' and lager. This is his first novel but he is also the author of *'I'm Rivelino'*, also published by Byker Books, a hilarious account of the thirty odd years of hurt he has suffered at the hands of the Magpies. With the royalties from this book he plans on buying a Ferrari and having a proper mid-life crisis.

Praise for Andy Rivers

Maxwell's Silver Hammer
A belter of a book that packs more punches than a Saturday night out on Market Street. Gangsters, guns and gadgies galore, Andy Rivers weaves a cracking plot through the Byker badlands like a Geordie Elmore Leonard and is one of the few writers I know of who can type while wearing boxing gloves. I had two black eyes before I'd finished chapter three. A thumping debut from a barnstorming new talent.
Danny King

I'm Rivelino
Definitely one that any football fan is going to relate to. It's funny, fanatical and thoroughly enjoyable. Whoever you support you are going to recognise yourself and your friends somewhere in this book.
Lovereading.co.uk

Well written, funny and most importantly smacks of the truth; a truth that any true football fan will recognise. Any student of broken dreams will lap this up.
The Crack

Acknowledgements

Many thanks to everyone at Byker Books for their faith, support and for encouraging radgies everywhere to put pen to paper. To Lisa for not telling me not to be so stupid when I said I was writing a book. To me Mam for ensuring I was the best looking of her kids. To Danny King for his help, advice and confirming my suspicions about Southern boys and their drinking capabilities by getting lemonade in his pints. To Daz for looking after me all those years ago and also for making me look good every time we went out. To Mrs F the only teacher who ever got through to me. To Sheila Quigley for her sound advice on reducing the profanity count. To Mick and all the Back Page staff for continuing to indulge me. To Little Mush and Charva for being different to everyone else on the estate. To all the lads for not letting me buy a drink on my forthcoming 40th weekend (worth a try like...) I'm touched. To Newcastle United for giving unimaginable highs and desperate lows over the last forty years and thus providing me with a well of misery to dip into as and when required. To Col. To Stu at Tonto Books for putting up with my constant questions. And finally, to all of the naysayers and knobheads who laughed when I said I was writing a book and told me it'd never happen - fuck you.

Cheers.

CONTENTS

Big Friday

Billy

He's waiting in the alley under the bridge for me; I spotted that big, pretentious Shogun of his by Kwiksave. It's a contradiction of visions that just sums up the coke addled, muddled up prick quite nicely.

Vince Merry, he believes himself to be the top man on Tyneside, my nemesis for so many years. He's had my little brother put away for murder and burnt down his business, threatened my ageing mother with violence, killed owld Dave and now he wants me. Well now he gets me, all of me.

I'm at the entrance to the alley under the bridge, there's only one streetlight and I'm under it, darkness and shadows all around me, the fine rain is visible against the light and the wind blows sweet wrappers around my feet. I feel in my jacket pocket for the knuckle-duster, its chunky, solid feel is reassuring. Sighing softly I look up into the Newcastle night sky for what could possibly be the last time and wonder how it ever came to this. Over thirty years of keeping my head down and not offending the big boys, playing it safe and paying my dues every time and still, in the end, I have to fight it out with them. The streetlight is slightly comforting, it's got a warm yellow glow to it but it doesn't lift my mood, I would give anything to be cuddling up to Lisa now.

Growing up where and how I did I've always known that life's not fair, I constantly expect to have people shit on me, I accept this and probably deep down knew that one day it would come to this. I think I even half knew it would be with this wanker as well.

Weary and resigned to my fate I have to start this thing. I hope I finish it.

'Merry,' I call into the blackness. There's a rustling sound and two figures step forward into the half-light. Big Tony stands to the right of Merry, a tattooed behemoth, all broad shoulders, big neck and massive biceps, Merry himself is brandishing a big blade, again, I expected this.

My heart is pounding as the adrenalin rushes through my

body, my legs feel frozen to the floor and my internal system is asking the question fight or flight? Understandably my brain is screaming flight but my heart knows the score and is telling me that I must fight, I've got to put him to bed once and for all.

Looking at the knife, I go for the token question.

'Thought it was a straightener?'

He smiles at me without humour and replies, 'Grow up Billy, we're not at school any more.'

There's nothing more to say, it's time to start the endgame. Putting my duster on my right fist I smile back and step into the alley towards them.

Three Weeks Earlier

Carlos

I love this club, it's always dark, loud and full, the pills are just kicking in and we've timed it perfectly. Whooaahyafucka, getting some big rushes now man. Faces everywhere, people slapping me on the back and shaking my hand, saying happy birthday and that. The bar looks busy. Bodies all over the place; dancing, talking, groping or just holding hands. Can't see Billy anywhere though but he'll be close by. Probably ringing his lass to check the boys are all right, she's sound though, understands he's got to cut loose now and then so she just lets him get on with it.

Doesn't matter anyway that I can't see him, he'll be alright and I'm alright as well cos it's me birthday and you can do what you want on your birthday, it's in the rules man. Barry's got in as well, magic, half looked like Big Tony on the door wanted a word with him for a minute.

'Howay Carlos, you Spanish bastard, let's get into it man.'

He's a cheeky bugger Barry, love him to bits like, mind you I love everyone to bits when I'm full of gear like this. Fuckinell these rushes are getting bigger and heavier now, I'll have to dance in a minute or I'll be monged and sitting down all night.

I've been Carlos from an early age, once the other kids noticed I still had half brown skin in winter as well as summer. A couple of their mothers mentioned it at the school gates as well but me mam soon helped to cure them of that habit. Our Billy's got a different dad to me, different personality as well, still as close as fuck though. Oh that's nice. I am getting RIGHT into this now, can't see Barry any more either but fuck it where's the dance floor. Then I see her, blonde lass, tight arse, dancing on her own. About time an' all, I was wondering where she was, I hope her bloke's not in the vicinity.

Let's find out.

'Shaking that ass, shaking that ass, alright pet, looking good as usual, you on one?'

Fuck me on one? She's off her tits, speaking of which, what a pair she's got. The rushes are starting in me balls now and only getting as far as me knob, I can't hold back, bloke or no bloke. Eating each other's faces then coming up for air, realising the risk we're taking. Start to get into the music as the rushes pile in faster, DJ's doing well. Speeding up, up, up, making me feel like I'm going to burst; then slowing it right back down, everyone ready to explode into life again when the strobes kick in and then...

'BIG SHOUT OUT TO THE BYKER POSSE FROM BARRY.'

I'm looking up at the DJ booth and Barry's jumping up and down next to it with his arms in the air. Then I'm jumping up and down and waving back, I've got hold of Sharon and she's doing the same laughing her head off, this is class gear. Barry's waving to the other side of the room now, I look over and there's our Billy, he's just laughing and waving back at him. Then he sees me and we're giving each other the V's and smiling.

I love this club me.

Clarty

Catch my reflection in the mirrored doors, looking good, bulking up nicely now with the steroids and the training. I'm not just Vince Merry's little cousin now, I'm a boy in my own right, fucking big boy as well, it was that prick Carlos Reeves who christened me Clarty back at school a long time ago. It was all over that thing in the lad's toilets, it was just a misunderstanding but he said I was a dirty, scummy, little bastard and told everyone my new nickname was Clarty. I was going to get Vince to sort him out but I didn't want him hearing about what happened, he might have got the wrong end of the stick. So I let it go hoping the name would die a death and everyone would go back to calling me Clarky, it didn't and neither did they. Fucking Dago twat.

Billy

This club's a nightmare. I forgot what they were like.

At this time of night at the age of thirty-four I should either be in my local having a lock in and a conversation or tucked up in bed with our lass. The floor's sticky with lager and dried blood, there's no seats because people are standing on them and waving their hands about, no room to move and the chillout area's full. The music's shite as well, all that boom boom jungle bollocks, no proper house that you can get into. Looking round it's all young kids as well, half of them'll be at school on Monday, I can't see many older heads at all. This was the place ten years ago though, back when we were lads. I don't know where everyone's gone now, most of them don't get past the local in Wallsend these days or Jesmond if they're taking their lass out. Carlos's birthday though and the playboy's starting to feel his age so he wanted to come here. He wanted to celebrate the owld times, back in the day that type of thing, so Barry got six pills, meant to be owld school ecstasy but they're nowt like it.

The owld ones lasted twelve hours and made you want to dance, these last about two and make me want to have a shit. They're all right in a way like; you get little bursts and that. I only wanted one so I gave my other one to Carlos, fuck it, it's his birthday. Speak of the devil, he's wandering over now, got some lass in tow.

'Billy this is Sharon, she's a model.'

I had to work hard not to burst out laughing, this was just typical of the twat, blonde hair, big tits and probably as thick as mince, just his type really. Funny how they were always models and actresses as well.

'Yeah, nice to meet you pet,' I should be nice anyway, you never know she could be me next sister-in-law. Ha ha.

This Sharon bird just squeezes his arse and giggles at him, he looks at me jaw gurning, that big daft smile on his face and says, 'We're just dancing for a bit, see you later.' I roll my eyes at him and push him towards the dance floor, him and his new bird. Smiling at each other they head for the floor doing the walking to the dancefloor dance that all pillheads know and love.

Laughing to myself, I go to look for Barry.

Merry

I am not happy. This is my main club, it's where I make most of my money and takings are down again. This music's shite as well, even if I was full of pills like the rest of these dicks I'd think it was shite. Give me some Bryan Adams or some Bon Jovi any day. Proper music.

'Clarty, answer me something, if this club's as full as it looks and everyone in it has taken some sort of gear then why have I only got half the money I had last week?'

'Someone's ripping you off cuz,' he answers, he's got a mind like a steel trap that boy.

'Fucking brilliant that, you're like Inspector Morse you are,' the cunt doesn't realise I'm being sarcastic, 'you're paid to know about these things before they happen, so who is it?'

This place is rammed and as I'm talking some prick bumps into me, bad move the mood I'm in. I smack him in the back of the head and he crumples to the floor, his mate tries to say something but I'm not talking, I give him a whack and he goes down as well. A circle clears around me and the two bodies, the bouncers come steaming down ready to go but they've seen it's me and calmed down, picked the stiffs up and carried them out.

That's helped a bit, the pressure was building up in me and my fucking head was starting to hurt, someone was always going to get it before the end of the night. Clarty's wittering away to me about how he was ready to back me up there, what the fuck's he on about? I didn't need any fucking help. He's followed me around all me life, my mam and his mam are sisters so I suppose he's always looked up to me cos I'm a fair bit older than him and I've done well for meself. It gets on me tits sometimes though. I use him in the business now because he's quite sharp but he trades on me name a bit and takes liberties with people now and then. He's started bleating something again now, I've got to get away from this prick and get ten minutes on my own to think about what to do.

'Just find out who's fucking ripping me off,' I growl at him, 'I'm going to get a drink.'

Barry

Just got rid of the last of my pills, thank fuck, it's a risky business selling in here but I needed the cash. One last line for me on this toilet cistern then I'm out of here to enjoy the party.

CRASH

'What the fuck's your problem?' I spin round trying to brazen it out, 'You didn't need to kick the door in, I would have answered if you'd knocked.'

'You've been a naughty boy Barry.' Two of the bouncers block the doorway of the cubicle, shit, I'm in trouble now.

'Someone wants to talk to you.'

As I look past these two I can see another bouncer clearing the bogs, fuck, that means Merry's coming in here to do me.

'Howay lads,' I plead, 'just pretend I wasn't here when you came in, let me go through the window.' They just blank me, they're probably more scared of him than I am, mind you that'd be difficult at the minute, I can smell the fear running down my trouser legs. I wish Billy or Carlos were in here as well, Billy would be handy, I remember how he was down at Whitley Bay when we were fourteen, fuck me he was unbelievable. I can't get hold of either of them though, no signal on the phone down here. Bollocks.

Billy

Phew, fucked with the dancing now man, music's still wank like. Can't find Barry anywhere and Carlos is probably with that bird so I'll get a drink and have a chinwag with some of the lads on the door, I haven't seen some of them for a long time. Moaning about this music reminds me, I must get the stereo fixed on the car. It's fucking stuck on some disastrous cheesy rock station and I can't shift it, it's a nightmare if I've got no discs. Modern technology eh? Load of shite really.

Speaking of which, check me phone, our lass hasn't tried to ring has she? Nah, I might ring her later then, tell her I love her. Mind you, might go down better telling her that when I'm not pissed and buzzing. Fuck it put me sexy new phone away and it is a sexy new phone incidentally, does fucking allsorts, I'm at the door now anyway.

'Alright lads, how's it going? Is Tony about?' No he's not here either, fuck me where is everybody?

Sharon

Looks like he's here now, I can tell by the influx of five or so radgies who've hit the bar, all full of steroids and coke with tempers to match. He'll be around somewhere with that wanker Clarty.

I'd much rather stay with Carlos and dance, it's his birthday as well, I could give him a special present if that dickhead didn't insist on following me everywhere. He'll claim he's been collecting and he has to come here to get his money as it's one of his bigger places. I know it's bollocks; he could just get Tony to give him the money in the morning as he comes round anyway on a Sunday. The big stupid bastard just likes to make sure no one's talking to me. If only he knew.

Big Tony

Right then, time to make the first move, Barry's a good bloke, hangs about with the Reeves boys, I've got a lot of time for all three of them, especially Billy. I'm sure none of them would drop me in the shit, bit surprised to see them in here though. Actually, given their history with my boss Mr. Merry I can pretty much guarantee they wouldn't drop me in the shit, so let's start with Barry and see if he feels the same way as his mates.

I walk towards the cubicle and stand to the side of the open doorway then I nod the other two out of the bog, it's empty except for me and Barry. As I go to step in the door there's a scream and a flurry of bog rolls bounce off my face and body. I look up and Barry is flying at me with a toilet seat, instinct takes over, step back, lay over to left, right cross to the jaw, fuck I've knocked him out. No I haven't he's groaning, throw some water on his face, he's coming to now.

'What did you do that for Barry you prick?' I sound harsher than I mean to, he's been held in that toilet for ten minutes now and he probably had all sorts of pain and torture building up in his mind.

'Thought you were Merry,' he answers sitting up now.

'Aye,' I smile, that's answered the last question for me, 'that's what I wanted to talk to you about.'

Billy

'Where's your lass then pretty boy?' Carlos is looking frustrated, ha ha obviously time for some abuse big brother style I think.

'She said her boyfriend had come in and she'd better go to be with him or he'd just kick off.'

'Good of her that like,' I reply, 'letting you down easy I mean, instead of just telling the truth.'

He looks confused for half a second, 'What do you mean the truth?'

'Well,' I say, 'she telt me you were a shit dancer with a little cock.' Aye sympathy, that's what brothers are for.

He starts giggling and gives me a light dig. The two of us are just going to take the piss for the next hour now I can tell, plenty more birds in here anyway and he doesn't normally go short.

'Whoah here's Barry, I thought he'd gone home.' It looks like he's got a bruise on his face, I'll be asking him about that later, don't want to spoil Carlos's birthday though.

'Where've you been?' Carlos asks him.

His face lights up, 'Getting the beers in man,' he says producing three Becks and three tequilas, 'here get this down your neck, happy birthday.'

He's a proper happy go lucky fucker Barry is; we've known him since school. Him and Carlos were in the same classes and started hanging around together after Carlos clouted a couple of lads that were bullying him. He blossomed after that, came out of his shell and stopped being so nervous. I remember when he was about seventeen, he was in court for drunk and disorderly and indecent exposure, basically he was having a piss in a subway. We worried about him breaking down in the box and embarrassing himself but it was funny as fuck in the end. Because it was just a magistrates he was only going to get a fine, but it was still the first time any of us had any real run in with the court system so he was all suited up and looking sorry when he went up to the box. We sat in the gallery a bit twitchy for him but then the magistrate asked him to explain himself and he just went for it.

'Your Honour,' he started, his voice was a bit reedy and he sounded nervous, his body language was shite, he was almost slumped over the stand. He kept on anyway though, 'In order to give you the full facts of this story, you must first understand my circumstances.' He looked at her to see if she was reacting in any way, she nodded at him to go on and his eyes lit up. He straightened up and looked directly at her, then took a deep breath and began.

'I have been unemployed since leaving school and am desperate for a job. My record will show that I have applied for many positions through the Jobcentre without success. It will also prove that without fail I have attended every Restart interview and went on every Jobhunters course, again without success.' What he didn't say was that he made a point of failing interviews because this would have fucked up his real job of burgling shops at night times.

'The reality of this failure to gain regular employment has led to my living in reduced circumstances.' He paused for breath and to gauge the mood of the magistrate, his voice tailing off in supposed shame at his predicament. Me and Carlos just looked at each other trying not to laugh; the fucker was minted and had the most cash out of the three of us.

'Please carry on Mr. Patterson.' The magistrate almost pleaded with him to continue.

'Well,' he said, realising he had her onside and gaining in confidence, 'I'd been on my daily visit to the Jobcentre and had noticed some vacancies that had just been put on the board. I rushed home and wrote my letter of application, taking great care with it, so much so in fact that I re-wrote it three times, my desire to become a productive member of society is so great your honour.'

She smiled at him indulgently and Carlos nudged me and giggled, 'I swear, he's like the son she never had.'

The prosecutor's jumped to his feet by this point, 'Objection, what has this got to do with a charge of indecent exposure?' Which, to be fair, he had a point but the magistrate just looked daggers at him and held up her hand, palm out.

'Over-ruled, this gentleman is explaining the circumstances and background to this charge, he is entitled to that don't you think?' The prosecutor sat back down harrumphing to himself and the magistrate turned back to Barry smiling and said, 'Please continue Mr. Patterson.'

'So,' says Barry, 'I had to post this letter but there were no stamps in the house, as I said your honour, my parents and I live in vastly reduced circumstances. As I didn't have any money I decided to head down Shields Road on the off chance I would bump into someone I knew who would buy me a stamp.' He looked sad at this point and turned his eyes to the floor, lowering his voice he said, 'I'm prepared to embarrass myself to find work your honour, even to the point of begging for a stamp.' Now I'm no expert on psychology but even I can see her heart going out to him. Mind you it should, the twat deserved a BAFTA for this act.

'Me mam was at work so I couldn't bother her, but I knew me dad had received his girocheque that morning so I started my search in The Blue Bell at the top of the road. When I looked in the door he wasn't there but one of his friends was and he insisted on buying me a pint. I didn't want to offend him by refusing even though I do feel bad about taking charity off people.

The same thing happened in the next five pubs I looked in and whilst in the sixth one, The Heaton, I was starting to feel the effects of all this generosity. Then I saw an old acquaintance from school and asked him if he had any stamps and he replied that he might have some in the house. So with letter in hand we went to his flat at the bottom end of Byker. There were a couple of other people there and a strong smell of what

I believe were drugs your honour. Now I'm not the type of person who would partake in or condone the use of such things but I believe in live and let live so I didn't say anything. I went to the toilet and when I came back a can of lager was thrust into my hand, again, not wishing to appear ungrateful I had to drink it. My friend informed me he didn't have any stamps so I resolved to quickly drink the lager and resume my search as soon as possible so as not to miss the post.

After leaving the flat I started to feel the effects of the speedy drinking of the lager and cannabis that I must have passively inhaled. I'd started to wobble a bit as I walked up the road and was aware that I was slurring my speech as I approached the subway under the metro line. I saw a young couple in there, about fifteen or sixteen your honour. To them I was probably a worrying sight and as I approached them in my dishelleved state they must have feared a little for their safety. From my point of view I thought I was okay and was just going to ask them if they had a stamp.

However, and I can completely understand this your honour I really can, they just saw a drunk starting to ask them for money. I'd just got as far as, 'can you lend me a...' when the young lad lashed out, kicking me in the crotch and shouting 'leave us alone.'

The blow bent me double and sent me staggering back against the wall as they ran off. You'll have to take my word for this your honour, being a lady and that, but the pain was immense and led me to check everything was all right down there. As I was doing this a police car drove past, put two and two together and made five, that is why I am before you today and that is why I pleaded not guilty.'

At this point, stifling giggles at Barry's frankly fucking unbelievable performance we looked up at the magistrate. She was smiling in sympathy, her eyes sparkling. She'd only fucking bought it, he was going to get off. Then in true and typical Barry fashion he kicked the arse out of it, saying proudly, 'And that your honour is why my application for the police force was never received.'

The whole court burst out laughing, even the coppers were pissing themselves, everyone in fact, except the magistrate who had a face like thunder and who was now realising what a mug she'd nearly been. The hammer came down, 'Fined £250.' and that was that.

Well not quite. Barry had one last go, 'As I've stated previously your honour, I'm unemployed and would ask if I can pay this fine at a rate of one pound a week?' She just looked at him unblinking, relishing her chance for public revenge and said firmly, 'Mr. Patterson, this is not Littlewoods catalogue, you will pay at a rate of five pounds per week.'

The court was in uproar again as Barry was sheepishly led out of the dock and one of the coppers turned to me and said, 'Reeves, thank your mate for the best laugh I've had in ages.'

That wasn't on in my book. We're allowed to laugh at Barry cos we're his mates but no one else is. I looked the prick up and down and then just shook my head at him and followed Carlos out of the door.

Merry

Right, had time to think now and had a couple of lines for confidence. An example is needed if I'm going to stay in control and the best examples are the frightening ones, if people are scared of you then anything is possible.

'Clarty, get the other lads, we're going out to have a word with Big Tony.' Look at him, chest out, strutting around, ordering everyone to get up and move out. He fucking loves it hanging onto my coat tails like this, still, he has his uses.

'And Clarty, make sure someone stays here with our lass so she doesn't get hassled off any of these fucked up ravers.'

Right, straight in, maximum aggression. I'm psyching myself up as I storm outside. I've got Tony by the throat in the alley outside the club, not so fucking big now by the way.

'Who's selling in here Tony?' His, no my, bouncers looking on, they wouldn't dare jump in against me.

'There's only your boy in here Vince, I swear I haven't seen anyone else.' He's shitting it, I can tell and that relaxes me.

I'm always dubious of disciplining this big fucker, it would be a hell of a fight me and him. I let him go and take a step back, my fucking temples are throbbing and the adrenalin is making me shake as it races through my body. Some people make the mistake of thinking it's your bottle going or you're scared but I've read up on this, it's just a natural chemical reaction in your body and if you use it right you can be unbeatable. I always use it right.

Clarty pipes up, 'Make an example of him cuz, fucking head doorman and he doesn't know who's in here.' Tony is glaring at him, I don't blame him though, Clarty has a point, he loves to emphasise the cuz bit in public as well. There's a crowd gathering, even if he's not ripping me off word will soon spread to whoever is. I'm getting tunnel vision as I move my right leg behind my left and line him up.

SMACK - I hit him with a powerful right hook, I must be out of practice as that normally sparks them clean out, Tony staggers back but doesn't go down.

'I swear Vince it's not me,' he's pleading now, 'you know I've always been loyal.'

'That was just a warning Tony, any fucker rips me off and they get buried,' his head's down and he's agreeing with me, all submissive. I'm glad that's over like, I handled it well, just need to sound confident now and the Chinese whispers will do the rest. At the end of the day I've just clouted one of the top fighters on Tyneside and had him beg me not to do it again. If any proof was needed that I'm still number one then that was it.

Sharon

He's full of hell again, too much cocaine probably. Apparently he smacked two lads earlier. That's one of the things I most hate about him, he makes people so impotent. I bet they just took it rather than fight back, like a deer being eaten by a lion, nothing they can do about it. He does the same to me, I just don't have a personality when he's around, no voice, nothing.

Maybe that's why I like being with Carlos, he wouldn't be scared to defend himself against anyone, least of all Vince.

Big Tony

I saw his punch coming a mile away; he was lining me up even before that weasel faced cousin of his joined the conversation. His day's coming, but for the time being he needs to think I'm on the team.

Enjoy it while you can arsehole.

Billy

Chucking out time, good, I'm fucked. Barry and Carlos have both pulled, two loved up airheads draped across them, I'll just say goodnight to the lads on the door. Fuckinell Merry was in the club, he's coming out now with his lass. Bollocks, he's left her and he's coming over here, says he's got a proposition for me.

He's just getting past the usual pleasantries when his lass starts getting loud with his cousin Clarty. We both look over at the same time, oh shit, that's the bird Carlos was with earlier, what's she saying? Something about knowing Carlos and she'll smile at who she wants to, Clarty's giving Carlos the wanker sign now, oh fuck. Carlos has started coming ahead at Clarty, he's all stanced up and ready to go then Merry growls in my ear, trying to sound hard, his foul breath polluting my eardrums.

'It can't happen Billy, not my cousin, not in public.'

'Square go Vince,' I say, 'they're both grown ups.'

Merry's playing the don again, 'I said no Billy, it only happens if my man wins and we both know that's debatable where Carlos is concerned, stop it now.' I look the cunt straight in the eye, his pupils tiny and the whites showing a tinge of red, too many steroids in my opinion.

'Don't know if I can mate,' playing for time, they're both at punching distance now. I hope Carlos knocks the prick out.

'And I don't know if I can guarantee your mother's safety

on that estate Bill, it's a rough old place and you two can't be there all of the time can you?' The absolute fucking sheer joy of knowing he's got me by the bollocks shines from his voice like a sunbed in Sunderland. The shitbag's played his ace card again, the usual one, and I know I have to stop it.

Carlos

I've had a good night and a good birthday, pulled as usual and heading for home. We've stopped for a minute while Billy says tara to the bouncers and then look who it is, Vince Merry walks out with his lass, the lovely Sharon. Bit silly of me to be doing it really but I'm not scared of the prick, never have been, the repercussions are a bit naughty though.

She gives me a smile and I give her one back, but unfortunately Merry's bum boy cousin catches it and the look on his face means it's going back to Merry any minute now. That paranoid twat will have invented a full-blown love affair in his head by the time he gets into his taxi, he'll stew on it all night and be looking for me in the morning. I'd better nip this in the bud right away, Clarty's still looking at me with a smile on his lips, 'What you looking at?'

He's just staring at me, grinning to himself, I don't like him anyway but now he's getting on my tits.

'What's your fucking problem knobhead?' I growl.

He looks at Merry then grins back at me and slowly gives me the wanker sign, confident that I wouldn't dare do anything to the boss's family. He doesn't know me very well.

'I'm talking to you, you fucking knob jockey,' I'm upping the aggression now, this usually shits them up and they're beat before we start.

Starting to walk towards him, aware that the normal people emptying the club are stopping to watch two big blokes about to go at it in an alley.

'Last chance steroid freak, what's your fucking problem?'

I'm moving in now, eyes locked, adrenalin pumping and the dance moves already choreographed in my head, honed through years of practice.

The realisation's just hitting him that I'm not playing and he's starting to move into position; too late muppet. I'm just lining the spanner up to leave the planet when this voice comes out of nowhere.

'Leave it Carlos, there is no problem, he's just pissed,' it's our Billy, 'Barry, get the lasses, we're going home.'

'I'm going nowhere Bill, this wanker's having it,' I reply, surprised at his intervention, he normally stops me killing them, not hitting them.

Then, 'We're fucking going right now charv so shift yaself.' There's a hard edge to his voice that only comes out now and then. When I hear that I do as I'm told, Billy doesn't get arsey as a rule so there'll be a good reason for it, probably something to do with Merry.

I drop my hands and walk off without a backward glance, still playing the part, Clarty'll be so pleased to be alive he'll have forgotten about the smile between Sharon and me so she'll be alright now. They'll all think I'm pissed off with Billy but it's all part of the game, we'll be drinking and laughing together back at mine in ten minutes and those twats will have something to talk about for a week. Everyone knows that Clarty needed his cousin to stop me doing him and that'll be around the town before I'm even home, so really, I've beaten him without throwing a punch, no coppers, no comebacks.

Class.

Barry

Looked like it was all ready to go off there for a minute, I was ready to help the boys as well, I'd have got straight into Merry's men, Merry's men? Must think he's Robin Hood the prick, robbing bastard more like.

Tony caught my eye when it was about to go off, he just shook his head telling me not to get involved. I'll need to talk to him about that sometime, just because I work for him now doesn't mean I abandon me mates.

Clarty

Vince is having a go at me telling me not to put him in that position again. Well I will definitely be seeing Carlos Reeves again, whether Vince likes it or not. People need to start giving me respect. Everyone thinks he can do me now and that I had to get my cousin involved to get out of it; I'll have to put them right about that, this isn't over yet dago boy, not by a long way.

Lisa

Mmmm, sounds like Billy's home. Four in the morning? I didn't think he had it in him. Maybe I'll have to get him to take me clubbing one of these days. He's coming up the stairs now doing that tiptoe walk that sounds like a herd of rhino charging and saying ssshhh to himself then giggling.

'Good night pet?' I ask as he stumbles in.

'Aye,' he slurs, 'clubbing, nearly a fight, Merrysh a prick. Back to wor kidsh and a couple of pints. I love yee pet.'

Ah the magic of strong lager on strong men never fails to amuse me. Mind you I'm the same, a couple of Breezers and that's me in love with the world. I love Billy anyway though; I'm even going to make him a breakfast in the morning, well in about four hours.

Clunk

Clunk

That's his shoes off then.

Sharon

Clarty is a fucking nightmare, I'm sure he fancies me himself. It's lucky Vince didn't catch on to what he was implying or there'd be hell to pay. That big twat just came in and slumped onto the bed next to me, now he's snoring like a pig, it's lucky I don't rely on him anymore. I've got needs and he can't satisfy them so I'm shopping elsewhere these days. I could do with Carlos being here now actually.

They went back to his for a little party and he'll be shagging that tart he was with, the lucky bitch. Still we've got our arrangement and I'll have to live with it. I wish he was here though, just thinking about him has put me in that frame of mind. Still I've always got my little friend in the drawer here, nice and quiet, Vince won't wake up anyway, thank God.

Tuesday

<u>Spanish</u>

They all call me Spanish round here, it's not the most imaginative of nicknames but better than half-caste. My real name is Miguel or Michael but my dad was, surprisingly enough, Spanish and even though I was born here in the cold, industrial northern capital of geordieland, I inherited his dark skin and good looks. I also inherited the Madrilèno appreciation of beautiful things; women, wine and days like these. It's warm, bright and full of promise and it's taking me back as I stroll to court.

It was a warm day like this in, ooh must have been about 1980, and summer holidays so must have been about August then as well. The day my boys came of age. I was strolling down Headlam Street towards The Stags Head as there was always a couple of faces in there that owed me money and always a couple of barmaids that'd help me spend it. I generally came down that way anyway in case the boys were about. Their mam wasn't keen on me being too involved with them, only one of them was naturally mine anyway like but it made no difference to me and I always tried to treat them the same.

I used to make a point of taking them out for the day now and then, usually down the coast cos they loved it down there, big beach, fresh air, rides and arcades. I made sure they had a good time whenever I was flush and it gave their mam a bit of a break. It was a strange arrangement for Byker back then, single mothers and part time dads, but it's fucking commonplace now, it's stranger to have two parents that are married to each other. I think Val was the first round here, she didn't give a fuck though and at least I wasn't far away when she needed me.

Yeah the world's moved on from the seventies now, new millennium, new values and all that. I'm fucking glad we got rid of new romantics though; what the fuck was that all about, blokes with make-up on? Mind you, young Beckham's on a mission to resurrect them I reckon. Anyway, that day I saw the boys but didn't get the chance to say hello to them or take them for a game of pool. Carl and William their names are and they were ten and eleven back then and must have been down to the baths. They did that a lot in the summer holidays as the pool was only at the bottom of the estate, I could see them walking up the hill together in the sunshine, their towels rolled up and their wet T shirts hanging over the back of their raggy arsed jeans.

They were chattering loudly about football and games as they rounded the corner to home. They were always big on sport them two, always on at me to take them to Newcastle matches. I don't know why, they were shite back then cos McGarry fucked that team but then Cox came in and the place eventually took off.

Anyway, because I'm halfway down the street I could see this bullying shit standing just ten yards from their house. He had a bit of a reputation on the estate in those days, he was a big fucker for his age and he put himself about a bit. I can still see his face in my mind's eye and he couldn't believe his luck, he was beaming as he realized that his two favourite victims were about to walk straight into him. I knew then that Carl and William could be a bit cheeky, Jesus you should hear them now, but this prick was about fourteen or fifteen years old and at that age he should have been above picking on much younger and smaller boys. If he was wanting to make a reputation he should have been looking up the league not down it. Just my opinion like and it doesn't seem to have harmed his career much at any rate. Anyways he just waited long enough for them to take another couple of steps before he jumped them. The two lads didn't even know he was there until the first punch hit them and he lashed into them as he always did. They just reverted to type by covering up as best they could, hoping it would be over soon. They were screaming and shouting and trying to wriggle out of his grasp as he was holding and punching them, then William broke free and ran for home shouting, 'Mam, mam.' Carl was a bit chubbier then, not like now, and was trapped by this bigger, heavier bully and couldn't escape. William had reached the back door as Val opened it.

I was starting to move to help the boys out, as I knew, without a shadow of a doubt, there was no bloke in there to sort this out, when events overtook me. In one instant Val had taken in the scene, realised what needed to be done and had acted. Slapping William across the face she had shouted, 'Never leave your family in trouble son, get back over there and fight him.'

I know those two very well, have done all their lives and they were typical young lads then, happy go lucky and a bit cheeky, but something changed in them that day. William, crying, ran back into the fray punching and kicking, his mother stood at the back door watching and ready to act in case things went too far. Reacting to his brother's aggressive reappearance Carl did the same, throwing away his fear and lashing out wildly, so I waited a bit longer to see what happened thinking it'd be good for them to fight him off on their own.

The bully boy was a bit slow on the uptake, but after about twenty seconds of taking punishment from two previously meek and mild little lads he realised there'd been a shift in the balance of power and he didn't like it. He's only got two hands and he couldn't block all the blows coming his way so he soon disappeared down the street, his face twisted in pain from some wild kicks and punches. He was followed by some choice words and insults from the lads as they congratulated each other an' all. In fact I remember teaching them a few of the words ha ha.

I watched their mam at the back door and I knew what she was thinking even then. She knew, as I did, that in this town, on this estate, in a house with no father her boys would have to fight for everything they would ever have, and I mean everything. So as Carl and William walked back into the house, their little, boyish faces set hard into what they thought were manly, tough guy, expressions they gave their mother a kiss as they passed in gratitude for the important lesson they had just learned from her. It was definitely a rite of passage they'll never forget.

It made me think that I needed to be helping them toughen up as well. After all, as the dad that's my main job isn't it? So I saw my mate Dave who ran Byker Boxing Club and the rest's history. Carl took to it and rose rapidly through the amateur ranks winning a clutch of junior and county titles, then he turned pro and got as far as fighting for the British Light Heavyweight title, that didn't go so well though and he retired after that.

Billy? Well, he was never one to fight by the rules and preferred football anyway, neither of them was ever bullied again though, which was the main thing.

I'd better get a move on though if I'm going to catch Carl in court.

__Maxwell__

My head is pounding and I'm running late, bloody Round Table do last night, I drank far too much as usual and now I'm paying for it.

The sun's shining right in my face and the traffic's crawling, I knew I shouldn't have come this way. The Tyne Bridge is always like this on weekdays. Nearly nine o' clock now and not at court yet, first case is scheduled for half past, I've got no chance of reading my notes beforehand. I'd best ring ahead; 'Yes, Judge Maxwell here, I'm running late, had a puncture this morning then got caught in the traffic over the bridge.'

'Yes, postpone my first case, who is it?'

Oh that name rings a bell. 'No, don't know him, okay then traffic's moving now I won't be long, I'll be in time for the second case.'

Carl Reeves eh, I haven't seen him for a long time, not since him and his brother were lads, must be going on twenty years now. As I recall it had been a shit day and I'd gone out for lunch to get away from my disapproving colleagues. My last two clients were obviously going to prison and the legal aid fees the firm would acquire for representing them wouldn't cover the petrol I had used, never mind the hours I'd have put in and I wasn't covering myself in glory in my new position. I couldn't face going back to the office on such a nice day so I'd got a sandwich from the bakers and was sitting in the car with the radio on low whilst reading the paper when I'd heard a commotion up the street.

When I looked up I saw the Reeves boys entangled with a much bigger lad. They seemed to be taking some punishment and my first thought was to get out of the car, then I stopped. The Spaniard was further up the street on the other side of them and if things got out of hand he'd surely intervene. Young William then managed to break free and run for home; I followed his path to the door and looked straight into the eyes of his mother, she stared back at me with a face like thunder and I had to look away.

When I looked back William was streaking back into the fray like a heat seeking missile, all fists and feet, the big lad was surprised by this and caught off balance, so like all bullies when confronted with resistance he ran away. When I looked back at their mother she was smiling at the other one and shutting the door, it suited me anyway, as they were nothing to do with me by then. Not anymore.

The Spaniard glared at me as he walked into the pub and I was tempted to hang him out to dry in court but I needed to keep him out of prison just to start justifying my position within the firm. That was when I decided to bend from my morals slightly and I made a deal with someone to get him off the hook. My contact was a good Lodge man on the force who was of the same mind as me; neither of us was staying in this shithole forever and had no intention of being dragged down by scum like these. Yes, that day was the making of me; I broke free of the past and embraced the future, definitely a good move.

I'll have to turn this radio off, it's not making my head any better. Some nonsense on there masquerading as music, local band apparently - Radgepacket or some such nonsense. Where on earth do they get these names?

Carlos

There's a few familiar faces at court today, seen a few from the past as well. I'm up first at half nine, should be on the phone to Sharon by ten and on the job by eleven. It's a nothing charge, handling stolen goods, shouldn't get more than a fine and a slap on the wrist. Nothing to worry about at all, that's why I told our Billy not to bother coming, he had a few things to sort out work wise this morning so there was no point in him hanging around here.

Fuck me, there's little Davy McKenzie. I haven't seen him since school, he's a good lad is Davy, I'll have to say hello. I heard he works as a mobile security guard for a big firm in North Shields. I can't imagine what he's doing here like, the bloke's as straight as they come, must be a witness to something. Mind you he looks like he's shitting himself. Look at him, poor little bastard all suited up for the judge while all of the regulars are in their best tracksuits. I'll sit with him for a bit in case they're getting at him, shouldn't have witnesses in this section it's fucking stupid.

'Alright mate? Long time no see, you still with Suzie?' Suzie and him were childhood sweethearts, together all through school, 'I heard you've got a little un now.'

'Carlos,' he jumps up, genuinely pleased to see me, shaking my hand. 'Yeah mate, still with Suzie, got a son David, he's nine now, what about you? How are you and Billy keeping?'

'Smashing mate, we're ticking along you know how it is, what you here for?' I ask him.

He settles back into one of those miserable, uncomfortable seats looking ashamed of himself. 'Conspiracy to rob,' he says, 'I was the inside man on a warehouse robbery, I've pleaded guilty though I won't waste anyone's time.'

He can't even look me in the eye. I am absolutely fucking gobsmacked at that, little Davy a villain, no way. This can't be right, he would never even come shoplifting with us at school and he got loads of stick for it but would never give in; our Billy always respected him loads for that.

'What are you expecting then?' I say, struggling to get this straight in my head; one thing is certain he's obviously going to be doing a bit of time.

'My solicitor reckons about twelve months, first offence, never been in trouble before, that's normally taken into account isn't it? The firm gave me a good character reference as well and they've said that if there's any vacancy when I come out they'll consider me. Good of them really in the circumstances.'

I am really confused, 'Why did you do it Dave?' I ask him, 'You've worked there for years and had a good number and you've got your lass and the boy. I know for a fact you've never been that way inclined.'

'Well,' he replies, 'you know that Vince Merry bloke, runs half the town.'

'Yeah, I know him,' I reply, an uneasy feeling starting to form in the pit of my stomach.

'He came to see me one night at the pub, said he had a proposition for me. I don't know if you remember him from school but he's turned into a scary bloke.'

'Yeah,' I said, 'I've seen him since a few times, he's a big lad nowadays.' I think I know what's coming.

'Well he had this other bloke in tow, his brother or something I think, he just sat there staring at me. Apparently he went to our school as well, I don't remember him though. Do you know him? I think he called him Clarty, a year or two below us he was.'

'Aye, I know him as well, he's a wanker,' I say, hoping someone hears and it gets back to him, 'go on.'

'They sat me down in the lounge and told me they were doing a job on this warehouse I was guarding, it's a bonded one see, full of booze and tabs.'

I'd read about this in The Chronicle. It was a biggish job, a couple of hundred grands worth of gear, the town was flooded with it for a month and it cost me and Billy some money and set our little project back a bit.

'How did they persuade you then?' I asked, already having a very good idea.

'They offered me five grand at first, then when I said no they pulled a couple of photos out of young David going to school. I didn't really have a choice then, did I?' he says his voice starting to quake; he's on the verge of losing it.

Bastards. It's alright calling in volunteers who know the score and are up to it, but forcing people into it is bang out of order. Now this poor fucker's going down and it'll change him forever.

'I'm worried that they think I'll grass them up,' he goes on, 'I don't care about myself but our lass and young David don't deserve any of this Carlos.'

'First things first Davy,' I say, 'I'll come in with you and then make sure word gets back to Merry that you're not a grass. Now secondly, whatever happens inside, keep yourself to yourself, keep your head down and do NOT show any weakness to anybody or they'll eat you alive. 'I'll find out what nick you get sent to and between me and Billy we're bound to know somebody in there. I'll call by your house as well and set your lass's mind at rest about Merry and his mob.'

It's all I can think of but it seems to cheer him up. Then I get some news that cheers me up. My brief explains that my case has been adjourned and as the Crown Prosecution Service has now run out of reasonable time to prosecute me, it's being dropped in the public interest - fucking magic. I've noticed a couple of Merry's boys hanging around the place as well, obviously making sure of Davy's silence but I'm not going to mention this to him. Instead I decide to hang on and see what happens. I'll ring Sharon when I come out, Merry'll just have to have his tea late tonight.

Lisa

I've went over the books three times now, twice last night and once again this morning. It's obvious; someone's got their fingers in the till. I'll deal with this myself though, Billy doesn't have to know unless the person concerned gets silly. Couldn't say for certain who it is but I've got my suspicions, maybe time to set up a sting, I'll speak to a couple of the regulars.

Milo

Some familiar faces in here, I've had a good look around on my way in and there's definitely some scum on the loose. I think I caught sight of a Reeves brother down the hall, can't think of his name; the half breed one, Pedro, something like that. I need to pop in and see Maxwell before he starts the case, not strictly anything to do with me as Chief Inspector, but, I have a vested interest in making sure justice is seen to be served. An example needs making of these people if we are ever going to arrest the moral decline of this country, and more important-ly, it'll help to sell my book.

I started my memoirs twelve months ago when I decided to retire. As a Chief Inspector in Europe's leading party city I could have filled twelve books with tales of celebrity misde-meanours, particularly premiership footballers. I know for a fact of one club in the area that regularly contributes to the retired policemen's fund in an attempt to keep their players out of the papers. I'm not sure if I can include that though, the publisher's a bit twitchy about the legalities of it.

What this means for me is that I need a big juicy story to sell the book on the back of and this warehouse job is all I've got. There was plenty of violence used on the night shift staff that were there, a shame no one died really but there you go. Turned out the night security man was in on it, he didn't seem the criminal type but it takes all sorts. He wouldn't give up the names of any of the gang involved either, says he doesn't know them and they just approached him in a pub. I'll have to make sure Maxwell doesn't fall for that, I need a big sentence and it needs to make the national news. My sound bite's all ready for when a camera crew stops me outside of the court. I discussed it with my publisher last week. It's got to look like it's come off the top of my head and is spur of the moment, when in reality it's the title of my autobiography, and has been for some months.

'Don't. Do. The. Crime.' I say it to myself, emphasising each word as it'll look on the cover. It's an old, outdated concept but it looks good. We'll stick a by-line underneath, '*Not in MY city...*' with a photo of me looking serious. The ironic thing is that if you know what you're doing you can do the crime. I've made and spent a fortune from it over the years.

Now then, where's Maxwell?

Maxwell

Right, a quick look at today's schedule and we're off. Oh it's the warehouse job, security guard on the inside, hmm it seems he wouldn't give up the others. Judging by his advanced age that makes him a complete novice who believes everything he's read about honour amongst thieves. You've got a lot to learn my friend; they'd have sold you out in a heartbeat. He's pleaded guilty though, which is handy, saves a lot of time. He appears to have gotten a good character reference from his firm as well.

About twelve months I think.

Billy

Bit of a result that was, sorted everything out with the boys and got them on their way early doors. Quick time check, they should be round about Doncaster by now, Zeebrugge after dinner and home for last orders. I'll meet them at the lock up in the morning. Job done. As a reward for my early start I'm treating myself to breakfast at the Cavern Café. It's one of those lovely windy, sunny mornings we get in Newcastle at this time of year, the type of weather that takes your skin colour from blue back to white - smashing.

Strolling down Shields Road it's sad to see how the place has declined. When I was a teenager, back in the eighties, there was ten bars on this road and it was lively as fuck on a Friday and Saturday night. The road was always heaving with people; the pretty boys and the muscle men, the young girls and the owld slappers, smells of perfume, kebabs and that horrible fucking poser gear Kouros mingling as one all down the road, it was a quality night out. Me and the lads all done up in wor best gear; Pepe or Le Breve jeans, Pod loafers, acid house shirts and some gel in your hair, I had some then like. I remember Barry turning up in a suit once, we fucking laughed him out of the bar, he had to get a taxi home and get changed before we'd let him come out with us.

Aye, Friday night seven o' clock on the dot, start at the top of the road and work your way down to Baxters and The Ford, the two disco bars with a late licence. Usually kicked off at some point, mind you, Grabber was on the door of Baxters in them days and no fucker messed with him. I remember wor Carlos once in there, this lass was trying to get into him and he was a bit cocky about it, he was putting it about in them days as well. Anyway, he asked where she worked and she said, 'The Cat and Dog Shelter up the West End.'

He just casually turned back to the bar replying, 'I wasn't asking where you lived pet.' Me and Barry creased up and she just stood there livid. I didn't feel bad at all about laughing at her cos she'd knocked me back the week before. Mind you it was funnier still when her mate swilled Carlos, I'm giggling to myself now thinking about it.

Aye, the road's changed an awful lot in the last twenty years and not for the better either. It used to be full of good shops; butchers, fishmongers and greengrocers. There was even a department store, a real one that dealt in good quality gear the old fashioned way, like Grace Brothers and that. It's been turned into student accommodation now and the whole road is just full of second hand and bargain shops, fucking heart-breaking really. Those students get right on my tits as well. There was a squad of them in The Raby last Christmas Eve, all dressed up trying to be wackier than the next twat. They look down on you cos you're from a council estate and have to graft for a fucking living. Someone put The Beach Boys on the jukey and next thing you know one of the pricks is lying on the floor and his mate's only standing on his back pretending to surf and they were all cracking up like it's the funniest thing in the world.

'God Tarquin, you and Richard, you're so zany.'

'Yah Imelda, in Sociology they call us the Mad Dogs because we're so wacky.'

Crazy John in the lounge showed them what mad really was when he started nutting the pinball machine and breaking glasses over his head, strangely enough they left quite soon after that - wankers.

The ironic thing is I always wanted to be a student, mainly for the shagging - only kidding. I know I was clever enough and I would have liked to have made something legit of myself but it wasn't to be. When I was at school in the eighties it was when Thatcher was in charge. The whole mantra of the country was that 'greed is good' thing. There was meant to be opportunity everywhere if you were quick witted and dynamic. Unfortunately, the main rule that applied was that you had to live in London as the North East didn't officially exist. It was hard to be dynamic on free school dinners and no pocket money. Still, I was quick witted but then I had to be, living on a council estate in Newcastle in the eighties and being the man of the house at the grand old age of fourteen. I learnt fucking quickly how to stay alive and how to keep out of trouble.

So, I left school and went on a YTS in computer programming for two years. Computers were a thing of the future apparently, which to be fair they were, I mean look around you now, twenty years later and Bill Gates owns the world. The problem then was they were evolving so fast that by the time I completed my course everything I'd learnt was obsolete. The funding for the Information Technology Centres up North didn't stretch to the new computers and systems being used in industry, just these real old-fashioned miniature mainframe things and BBCs. They probably got all the top, up to date gear in London, which is why all of those boys down there who aren't now celebrity gangsters or market stall holders went on to make millions while I'm a pretend baker who sells dodgy baccy and beer. Still it's my own fault, Norman Tebbit did tell us to 'get on our bikes' and leave our homes and families to look for work; we just selfishly ignored him and decided not to turn our backs on our birthrights and heritage so now we have to pay the price.

Mind you Lisa's uncle Ron's okay, a proper fucking old school, Millwall geezer. He sort of took on the guardian mantle when her dad died. They're much the same as us the working class lads down there, they got shit on as well, you want to see some of the estates they live on. The first time I went down there to meet him I was well impressed, he's a very well connected man but with none of that 'I'm a gangster' bullshit. You can tell he's well respected and has a lot about him just by the way he dresses and carries himself. He's always suited up, got all the gold on his fingers and the Brylcreem in his hair. He looks like an ageing businessman until he smiles, and then you can just about see the Millwall tattoo inside his lip. CBL, that means Cold Blow Lane like, it's where they used to play before they moved to their new plastic stadium, like I said, proper fucking old school.

I went to see him cos I wanted to ask his permission to marry his niece, with her dad gone he was her protector if you like and if I was going to replace him he wanted to check I was up to the job. We went in his local, The Red Lion - it seems to me that at least half the pubs in London are called The Red Lion - and it's only a fucking Bushwhackers hangout. His local is used by one of the top football firms in England and he's took me there on match day; looking back I think it was a kind of test. I walked in as he took a call outside and it's wall-to-wall hard cases. I'm not talking teenagers who run away or who are hard when it's six against one, I'm talking forty and fifty year old ex dockers mixed in with the twenty and thirty year old bouncers and bodybuilders. Basically, proper blokes. The bar went silent as I walked in and I was shitting myself, they were working out if I was an undercover copper, a rival hooligan - I think they were playing Cardiff - or just a fucking idiot.

I got to the bar, trying to play it cool and looking like I didn't give a fuck who they were. Then as soon as I ordered the bloke next to me just shouts, 'He's only a facking Geordie chaps,' and a couple of them started moving towards me. I'm twenty-one years old and I can handle myself; I know I can. These blokes though, they're serious fucking fighters. None of this giving it the big one when you're mob handed and then on your toes if the gadgy fights back; these fuckers just go to town whatever the odds.

A couple of them are coming towards me and I've taken up the stance with a glass in my hand but in my heart I know I'm going to die. I'll make sure the first one in remembers me though, every time he looks in the fucking mirror.

Then Ron comes in puts his palm out to them and says very calmly, 'This gentleman is my guest, anyone who has a problem with that also has a problem with me,' fuck me they couldn't crawl up my arse quick enough. They were all shaking my hand after that asking me about Newcastle, a couple of them mentioned the Gremlins but, not wanting to push me luck, I kept out of that. Anyway they all fucked off to the match and it left me, him and a couple of older blokes in the pub, so we started to chat about Lisa and me. I should have realised how serious he was taking this marriage proposal because he missed the match to discuss it with me.

He asked what I did, how I did it, who I knew, if I'd been inside and all that type of stuff. Then he brought up the night me and Lisa met and asked why I'd hammered her then boyfriend. There's something about the bloke that makes you spill your guts to him, I just told him I loved her and couldn't watch anyone hurt her, how it filled me with rage and that if there'd been no bouncers about I'd have killed the cunt with my bare hands. He seemed happy with that and ordered a couple more pints then turned to me and said, 'Billy, my family is everything to me, I haven't got any kids and when my dear wife passed away that left me with Lisa. If you ever hurt her I will kill you do you understand?' I just nodded, I expected something like this to be honest but the way he said it, so calm and matter of fact just fucking unnerved me. Then he shook my hand and said, 'Welcome to the family son.'

I've been down there at least four times a year since and he's always up here. I get on great with the bloke, so does Carlos, he fucking loves our kid cos he gets him tickets for fights and that down the smoke. Might give him a bell actually and see when he's next up, he hasn't seen the boys for a while; yeah I'll ring him this weekend.

Here we are then, I'm at The Cavern and I take a minute to stand and look down the road. There's shite and debris blowing about everywhere, boarded up windows and cracked panes, this is my history and it's been allowed to die by the pricks in charge. Numpties in shell suits shuffle by, some of them swigging Special Brew on the march, must be giro day.

Teenage charvas hanging about on the corner looking for victims. A middle-aged bird goes by with her shopping and catches my eye, Emma she's called, Emma Redgrave. She used to be the barmaid in The Blue Bell before it got shut down and turned into a bike shop, she gives me a smile of recognition and I smile back. The charvas are looking her way and thinking about moving over but I catch their eye, I'm shaking my head at them and they know that I know the score. They turn away looking for a softer target, Burberry caps showing a glimpse of tattooed necks, body language showing all of a scarred personality.

Maybe it was always like this here and because I was part of it I just didn't notice. Personally I think the deprivation of the seventies and eighties has led to this as third generation unemployed families just don't give a fuck and take what they can, wherever they can get it. I grew up on this estate and have great memories of it though, summer holidays that went on forever. The caretakers' strike so we were off school. All the power cuts and everyone pissed and singing by candlelight in the pubs. Playing football all day on the field. Kick the can. Going to the baths and the pictures on alternate Saturday mornings with Carlos. I look down the road at the old picture house, The Apollo was brilliant. We used to sneak into the eighteen certificates when we were young; I saw Star Wars, Flash Gordon and Jaws there, proper films that filled you with excitement and suspense.

What's it been turned into? I'll tell you, a fucking McDonalds. How ironic is that? An icon of proper youth and childhood like The Apollo turned into a bloated twenty-first century version. Where once dads used to take their kids to the pictures at the weekend, now they go to McD's every second Sunday when their access allows it. Anyway, I could stand and reminisce on this road all day but fuck that man... it's time for brekky.

The breakfast in here is absolute class and because they know me I always get extra as well. Mind you, I'll have to start training with our Carlos a bit more, put a couple of pounds on just lately. He'll be here in a minute for his shredded wheat and wholemeal toast, shouldn't be a problem with his case.

'Cheers pet,' look at that a free paper as well, they love me in here. Back pages first like all proper blokes. The Toon's new hotshot cockney striker has decided it's too cold up here and he wants to go back down South, obviously it'll be nothing to do with agents or money, mercenary tosser. Where's the old school mentality? Where's the modern day Kenny Wharton or Peter Jackson? Proper blokes that got on with it and fought for the shirt and the city.

Mind you, I've heard a couple of whispers that this particular playboy footballer has been partying a bit hard since he got here. It could well be the club getting rid of him, let's just say that it snows every day where he lives and leave it at that. Let's see, nothing in the announcements, court report and no real news. Not much happening at all in the region's capital today, although, the front page makes interesting reading.

Major East End Re-Development

A billion pound blueprint to breathe new life into a huge part of Tyneside was unveiled today in the UK's biggest inner city regeneration project. The scheme involves thousands of new homes and major commercial investment including an international Housing Expo, which would be the first of its kind in the country.

The City Council are hailing the idea as a new approach to regeneration which aims to spread the prosperity of the city centre eastwards into Byker, Walker and Wallsend. The 15-year project costing around £750m will be the biggest inner city regeneration project in the UK funded mainly by the private sector.

Plans include 2,500 new homes for families, students and key workers such as teachers and nurses with a mix of social housing for rent as well as for sale.

The other major scheme is a Newcastle Housing Expo in Wallsend, which will showcase the best contemporary ideas in urban living and housing design. Around £400m will be invested into the project, which would initially involve build-

ing 300 new homes and refurbishing another 150 in phase one.

The Council says there will be no more demolition, except in areas already earmarked for clearance.

The Council plans to proceed with the development of Tyne Bank in the Byker area as a 'district heart' with a new customer service centre, library, health centre, children's centre, re-developed school and new shops.

Though both schemes will need a major injection of private sector cash, council leaders say there is no shortage of potential developers and most people in the East End back the Expo proposals.

Executive member for Development and Regeneration, Coun Paul Allum, said: 'Developing the East End is a major challenge but we are absolutely confident that this time the council has the right approach. Quite simply, Newcastle is on the up, there is substantial interest in the commercial and residential development sector and we are a city with a bright future ahead of us. We have enjoyed overwhelming success in regenerating the Quayside and city centre and we now want to expand that success eastwards in a way that will attract the private sector to invest in our local communities.'

About time, it'll be good for the area, mind you I'm still moving me ma out first chance I get. There'll be a lot of money sloshing about there though; I wish I had a couple of quid in it. Oop phone's going, I'm a bit embarrassed, that Stone Roses' ring tone's a bit outdated now, still a class tune though.

'Carlos, what's happening?' I'm moving outside, I don't like having conversations in earshot of other people.

'Case is dropped! Fucking result charv. Who? Davy McKenzie, aye, what's he doing there?' This is fucking mad, little Davy never broke a law in his life; I'll bet he even paid the poll tax when that was about. Merry is an absolute bastard.

'Right, see you later then.'

If Carlos is staying at court then I may as well have one more cup of tea. No more tabs or bevvy to distribute, all the money paid out and banked up and I don't have to be at the shop until cashing up time.

'Stick us a couple of slices of toast with that tea pet.'

I'll have to start training again.

Milo

'Mr. Maxwell, how are you?' God, he's looking old these days.

'Very well, Chief Inspector, very well.'

'Good, good,' we've played this game too many times now, he knows I want something and he wants me to come out with it, I can tell. Well I'm too long in the tooth to play it his way.

'Have you time for a coffee?' I may as well keep him in suspense a bit longer and get a drink out of him.

'Yes, come to my chambers, I have to look over some case notes anyway.'

'Oh, I'm not interrupting am I, when are you next on?' I try to look suitably impressed by his importance, I know his vanity and I know he likes it.

He's smiling benevolently and I know he's in a good mood; he looks quite smug about something, I'll ask him about that as well before I call in my favour.

Maxwell

I'm pouring the coffee for Milo when he finally asks me about my good mood. I could see he was working up to it and I just can't contain myself once I get started, this is rash I know, but it can't hurt to let him know how far I've risen in this world before he starts making demands.

'Firstly Mr. Milo, a bit of background, you may or may not know this but traditional council houses and estates as we know them are diminishing throughout the land. In a nutshell this is because of the Arms Length Management Organisations brought into play by central government. Local authorities have to hand over their housing stock in order to get their hands on government funding to modernise the properties and estates. There aren't any council houses left in Newcastle; they are all run by an organisation called Novocastrian Homes.'

'With me so far?' I glance at him as he nods his head, painfully slowly. My god and this man is in a position of power.

'Well, Newcastle has been earmarked as an area of massive investment, and I mean massive, there is going to be a huge regeneration project to ensure numerous homes for key workers throughout the region. This entails the buying up of old, run-down and vacant council houses in key sites from the council through Novocastrian Homes. Given the state of the housing market in the North East and the rate of inflation the profits will be huge for the developers so they can make a reasonably generous offer to the council for the homes they want.'

He's nodding furiously now, 'So will anyone connected with Novocastrian Homes be making any commission on these deals?' he says questioningly.

Do you know I do believe he's got it, 'Yes Mr. Milo they will,' I reply gleefully.

'These are obviously completely legal and above board, no bungs or sweeteners, and all commissions and bonuses declared to the taxman. Obviously this hinges on the right sites being vacant and any existing tenants being prepared to move, but when you have the right contacts that can always be arranged.' The look on his face means I've said too much, time to get back to business.

'Now what else can I do for you?'

Val

I hope Carl's okay today, Billy says it's nothing to worry about but I don't want him to go to prison, he's such a headstrong lad he'd probably get into more trouble once he was in there. I worry about them both all of the time if the truth be told, Billy holds it all in and always seems in control but I know he's always thinking about things. I know they both worry about me on this estate as well and want to get me a house down the coast, Tynemouth somewhere like that.

I'd like to live down there but the chances of getting enough money to do it are slim and I'm not getting any younger either. There is one way but that would mean raking up a few things that are better left in the past. I might look into that and see if there's a way round it but I'll keep it to myself. First, I'd better ring Billy and see what's happening with Carl.

Spanish

Nearly bumped into Milo on the way into court, just thought I'd check on our Carl, he reckons he'll be okay but you never know and there's a few faces in Durham I could have a word with if needed. Turns out his case was adjourned but they'd run out of time to prosecute so he's off the hook, good result.

Stayed in court with him to see his mate get sentenced, fucking five years for a first offence, no way is that right. Carl was going mad in court; he got thrown out in the end, shouting abuse at the judge as he was thrown out. I knew the judge, Carl doesn't know that I used to know him but I did; he was my brief back in the seventies as well as other things. He nearly had me put away he was that incompetent, lucky the prosecution lost that witness statement or I'd have got five years as well. I looked him right in the eye after he'd passed his sentence today, the lad's breaking down in tears and he looked straight at me and smirked. Prick.

I saw that Milo sliding out looking pleased with himself as well. I remember when that fucker was a plod, he was the arresting officer actually when Maxwell defended me that time. I think he's well up the ladder these days. Better give Billy a ring and let him know that Carlos is in one; he takes some stopping when he's in this mood.

Milo

Well then, job done. Maxwell came across in the end, took a bit of persuading but a favour's a favour. I'm surprised he was so awkward about it really; as far as he's concerned I took a big risk for him back then. He thinks it was me who lost the witness statement so that Spanish could walk, when in reality I passed the blame on for that and someone else had their career put on hold, but he's not to know that. We all knew Spanish was guilty as sin, he always was, but Maxwell was desperate, fresh out of law school and into his first job; it was his first big case and he wasn't covering himself with glory with his new employers. Anyway, he asked for help on the promise of a favour returned when he was higher up the chain, always did have his career all mapped out did old Maxwell.

I saw Spanish on the way out, I don't think he saw me, too concerned with that head the ball son of his. That boy's going to get into serious trouble one day if he doesn't rein that temper in. I'd better get ready for the press, get myself quoted and on the national news tonight then ring my publisher.

Merry

Where the fuck is she now? Why's her phone switched off? That bird is never around when I want her. She left a message saying she's gone out with her mate, probably spending my money in town and she knows we're going out tonight. When she does turn up she'll spend hours getting ready and we'll be late, if I didn't love her I'd kill her.

Good result today Davy keeping his mouth shut. Five years was far too steep though, he'll have to appeal, they can't increase it anyway so he's got nowt to lose. I heard that Carlos was there with him, I'll have to keep an eye on that as well, I don't like the thought of that cunt knowing my business. The boys said he was blatantly badmouthing our Clarty as well. If he keeps it up he'll have to be dealt with, I can't allow him to make me look weak but if I do it it'll have to be done properly because he's a dangerous fucker.

'The number you are calling is not responding, please try again later,' turn your fucking phone on you cow.

Fuck it, I'm going to see Joanne, she won't give me any of this headache shite either. She'll come across how I like, when I like and where I like.

I might take a present for the boy as well, although maybe not, she doesn't take him to work and it would get nicked if she left it there.

Cheered up now, the thought of a shag in the very near future soothing my mind, where's me car keys?

<u>Billy</u>

I don't know what Spanish is on about, he said Carlos had lost the plot earlier and was going to be roaming round town looking for bother. I got myself ready to take him for a pint and calm him down when he turns up at ours anyway. Lisa cooks a bit more food for him and he had his tea with us. He's good as gold; joking with Lisa, on the Playstation with the boys and watching the football with me. He's obviously worked his frustration out somewhere, must be shagging knowing that fucker. I'm not asking him though; he'll get all smug and not tell me anyway.

I'll find out soon enough.

Saturday

Merry

'Sharon,' what the fuck is she doing in that bathroom?

'Hurry up man, I've got to get ready shortly,' she knows I can't be late for this appointment.

I'm putting my plate on the pile in the sink when she finally appears in the kitchen, looking fucking good an' all mind, if I didn't know her better I'd say she was playing away; she'd better fucking not be.

'About time,' I growl and stomp off up the stairs.

While I'm shaving I get to thinking about her and how we met, we've been together about seven or eight years now, she wasn't long out of school, must've been about eighteen. I'd made a name for myself by then and she was impressed when I paid her a bit of attention. I first saw her in The Ritzy with her mates and I sent a bottle of champagne over; she nearly wet herself with excitement. Later on that night I smashed two blokes to bits in front of her and she was mine. I think she got off on all the power I had and people crawling up my arse. She used to love going out and seeing bouncers shitting themselves and waiters moving people to give us the best table. I love her as well like; can't understand how we've never had a family yet. Mind you, there hasn't been a lot of bedroom action going on just lately; I've been a bit tired with all the late nights and running round the clubs keeping an eye on things and by the time I get home she's asleep.

I don't think she realises what my life's like sometimes. Take last night for example; I get to Maddos Club and there's no one on the door, just a receptionist taking the money, all the bouncers are inside in a stand off with ten lads. Now, the manager's there and he starts giving it to me about sorting it out quick or he's getting another firm in. I can't afford to lose the contract so I steam into the cunts and the lads all follow me; there's claret and teeth everywhere but we get them out. Then the manager gets me in his office and starts fucking screaming at me, 'You can't do it like that,' and all that bollocks. I just said to him, 'You wanted them out, I got them out. End of.' Then he starts saying he's ringing head office and we're going to be out as well. I was still a bit high off the fight earlier and I'd done a couple of lines anyway to keep me awake so I was rushing a little bit as he pushed past me to get to the phone. I grabbed the fucker by the throat and lifted him off the floor and then slammed him into the wall. Putting my face right into his I just told him that no one in this town fucks with me and if he wants to try it then he'd better start thinking about moving. He changed his mind then.

Now that's a normal sort of night for me. Usually I get home buzzing and ready for action and she's spark out. Honestly, she doesn't know the fucking half of it. If our Clarty wasn't such a wind up merchant I'd give him a bit more to do. I might have to anyway, we're not going to have any sprogs if we don't have sex are we? I mean I get it when I need it off Joanne but that's just fucking a whore, it's just a release for everything; when I'm with Sharon it's the real thing. Same with the family idea; Joanne's got a fifteen year old boy she claims is mine, I mean he might be but legally I'm not recognising him. I give her cash now and then to keep her quiet and I wouldn't see them in trouble but he's not really my boy. Not really, she's a pro for fucks sakes; he could be anybody's.

No, I want a proper family with the woman I love and she doesn't need to know about anyone or anything else.

Ron

It's about time I made another pilgrimage to geordieland; we're up at Sunderland soon so I could kill three birds with one stone. See the family, watch the mighty lions destroy them sad pretend geordies and visit Tel.

I remember when he was sent down, I knew it was coming but even so I was absolutely bleedin' gutted, life imprisonment and a recommendation of at least twenty-five years. His missus broke down sobbing she did; I got one of the lads to bung her a grand and told her she'd get four hundred a month to help her keep it together.

As I was walking out the court one of the CID whispered to me, 'You're next Carter.' I just looked him up and down slowly, taking in every detail of his appearance and face. He swallowed a couple of times and went white as, taking my time, I said, 'If it's you that comes for me sonny you'd better have kissed your wife and told her you love her that morning.' The cheek of the barsteward, his guvnors had all bought bleedin' timeshares out of me even then and that was twenty odd years back, god knows how much the slags have had off me since then.

Yeh, it'll be good to visit old Tel, keep his spirits up, I'll get on the blower and sort it out.

Sharon

The look in his eyes when I came down the stairs then, I almost thought he knew. I've never done anything like this before but I need it to keep happening more than anything. I used to think I loved him, I know I loved all the attention he gave me and the way everyone did as they were told. I've grown up now though and I want a proper relationship. I want to be with someone because I love them not because I'm scared of them. He was on about kids again last night; I pretended to be asleep when he came in and when he started talking I kidded on I was drifting back off and in the end he gave up. I'll have to shag him again soon but I'll spin it out for as long as I can while I work out what to do for the best. God, I hope he never finds out that I haven't stopped taking the pill, he's such a violent short tempered bastard I think he'd do me some serious damage.

'You look lovely babe,' I lie to him as he comes back downstairs, nice designer suit but he makes it look cheap and nasty, all misshapen on those freakish shoulders.

'Do you fancy meeting for lunch?' I ask him, already knowing that he won't be able to.

'I can't pet,' he replies tapping the side of his nose and winking at me, 'important meeting, know what I mean?'

I knew that you big, stupid thug.

'Oh well,' I pout at him, 'I'll have a look round the shops instead.' It's what he expects me to say.

I'll actually be in a hotel room having a decent jump for once, probably best not to mention that.

Billy

Taking the boys to the match today, can't wait. I promised them this if they got good reports from school so they grafted their little arses off and got some good grades and things; our lass was well pleased. As well as that Peter got moved up to the top set in maths and Kenny has been made captain of his primary school's football team; you can't fault them for effort. The real bonus though is if they stick in at school they'll have a future and they won't have to live like me and Carlos did when we were younger.

Lisa and me were discussing them last night when I took her out for a meal; bit of a surprise like, I'm an old romantic really. Anyway, I want them to start boxing at Carlos's club, more for the discipline than owt else but she's not too happy about them fighting and getting into that way of life. She wants them to use their heads before their fists and I agreed with her on that and told her so, but she also reckons if they've got me, Carlos and uncle Ron they don't need to be fighting. That's all well and good but we won't be around all the time will we. There will undoubtedly come a day when they need to be able to punch their way out of a situation, probably in a pub or something. Anyway, she was definitely coming round to my way of thinking so I left it at that and got stuck into the pasta and tiramisu, then we got pissed and had a right laugh.

I am proud of my boys and the way they're turning out. Obviously as their dad they look up to me so I've told them to learn as much as possible about things that interest them and to try and stay away from crime and drugs. A bit hypocritical of me I know but I know all about these things and where they lead. At the end of the day I break the law so they won't have to, mind you they don't know about that. The lads think I'm a baker by trade and that I got lucky buying the old bakery on Wallsend High Street. The reality is that it's really an excellent way to wash through the money we make from the duty free runs and if any coppers are interested in how I own my own house, well, I've got a thriving bakery business that turns over a profit of thirty grand a year. As it happens the actual bakery makes fuck all, I run it at a loss most weeks but it's the best front in the world cos everybody always pays cash in a bakery don't they? I almost give the stuff away and bank the other money through the tills.

Me and Carlos started doing the tabs and booze runs a few years ago now, everyone goes to France and there's always loads of hassle at Calais isn't there? Well not us. I soon worked out that the Hull to Zeebrugge ferry was a lot easier. Longer on the water but a lot less driving from Newcastle and virtually customs free, you can get your stock in Holland or Belgium depending on who's cutting who's throat pricewise at the time and Bob's ya uncle.

We started making enough money to expand and now I've got four tranny drivers making three trips a week each, me and Carlos don't have to bother doing it ourselves any more. We supply a fair few of the pubs and clubs around this neck of the woods and it's nice regular money. Obviously like every other business there's competition but we carved out our own area and have a good relationship with the other operators in Newcastle. Don't make a fortune like, but enough to make all our lives, the drivers as well, a lot more comfortable. No hassle, don't step on anyone's toes, life's sweet.

Me and Carlos are saving up to buy a house between us in Tynemouth to move me mother into, that's her dream of retiring down there. It's our dream as well cos the estate's full of fucking refugees and charva types now, there used to be a bit of community and even a sort of rogues' code of conduct but that's all gone over time.

A couple of years ago some cheeky fucker followed her home from the post office and as she put her bag down on the kitchen worktop and went into the living room he put his hand in the door and swiped her bag. There was a time when those types of things didn't happen on our estate, you only nicked off the people who could afford it. I don't know what's happened to the younger generation I really don't.

Anyway, unfortunately for that prick Carlos and me are still well known in Byker and have a lot of friends and contacts. I soon knew who he was and the next day her bag was on the doorstep with a letter saying sorry and in it was double the money that was taken. Carlos had bruised knuckles for a couple of weeks but he said it was worth it.

The wanker's moved away since.

Milo

I've been sitting in the multi-storey in this car for ten minutes now, if he doesn't turn up soon I'm going to go and leave him sweating on what'll happen. I hate poor timekeeping, I'm a busy man and he should know this, the longer I sit here the more chance I have of being seen. What Maxwell said the other day about making a fortune has stayed in my mind for some reason, it seems that he must have some knowledge of where the developers are looking for sites and then he ensures that the sites become vacant, now how does he do that? More importantly how do I get a piece of it?

I'll need to ponder on that one. Must ring my agent later as well, he left a message for me last night about the book not being explosive enough, he said it needed one last kick or shock in order to sell, hmm, something else for me to think about.

Here he is now the big ape, he's soaking, it looks like it's pissing down outside of the car park. I watch my window move smoothly down, thirty thousand pounds of craftsmanship this vehicle and it's absolutely wasted on this idiot.

'Get in the car,' I say as he starts trying to apologise. I stop him with a curt, 'Shut up and give me the money and don't raise the envelope above the dashboard this time.'

'I'm sorry I'm late,' he mumbles.

'Don't ever keep me waiting again,' I snap at him and just for a second I can see the anger flare in his eyes, 'don't fucking look at me like that either,' I put him back in his place.

I can make or break this clown, retiring or not, and he knows it. I've guided him for the last ten years; told him where not to be on certain nights, told him which dealers had just been put away and where there was a supply chain vacuum. It was me who told him to start his own security company and it was me who approved his licence, he needs to be reminded of that sometimes.

Sensing my anger he butts in.

'Look,' he says, 'I'm sorry, I was taking a call from your mate Maxwell, the judge.'

'Good friend of yours is he?' I reply, seemingly unaffected by this news but my mind has started working overtime.

'I do a bit of work for him now and then,' he says with a wink, 'you know, a bit of debt collecting and house clearing.'

Aha, a little light comes on above my head and the penny drops. That's answered one of my questions about Maxwell and I'm definitely going to find out about the other one. If this is juicy enough, and I think it may be, then I may well have an explosive end to my book.

'Whatever,' I say to Merry, 'now you've taken up enough of my time, I'll see you next month.'

'Can't you drop me off?' he starts to whine.

'No,' I reply, 'the exercise will do you good. Now get out, I've got police work to do.'

Billy

Norwich today, they're fuck all really, no problems on or off the pitch. I've kept me eyes open in case there's any boys in town looking for it but there's nowt to worry about. Noticed a few of the Gremlins looking a bit bored by The Monument, Sunderland are at home today as well. I'm surprised they aren't down there causing havoc, mind you the lads I saw were just fringe men not the main players.

Could of swore I saw our Carlos as well just now when we came out of Burger King on Northumberland Street. I'm sure I clocked him, head down striding towards the metro station on the other side of the road. I shouted his name but he never looked back, it mustn't have been him. The lads never noticed either; I'll give him a ring later, see if he fancies a pint. Mind you if this weather keeps up I might well stay in tonight, freezing and pissing down; the things you do to follow this shower of shite.

'Howay then lads,' I say, 'they can't start the match until we get there, so we'd best hurry up.'

'Really dad?' our Kenny looking all wide eyed and excited, still at that stage where he believes everything his old man tells him.

'Don't be daft you muppet,' Peter jumps in with both feet, only two years older but already more cynical than a room full of journalists. Kenny doesn't like being made a knob of, especially by his older brother and they look like they're going to fight so I act quickly and get them both in a headlock and start shouting, 'Two daft lads for sale, twenty pence and a pickled egg.'

They're wriggling about embarrassed and shouting, 'Get off,' but eventually they just start laughing and tell me I'm mad. People are looking but we don't care and we're just giggling together, it's like I'm the youngest out of the three of us.

I love days like these when things are simple and there's no real shit to deal with, even when it's raining.

Sharon

I'm taking a real chance getting a taxi to the hotel but the weather's horrible. I got the bus into town and then used a black cab off the street; if I'd used a local firm the news would have got back to Vince before I'd got my knickers off. It seems strange sneaking around like this but exciting at the same time, the way it was at first with Vince, that's like another life now. I can't believe I was so young and stupid to fall for all that 'I'm the daddy' shit. I'm fairly sure he's at it with someone else as well, no definite evidence just signs really, different smells on him sometimes, like cheap perfume that type of thing.

Actually I hope he is and I hope he leaves me for her, that would leave the way clear to see where this thing was going with my lover boy. When we first started this a few months ago I made sure that I found a hotel out of the way on the edge of town. I obviously didn't want to be spotted going in there.

God I'm excited, I've fancied Carlos for years and years. It's brilliant every time and afterwards we even talk about stuff, that's never happened with Vince. I think I'm falling in love with this man but I can't tell him though, he's a love them and leave them type of bloke and if he thinks I'm getting too serious he'll be leaving.

Still here I am, check in, get settled and wait for 'Mr. Smith'.

Maxwell

It's been a long morning and I've attended a number of meetings; the Law Society, the Rotary Club and the most important, the board meeting at Novocastrian Homes.

Everything appears to be progressing nicely, bonuses and dividends on track. The chairman even pulled me to one side afterwards and congratulated me on my foresight in clearing the homes we have in the earmarked streets of Byker just in time for this huge revamp. He also seemed to think it was lucky that the majority of them are lying vacant at the right time but as I told him, 'You make your own luck in this life Mr. Chairman.' He doesn't know it yet but come the handover date every single one of those homes will be vacant.

The light's flashing on the phone; it's probably my latest bit of trade, I do slum it sometimes. I'm seeing him tonight and he probably wants to know what to wear, well not much my good man, not much, I'm in the mood, money always does that to me. Oh, maybe not. This voice is harsh and unforgiving, it's certainly not him, hmm, someone I thought I'd left behind. Wants money owed and is coming to see me tonight to get it. I'd better call him and cancel tonight, it'd be best not to have any complications at the minute and I think this situation can be dealt with quickly and cheaply.

__Carlos__

That was fucking excellent, I'd never been in this hotel before we started this, but it's nice. She always has a really good time as well, I make sure of that, usually have to peel her off the ceiling when we've finished and today was no exception, I'm fucked now like. The best bit for me was coming just as Newcastle got the winner on the radio, like a double victory, a real six pointer. I'd better not tell her that though, I don't think she'd appreciate it.

The funniest thing though was when, after we'd finished and she was having a tab out of the window, the DJ played that Radgepacket song 'Gigolo Doorman' - you know the one, it was on the telly a few weeks back: -

Take your pick of the fake tan clique
As they're herding around your door
Hear their chatter, stilettos clatter
You know you're gonna score

Pull in your gut and flex your pecs
You're just so attractive to the opposite sex

Big Bad Norman
Gigolo doorman
Legend in this town
In reality, you're just a steroid freak
A pumped up BEEPing clown

Anyway, so she's listening to it going, 'That sounds just like Vince,' and I'm pissing myself because the lad who wrote it is a mate of our Billy's and he actually did write it about Merry. I'm not telling her though, I really wouldn't want to piss her off, I like our sessions and I'd like to spend more time with her. I've never really been into proper relationships, just one nighters, it's easy when you're a combination of sportsman and local celebrity, but this is different, I miss her when I can't see her.

Anyway, best not to push it. Even though Merry's a dick and he's fucking about behind her back she seems happy enough the way things are and it's better to have some of her instead of none. Taxi home now, bit of scran, a shower, shit, shave and a couple of pints tonight, think I'll give Billy and Barry a bell and stay local.

Billy

Tried to ring our Carlos when we got the winner in the ninety third minute but his phone was off, his battery must be out of juice. The lads really enjoyed themselves as well. They haven't realised yet that I always pick a match against a shit team for them to come to so the chances are we'll win, they'll have a great time and they'll work hard at school so I bring them again. Piece of piss this parenting lark. As it's been really cold and wet today, I decided at half time I was staying in tonight, fuck it; dvd, chinese and maybe a bit of good old fashioned romance on the settee.

Failing that Match Of The Day at half ten.

Sharon

I've never had a man do things like that to me before, I could have easily stayed in that room with him for the rest of my life, it was love making instead of just sex. I know I'm on the verge of falling madly in love with Carlos already but I can't say anything. Vince would kill him and probably his brother as well, that's if he didn't run a mile from the commitment anyway. It's so exciting but so depressing at the same time, really it's a no win situation and I can't see a way out.

Clarty

Oh dear, looks like Sharon's been a naughty girl. Now why would she be going into a hotel on her own when she's got a perfectly good house with my dear cousin in Benwell?

And then, lo and behold, fifteen minutes later, Newcastle's very own Rocky turns up grinning like a dog with two dicks. I hate that twat. I hate the way people lick his arse. I hate the way people flock round him and more than anything I hate his big fucking stupid dago smile. He thinks he's the man because he won a few fights in the ring, I'm a better fighter than him, boxers are fuck all. I've just never had the breaks he had, I know his brother did all the fighting for him when he was young, I'd kill the prick in or out of the ring. Maybe we'll find out one of these days. I could take him easy and when I do I'll do it in front of his mates and hangers on. Just for now though I'll keep an eye on Sharon, I can see a double header coming off here and I'll maybe get the chance to fuck both of them one way or another.

Better get ready now, collection night round the town. I hope Vince doesn't get pissed and start telling me how much he loves her and wants kids with her again tonight, I might not be able to stop laughing at the stupid bastard.

Big Tony

Saturday night, another busy one in the party city, fucking sick of hen and stag nights turning up from elsewhere in the country though, can't they go and puke in their own streets? Here we go again, 'Alright ladies, looking good, are you enjoying yourselves in geordieland then?'

One of them, fit as fuck, miniskirt round her chin, looks like she's gagging for it.

'A want to snog a jordee,' she can hardly get the words out she's that pissed.

'Where you from then pet?' go into professional geordie mode, well that's what she wants.

'Barnsleh,' she answers, leaning against the wall.

'Well then pet,' this won't take long, 'why don't you and your mates go in for nowt, get yourselves a drink and then you come back out here and keep me company for a bit.'

Yeah they like that idea; off they go, wobbling in, like wildebeest walking into the lion territory in the Serengeti. They'll be stalked round the building and the stragglers picked off one by one, then they'll wake up in the morning with their knickers in their pocket and a thumping hangover, ringing their boyfriends saying Newcastle's over-rated.

The other bouncers are laughing at me, don't know why, they've got to cover the door when I'm shagging her in the car park in ten minutes time. A nice stress reliever before that fuckwit Merry turns up, still won't be long now before I stop dealing with him one way or another.

Barry

Here we go again back to work on the nightshift, the club's warming up nicely and as soon as I get rid of this gear I'm out of here. Tony was asking about Billy earlier, said that Merry had been making noises about getting him on the team. I told him no way would Billy work for Merry, he won't work for anyone as it is, never mind that dickhead. I put him right about Billy and Carlos as well, everyone thinks Carlos is the muscle and Billy is the brains, which is only half right, Billy's the fucking muscle as well. Carlos and him looked after me at school, stopped the likes of Merry picking on me and gave me the confidence to come out of my shell. I hung round with Carlos cos he was in my year but outside of school I knocked around with both of them.

I can still remember the time down at Whitley Bay like it was yesterday, that was the last time Billy and Carlos had anything to do with Merry. It had all started out as such a laugh, we'd travelled down to Whitley Bay on the metro early in the day, spent money in the arcades, eyed up the local birds and then got nowhere with them; not even Carlos. We ate candyfloss and arsed about on the rides like you do. As mobs go we were pretty dis-united at the best of times and as there were only six of us that day we'd probably pushed our luck just by being so far from home.

Me and Carlos were the youngest at fourteen, you'd probably best describe us as charvas these days, all attitude and front, back then we were just yobs. Merry was the oldest at nineteen and was apparently one more knockout away from a GBH charge as he was constantly fighting in the local boozers. In between them a couple of Merry's drinking buddies Fat Kev and Munkus, they were soft as shite and crawled up his arse goodstyle; Fat Kev still does, I don't know what happened to Munkus. Then there was Billy, fifteen years old, streetwise and hard, Merry's two sidekicks went nowhere near him and left us alone because of him.

Now unknown to me, on our way into Whitley Bay via the metro station, Merry had noticed a newly concreted hole in the factory next door and he also realised it wouldn't be properly dry until the next day. The factory in question made sweets that would be easily saleable on the streets of our estate in Byker so he quickly decided that we would be hitting the place on the way back. Night was falling when we decided to head off, we'd done all our money in the arcades and had a good day out. When we got back to the station it was dark and that was when Merry broached the idea of 'doing' the factory. Billy wasn't too keen, he could already see trouble ahead, I sided with Billy and obviously Munkus and Fat Kev rammed their tongues up Merry's arse, this left Carlos to decide. I naturally assumed he'd say no and that would be it, I was even heading towards the platform when I heard Merry say, 'You scared then Carlos?'

As soon as I heard that I knew we'd be doing it, Carlos changed his mind quicker than a politician in trouble whenever his manhood was questioned. I looked at Billy and he was just muttering under his breath and looking daggers at Carlos. So, the job was on and we were doing it. We stumbled our way round to the back of the factory and found our first surprise of the night, there was another crew of lads there from North Shields who'd had the same idea on their day out. After a quick standoff between the two top lads it was agreed to split the job and Carlos and me were quickly put out of the way and posted on the front street as sentries. Not being used to this kind of thing we both found it quite exciting, in our heads we thought we were acting like real pros but anyone watching us would have sussed what was happening immediately. The way we were hopping about, looking up and down the street and then trying to look casual at the same time would have given the game away on its own but combined with the stupid little whistles we kept practising we may as well have worn signs that said 'we are crap - please arrest us'.

Anyway, despite our limitations the job was soon complete and both sets of lads had a bin bag full of sweets but it was about now that our master plan started to unravel as we hadn't actually thought about getting the stuff home. It was then decided by our glorious leaders that we should get the bus as travelling on the metro might attract too much attention - because obviously you wouldn't notice thirteen lads on a bus carrying a bin bag full of sweets. I looked at Billy at this point as even I could see this was a fucking stupid idea but he looked resigned to it, I think he knew what was coming and was preparing himself for it. Nobody really knew Whitley Bay that well so we mooched around the back streets in the dark looking for a bus stop as a number of curtains twitched and monitored our progress, then, when we'd finally found one, the inevitable happened and two coppers appeared out of nowhere. After they'd asked us what we were doing and where we were going they then asked what was in the bags; most of us had been edging away from the bus stop while they were talking and at this point decided to leg it. They grabbed hold of one of the bigger Shields lads and we sprinted along the sea front towards the arcades. Merry then made his second stupid mistake of the day shouting and screaming abuse at the coppers as we ran. It was all I could hear for the thirty seconds it took us to sprint to the arcades, 'Fuck off you daft bastards,' and, 'Come and get us then you cunts.'

Now at fourteen I was no expert on not getting chinned but the one thing I did know was the best way to get by was to keep your head down and say nowt, especially in a strange area at night. Predictably enough though he'd soon attracted the attention of the local casuals who quickly realised we weren't their mates and thought we were shouting at them. They mobbed up and followed us as we headed to the only other place we knew in the area - the metro station. The North

Shields boys had sensibly disappeared into the night air leaving just us six Byker lads running for the station and about forty Whitley Bay casuals hard on our heels. I just ran for my fucking life. As I ran I promised God that I'd be good for the rest of my life as long as he put a train in the station. God, as ever, took the piss by putting one in there that was on the other side of the track and going the other way. We sprinted up the stairs of the bridge between the two platforms in a melee of arms and legs, me and Carlos were faster than Billy as he was a heavy fucker even then, more so since he'd done his knee playing football for the school, so we stopped to see where he was and as we turned round Carlos got knocked out with a massive haymaker.

Now in Hollywood when you see this happen to one of your mates you steam straight in, spark everyone clean out then pick your mate up and make sure he gets home safely, his dad buys you a pint and his fit sister falls in love with you. Unfortunately I didn't live in Hollywood, I lived in Byker. I got smacked from behind and went down like a sack of tatties, curled myself into the foetal position against the walkway wall and hoped for the best as the kicks and punches rained down on me.

Eventually it stopped and I looked up, there was five or six of the cunts throwing digs at Billy who was just lashing into them, he was standing in front of us and wouldn't budge. There was a couple more of them on the floor holding their faces as the blood seeped through their fingers. Carlos was just starting to come round and I slapped him a couple of times to wake him up, as I did I could hear Billy screaming, 'LET'S FUCKING HAVE IT THEN, IS THAT YOUR FUCKING BEST YOU PUSSY CUNTS?' This Whitley bay mob had the numbers but none of them had the bottle to fight Billy, they were backing off at a rate of knots as me and Carlos got up. I asked Billy where Merry and his mates were and Billy replied, never taking his eyes off the retreating mob.

'They got on the fucking train and left you two on the floor, these wankers here are just what's left of the main mob, the rest of them caught sight of the Shields boys and chased them into town. How you feeling Carlos?'

'Fucking shite man,' he replied, 'they've broke me jaw.' Carlos wouldn't be chatting any lasses up for a while, do him good anyway, give his cock a rest. The Whitley boys had fucked off now and Billy turned to us both and said, 'Next time I say no, just fucking listen to me, as of now we are fuck all to do with Merry, remember that.'

I'd never seen him like that before, at school and in the street he was always in control even when he lost his temper, which was rare anyway. His eyes never went as wide as they were now. I keep getting interrupted in my thoughts though by people who want to buy pills and I've taken a couple myself so maybe I'm remembering this wrong, but, the more I think about it now the more I realise he was scared, that's why he fought like a fucking lunatic and wouldn't go down. If he had hit the floor then all three of us were fucked and I think he knew that, the fear drove him on and he just kept fighting. That's why he looked different to normal; I've never seen Billy Reeves scared of anything in his life. Anyway, whatever the reason, I owe him and if I ever get the chance I'll repay the debt.

'You what mate? Yeah tenner for three,' this shop's open all hours.

Lisa

I love cuddling up to Billy on the sofa, the boys are in bed and we've had a couple of bottles of wine and a lovely Indian take-away. I can even tolerate him watching Match of the Day while we do it as long as he doesn't make me wear a Newcastle shirt in bed tonight. I'm toying with the idea of telling him about the phone call from school yesterday about Peter; he's been fight-ing and has got some detentions for it. The school would like us to meet with the other boy's parents and sort it out so they don't have to, they haven't threatened suspensions or exclu-sion but they certainly implied it.

He's turned the football off and has a naughty glint in his eye; actually I think I'll tell him tomorrow.

Wed-
nesday

Billy

I love Wednesday morning in the bakery, no matter what I'm doing I always make a point of being in here. It's the day before pension day for a lot of the old dears who shop in here and a couple of years ago my then nightshift baker Pete asked if his nan and her mate could have some of the leftover stuff from Tuesday as they were skint. I like to think I'm a nice bloke so I said yes no problem. Next thing I know word's got round and a few more of her mates turn up as well. Then my gran hears about it and comes down with a couple of her mates and it just balloons out of all proportion.

Now on a Wednesday I get what seems like the whole of Wallsend's pensioners down here. I'm not even giving away the leftovers anymore; the nightshift baker has to do a special batch of bread and cakes on a Tuesday night for them. It doesn't really cost me that much and I don't mind doing it, I'm a bit of a believer in karma anyway and helping them out like this got me out of the shite a few months back. I've been investigated a couple of times by the law for my alleged smuggling activities, smuggling? It's only tabs and booze, it's not like I'm a gun runner or drugs mule is it? Anyway, they've been to the shop to check out my income, only thing is they turned up on a Wednesday morning, so I made a quick call to Carlos and had him and Barry up the street intercepting the pensioners, giving them all three or four quid and telling them to get what they normally would but pay for it. The place was manic and the coppers couldn't believe it, they were like a grey haired swarm of locusts. The till was ringing constantly and beeping that much that I nearly started dancing. After that the law just left me alone content that I was living as my income allowed and those pensioners, fair play to them, they were all telling the coppers how good my bread was and how they shopped here every day, it was great.

Me mam popped in this morning for some bits, I think she's skint again; I made sure Tracey filled her bag up. She asked if Pete had been in touch actually, she always had a soft spot for him. Young Pete, now he was a case. He was a bit of a long haired hippy type and was always singing about the place and eventually started this band up so I sponsored him through the bakery, not much like, just enough for a couple of guitars and to get some flyers made up. They started gigging around the normal studenty places and dodgy bars and have actually done okay for themselves.

He left the bakery about a year ago and they've spent the time touring all around Britain in the small clubs and that. Through this they've managed to get a reasonable following around the country and have released their debut album off the back of it. I helped him with the band name as well, I took him and his three mates to Carlos's gym one night and they watched Carlos sparring with this over enthusiastic bouncer. The bouncer was just swinging wildly at Carlos cos he was shitting himself and I shouted out, 'Watch your pretty boy face bruv this one's a radgepacket,' the long haired boys just fell about laughing and the band had a name.

Actually, I inspired one of their very first songs as well 'Strawberry Pie Filling'. I wandered into the bakery one night when Pete was working and I was a bit mashed, he was just singing away to the radio as he filled these strawberry pies and I was feeling a bit lyrical in a Happy Mondays sort of style. Next thing I know he's writing down the shite I'm warbling and telling me it's deep and meaningful and that it represents the contrasting outlooks of men and women, I just agreed and said he could have it for free. All I did was sing the first shite that entered my fucked up head about pies and strawberries. Still whatever floats your boat eh? I wish I'd written that bouncer one though, they've just got in the charts with that. Not many people know this but that song's about Merry. We saw Pete and his mates in Maddos one night when Merry was in there off his face; he was pushing lads about and bullying them to impress these fucking mini skirted bouncer groupies and they were loving it. Pete must have remembered it cos he told me it was about that prick last time I spoke to him.

Good on them though for getting a record deal cos they stuck at it. I must give him a ring actually and see when they're playing up here.

Clarty

I've thought on this for a while and decided tonight's the night to gain a bit more respect from everyone, it's about time Carlos Reeves was put back in his place. I normally go to the Powerhouse Gym on Elliot Street in the town but tonight I fancy going to Byker Boxing Club with a couple of the door lads, they're up for a bit of sparring if they get the chance.

Carlos

Always do your shopping on a Wednesday, no crowds, and no hassle. No fucker's got any money see, so clear aisles and fresh veg, fucking class man. I'm just dodging round the freezers really trying to decide what mass produced shite I can treat meself to this week. I always get some rubbish just to vary me diet a bit. I eat loads of fruit and vegetables, pasta, fish, chicken and wholemeal rice; all that good stuff. Every now and then though I like to just eat some easy to cook shite, don't we all? So choices today are crispy pancakes, turkey twizzlers, fish fingers or maybe some faggots, nah, scrub them, they remind me too much of the rent boy.

I can't concentrate anyway really, I like food and I like thinking about it but there's something more important on my mind. I don't know what's wrong with me but I just can't get Sharon out of my head. I'm constantly thinking about her, where she is, what she's doing and who she's with. I see her smile when I wake up, I hear her whispering to me when it's windy and when I'm on my own in bed at night, in that place between sleep and awake, I'm sure I imagine her kissing me goodnight. I think I'm going mental. I've never been in love before, plenty of lust but no love, Billy's always telling me about it and it sounds a bit like this. I'd ask him but he'd take the piss. It's got to be love cos I've knocked all the shagging on the head, I've elbowed a few regular lasses in the last couple of days cos I just don't want to be with them any more. I only want to be with Sharon but she's with Merry, the steroid-gobbling bag of wind and piss. If I thought there was an inkling of her feeling the same way about me then I'd take her and all the hassle and aggro that went with it. Fuck me, I am in love, it's taken thirty-three years but I got there in the end.

Think I'll just have the fish fingers actually; Jamie Oliver's not keen on them twizzler things.

Spanish

Durham nick's still the same. Terry hasn't changed either, still a big bloke, still got the same confidence in everything he does and most of all still got the same dead eyes. He's not the top man in this prison but no one, and I mean no one, fucks with him.

I was banged up with him for a couple of years back in the eighties. He was getting shit off a load of fucking mackems one day for being a cockney up here so I jumped in for him, we ended up sharing a cell and have been best of mates since. I visit him at least twice a year and have kept writing to him. I know he appreciates it cos everyone but his best mate Ron fucking deserted him after about five years.

The ironic thing is we're virtually related, his mate Ron is Ron Carter who is Billy's fucking uncle-in-law or something. He's heard all about Carlos and Billy's exploits over the last ten years through me and Ron and would really like to meet them. He's a big boxing fan is Terry so when I got him a video of Carlos's fights he was made up and the screws let him watch it to keep him quiet. I think he did a bit when he was younger and qualified as some sort of coach. I know he does a lot of training in here and coaches a few of the lads.

'You're looking well Tel,' I say.

He just smiles and then, 'They're talking about letting me out soon Spanish,' he's positively fucking beaming.

I'm genuinely made up for the bloke, 'Fucking excellent news that Tel, what's the score then?'

'It's still in discussion but my minimum tariff's up this year and I'm looking good for parole,' then a dark look across his face, 'I'd have to keep away from the kid and the ex-wife, restraining order apparently. The boy's grown up anyway and

I gave up on her years ago. I was thinking of keeping out of London altogether.'

'If you're stuck when you come out mate you could always stay with me,' like I say we're best of pals, even if he is a scary bastard.

'I might just take you up on that Spanish,' he says, 'there's only Ron in London who bothers with me, I feel like I know your fucking family better than mine.'

'Anytime mate,' I say. 'Incidentally, our Carlos has got a mate in here, first offence and he got five years, poor little fucker's as straight as they come. He'll be shitting it in here, can you keep an eye out for me?'

'No probs Spanish, as long as he's not into little gels or boys, I'll put the word out he's with me and he'll be alright, what's his name?'

'Davy McKenzie, he's not a paedo mate, I'd let you do him if that was the case. He was in on a warehouse job and he got five cos he wouldn't give anyone up, poor bastard didn't even want to do it, his kid was threatened.'

'Yeah mate, I know who he is, I'll sort it. The bloke who threatened him, was it that Merry geezer? I've heard his name about the place.'

'That's him Tel, proper wanker and bully, he's got a sneaky little cousin who lives off him and tries to play the big man. Him and Carlos had a run in not long ago and Merry had to stop it, just as well cos I know who'd fucking win.'

Terry just laughs and then the bell goes and it's time to move on.

'You okay for another Visiting Order Spanish?' He asks. The big lump's got virtually no one else, it's heart breaking.

'Anytime mate, and I meant it about staying with me, it'll be great.'

He's happy with that, quick handshake and I'm away. I like to see Terry and keep his spirits up but this place shits me up something chronic.

Merry

'You go in love, I'll just park the car and make a couple of calls.' Off she goes, mini skirted little arse wiggling into Asda. Jesus, my balls must be huge by now, I could quite easily do her over the car bonnet and fuck the law I'm that desperate. I hope her condition sorts itself out soon, I think that doctor's taking the piss. No sex for three months, I'd be knocking people out left right and centre if I didn't have my other release valve on the side.

I'll give her ten minutes then catch her up, I fucking hate shopping and I need to think about something so this'll be a good time. I think it's about time I gave Billy Reeves a ring, I'm not getting any younger, I'm not exactly surrounded by quality and I know he needs the money because that bakery of his isn't making any. I also know he's desperate to get his mother off that estate and living down the coast, well, I can't give him that but I've got a contact who could get him any council house in Newcastle and that's got to be worth him thinking about.

It's strange how things have turned out for those two. I remember when they were just snotty beaked kids always playing football in the street, we had our run ins then like and I had to show them who was in charge but you do when you're young don't you? I've always rated them both, in fact, if they had a bit more ambition they could have been main players in this town. They've always seemed happy just to know everyone though, be respected but not feared, fucking weird outlook that is. To me respect and fear go hand in hand, that's why I'll always be top dog while they'll have to rely on charity from people like me to get anywhere in the world.

Still we're from the same estate so I don't mind giving the lads a leg up as long as they're grateful.

Yep, that's decided, I'll get Billy's number and invite him onto the firm. Might have some problems with Clarty but I'll sort them when they happen.

Lisa

Bingo, I've just asked young June if she can lend me a fiver until later so I can get some milk for the tea room and she hands me the marked one. I wrote thief across it in ultra violet pen, the type you can only see under those lights; we've got one for forged notes in the shop. I gave the fiver to one of the old dears and told her to spend it in the shop on anything she wanted as long as she kept it quiet and now it's in June's pocket.

'June, give me a hand in the tea room will you,' I say pleasantly enough and walk over to it. June follows me in smiling and thinking she can have a tab, wrong pet you can't.

'Shut the door and sit down,' my whole demeanour and tone has changed and it's thrown her right off balance.

She looks shaken and white faced, 'What's the matter Lisa?' she's asking.

I just put the fiver on the table in front of us and say, 'You tell me.'

She just starts to cry and I don't need to say any more, she's looking up saying 'Sorry, sorry.'

'Too late I'm afraid,' I reply, 'I can't trust you any more. You've got a choice, you can resign and we'll leave on good terms or you can make me sack you and then I'll have to tell Billy that you've been ripping him off; your choice.'

'Please don't tell Billy,' she's sobbing now all sorry for herself, 'I'll just go.'

'No,' I say, 'what you'll do is you'll stop crying and write out your notice. Then you'll work for the next two days and if you so much as look at any money that isn't yours I'll chop your fucking fingers off. Understand?'

'Yes Lisa, I'm really sorry.'

'Yeah pet, sorry you got caught.'

Problem number one dealt with, now for problem number two. I've been to the school about Peter and the fighting. I'm thinking he's being bullied so I didn't tell Billy as he's got a real thing about bullies and fighting back, I know he'd over-react.

When I get there I find out that my son is the fucking bully and the poor little sod he's been picking on with his mates has finally snapped and landed him one. I've told him already he's grounded and his dad's going to be dealing with him as I'm disgusted with what he's done.

I'm telling Billy tonight and he can go and see the other boy's dad.

Sharon

I couldn't believe it when I saw him in Asda, it was all I could do to stop myself running over and jumping his bones there and then. I'm going to have to tell him how I feel at some point, even if I never see him again, he has to know, this is killing me. I followed him around the shop for ages wary that Vince was outside in the car and he never even noticed me the cocky bastard. He looked a bit pre-occupied, a bit of deep thought going on there; I bet it wasn't about me though. In the end I waited until he was in the freezer aisle and I bent right into the one next to him, miniskirt covering nothing and saying everything, when I came up for air he was grinning at me.

'Oh Carlos,' I said, 'what a surprise, I didn't know you shopped in here.' He just moved towards me with a mad look on his face, looked like he was going to snog the face off me.

As he got closer, I said to him, 'There's something I've got to tell you.' I was ready. It was all going to come out; how much I loved him, how much I wanted him and to have his children and how I would run away with him at the drop of a hat. Sadly as well, how I would understand if he didn't feel the same way and if he felt it wasn't worth the upheaval this would cause because of Vince. I didn't get the chance though. As I drew breath to say all these things his eyes widened and his gaze fixed behind me, then a great shadow fell across us and I knew Vince had come in from the car.

'Carlos,' he said, 'have you got Billy's number I want to talk to him?' then he turned to me and asked, 'What were you going to say babe?'

As Carlos was digging out the number I just mumbled

something like 'Your colour never fades does it you must use stand 'n' tan?' and shuffled away to the sound of Vince's laughter ringing in my ears.

Barry

'Keep your hands up.'

Fuck me this is hard, Carlos is slapping me around the place here. He's not even punching me properly but I'm bouncing off every rope, panting like an old man and sweating like a pig. There's the bell, thank fuck for that. Look at him, he's not even out of breath, mind you, this has got to be doing me good. He's learning me to box which ought to come in well handy for my new job and there's always the chance I might get a go at one of his many ex-birds if I get fit enough. Having said that, his exes tend to only like pretty boys.

I take the headguard off and then the gloves. I'm hanging them back in the cubby-hole on the wall when a couple of the younger lads Hammy and Muzza wander in; a pair of up and coming fighters there and no mistake, not just in the ring either. Could be useful them two. Owld Dave's sweeping up at the other end by the front desk, he's run this place for years. Carlos has trained here for over twenty now and when he won those county titles at junior level they loved it here. As soon as he turned pro and had a bit of cash Dave brought him in as a partner, the publicity he generated doubled the turnover in the place straightaway and even though he's retired people still come and sign up just to train with him.

Most people still remember that famous British Heavyweight title fight with George Scott. He was in trouble from the start, Scott was heavier and bigger and just jabbed the fuck out of him and Carlos made the mistake of trying to have a toe to toe with him and got battered. He wouldn't fucking go down though, he took Scott the whole twelve rounds and got some good digs in. The tabloids called him 'The Battling Geordie' and did a few days worth of features on how hard we are and how we don't wear coats up here. At the end, when he was being interviewed by Sky, they asked him why he wouldn't throw the towel in and he just said, and I can still remember it word for word, 'I learnt at an early age not to run away or give in ever, if you start giving up then you spend your whole life doing it.' You can see Billy in the background when he's doing that interview and he's just staring across the hall at George Scott with his fists clenched.

He wasn't stupid though Carlos, he retired while his face was still intact and tried to break into modelling and advertising and that. He got offered a few things and even had an agent but it would have meant moving to London so he said fuck it and went to work with Billy. He's still got the pulling power for the local wannabes and hard men, loads of bouncers train in here, not many tonight though, in fact there's only a couple of us in and the two teenagers who've just came in the door.

Carlos

I need this tonight after this afternoon's episode; it's good to punch things when you feel like a prick. Still, get it out of my head and concentrate on this. Decent session this is with Barry, he's getting better. He was fuck all at school and got picked on a lot until one day me and him were outside a class a bit early and Merry and his mob walked around the corner.

They got hold of him and left me alone, mainly because of our Billy I think; they were pushing him around a bit and trying to make him cry in front of the girls who'd just turned up and they were loving it the hard faced bitches. I stepped in then. There were three of them and they were all bigger than me but I'd been boxing for a couple of years by then and knew a couple of tricks, I smacked the nearest one and put him on his arse then stood between Barry and the other two. Billy had taught me how to make a fence between me and anyone else so I did that and told them to come right ahead if they wanted it.

They were fifteen and I was twelve but they'd just seen me deck their mate and I was big for my age so they weren't too confident about their chances. Then Billy walked around the corner with his crew and all of a sudden they had somewhere else to be. Since then Barry's been our mate, as he was in my year at school he hung about with me more but he's always been in awe of our Billy since the Whitley Bay thing when we were young. Mind you so am I, Billy's never been a match fighter like me, he didn't like the boxing much but put him in the street with his back against the wall and he's a fucking animal. The cunt won't stop until it's over one way or another.

It's getting late now and I'm about ready for going home. Dave normally locks up, so I'm thinking about an early night and a bit of rest when Barry points out Hammy and Muzza to me and I wander over to them and introduce myself. Billy mentioned these two as the up and coming boys in Byker and asked me to have a word with them about me mam's house; there's a little squad of dickheads hanging around the back of hers drinking and sniffing glue and she's a bit worried about walking past them, especially when it's dark. They're a good pair of lads these two, they know the crew involved and they'll have a word. I've promised them a bit of extra tuition when I'm about and they're well happy, job's a good un. I'm just having a bit of a crack with the lads before I go when the unmistakeable shadow of steroid freak falls across my nice, clean, pure and drug free gym. I look at Barry and he's staring straight behind me, he doesn't look scared just wary, this obviously means I'm not getting an early night.

Billy

Had a phone call from Vince Merry, incidentally I'd love to know how that knob got my number, he wants to meet me, says he's got a proposition for me. I didn't really fancy it because any proposition from him will be shite and end up in me going to prison just like little Davey Mac, but I can't just tell him to fuck off, he's moved up the rankings a bit since school. I haven't really got time for this either, I wanted to talk to Lisa about the trouble Peter's been having at school, he's battered some kid apparently and got some detentions for it. I wanted to tell him well done sticking up for himself and that but she just said it was a lot more complicated and I needed to talk to the other boy's dad. No problems with that, I'm a reasonable man and I'm sure after our chat he'll agree to keep his son in check. Anyway that'll have to wait until tomorrow as I've agreed to meet Merry in The Raby. There's no point mentioning it to our lass, I just tell her I'm going out for a bit and she's asked me to give her a ring if I'm not going to be late in case she wants some food bringing back. That's love that is, not where are you going or who are you seeing, just get us a Chinese will you?

I love her to bits I do.

Clarty

Nearly at the gym and one of the lads asks if I'm alright, got a few nerves but nothing I can't handle, 'I'm a face in this town,' I reply, 'a fucking boy of the first order and Carlos Reeves is going to need to realise that.'

The other lad's face drops at the mention of Carlos, he obviously didn't know what he was getting into, well it's too late now we're here. I bound up the dimly lit stairs to the gym, there's an old bloke sweeping up by the front desk and the place stinks of sweat. I thought there'd be more people here to see Carlos get taken down a peg but it doesn't matter word soon gets around. I'm psyched up to fuck and ready to tear the place apart. The first bloke I spot is that Barry wanker looking at me from across the gym then Carlos, his back to me, in the corner with a couple of young lads. They picked the wrong night to come training but they'll be all right if they keep out of it.

'Hoo, dago twat,' my voice echoes across the mainly empty gym and bounces off the far wall, he doesn't look round. The cocky bastard's ignoring me. I can feel my temper rising and I try to control it and use it, 'I'm talking to you, you spic bastard,' my voice is rising, I'm almost shouting at him but still he ignores me. I grab the old bloke and push him against the wall, 'Look at me now you half caste cunt,' I almost command him but he just carries on training the young lads with his back to me. This is a battle of wills I won't lose, he's embarrassed me already outside the club and won't do it again. I'm just about to slam the old fucker's face into the wall when one of the lads with me shouts, 'Hoo, Carlos man.'

Now he turns around to face us, that big stupid grin on his face, laughing at me again saying, 'Oh, did someone want me?' I'm looking daggers at the prick with me who shouted and he shrugs as if to say sorry. Turning back to Reeves I'm primed to launch into him and the boys beside me are growling and ready to go when he holds his hand up and speaks.

'What do you want Clarty?'

I'd have thought it was obvious, 'You need to learn some respect Reeves and I'm the man to teach you.'

'Well,' he says, 'you don't need to come down here mob handed throwing owld fellas about. I'll get in the ring with you any time you want, that's if you're up to it like.'

He's making me look stupid again. I'm not taking this, I'm a big powerful bloke and I won't be talked to like a cunt.

'Okay get in that fucking ring, no headguards and no gum shields.'

I'll show this prick.

Merry

Billy's at the bar when I get there, good for him, he knows his place and didn't keep me waiting, that's what I like dealing with, someone who knows the score. Big Tony's with me, I rang Clarty as well but he's switched his phone off, he'd better be keeping out of trouble the twat.

While I nip to the toilet Tony moves a couple of young blokes out of the corner table, I always sit furthest from the door with my back against the wall as you never know in this town. The blokes don't even think of protesting and just move away, heads bowed. This is one of my pubs and the landlord pays me five hundred quid a week to put my name up to potential troublemakers, which normally puts them off. If it doesn't prevent them from kicking off and acting like arseholes then a visit from Tony and a couple of the lads will do the trick. I've been accused in the past of acting illegally but the landlord called me, they all do. Mind you what they don't realise is that I cause the bother in the first place; give a couple of hundred notes to some up and coming young team and they'll wreck the bar, do it twice and the landlord's calling me, pays for itself after a couple of weeks.

When I come back I beckon Billy over, a few of the locals notice this and there's a bit of a murmur round the bar. Billy's well known in this town and most people don't associate him with me, he's known as one of the nicer blokes in geordieland.

'Billy, how's it going? Take a seat.'

Tony's back with the drinks, 'got you a lager Bill, that right?' he asks.

'Aye Tony,' he says, 'sound.'

I don't think they know each other very well those two but they'll know about each other so there'll be mutual respect tonight which is good, I prefer dealing with grown ups.

'So,' Billy's looking at me now, 'what's this proposition you've got for me Vince?'

I pause and just stare at him for a little while unnerving him a bit; I've read loads of those cockney gangster books and they all do the same things, I've tried to use some of their everyday stuff myself. Funny how they all claim to be the hardest man in London at the same time though and that none of them have ever lost a fight, maybe I should write a book? Yeah, he's blinked twice now, I've got him, time for my spiel.

'Tony, go and play on the bandit for a bit.' Tony stares at Billy for a couple of seconds, that's good as well. I don't want those two becoming too friendly just professional associates who'd sell each other out without a second thought, then he gets up and walks over to the bandit without a word. I look back at Billy, he's realised this is important and is all ears. Here we go.

'Billy I'll get straight to the point. I'm not getting any younger, the business is expanding faster than I can manage it and there's no one with any brains working for me,' I nod towards Tony.

'He's alright for certain physical things but any other job

and he's a bit dense.' Tony's good at punching people and nothing else. End of. Billy's looking interested already.

'The thing is I know you can think on your feet and have got some intelligence in there. I also know that your bakery is losing money and that you want you mother moving out of Byker.'

He's giving nothing away at all, just looking straight at me, those steely blue eyes fixed on mine. You know there are times when, if I was someone else, I'd find Billy Reeves a scary proposition.

'Anyway, I need a right hand man and I'm offering you the chance to come on board with me. I'll give you a grand a week and ten percent of any future money you bring into the organisation,' I saw that on Miami Vice yesterday on Sky Gold and I've been practicing it all day.

'What do you say?'

Carlos

This bloke is a proper mug. I can't believe he got in the ring with me, I'm an ex-professional for fucks sake. He's watched a couple of fights on the telly and thinks it's easy, the same type of prick who used to slag Frank Bruno off but would have been knocked out in two seconds by him. He fell for all of the pre-fight stuff as well. I made him wait until they'd addressed me properly before I'd speak to them and then I goaded him into getting in the ring. He was so scared of losing face that he was prepared to get in here rather than look scared in front of anyone and now I'm going to tear his fucking face clean off. The two boys with him don't want to fight, I know them both and one of them was here last week asking about joining up. Their body language when they came in was showing them off badly, they were not interested at all. I told Hammy and Muzza to fuck off if they didn't want to get involved but wild horses wouldn't keep them away from this, watching a live fight is better than all of the training books in the world.

The bell goes and we're off. As I expected he's tearing into me throwing punches left right and centre, all telegraphed a few seconds before he's thrown them. Piece of piss. I'm throwing the odd jab now and then just to see what he's got, I know the prick's never done any boxing before, in fact I doubt he's done anything but weightlifting, he'll be fucked before the end of this round.

Right then, strategy time, Ali the greatest boxer in the world, after me like anyway, he had a tactic called 'rope a dope.' Basically he'd back off up to the ropes kidding on he was fucked and take a load of punches off his opponent when in reality he'd be covering up that well none of them would get through and his opponent would be tired right out halfway through the round, Ali would then blitz the fucker and more times than not it would be game over. Well I hesitate to use the phrase 'rope a dope' on this clueless twat, it would be an insult to dopes and to the proper boxers that Ali put away, I think I'll call this 'hunt a cunt.'

About a minute in now and he's huffing and puffing, I'm just backing off continually, jab and move, jab and move, he's throwing haymakers from behind his head that are about a foot out, fuck me has this wanker ever had a fight? Think I'll practice me dancing a bit, might as well get some kind of workout out of this before I knock him out.

Billy

Tricky one this, numbnuts has just asked me to join the firm. He's sitting there playing Don Corleone again and come out with a load of shite about helping me out and getting me mam a new house. Prick'll want me to kiss his ring in a minute but that's more his cousin's line of work, know what I mean? He made a fucking entrance as well, got Big Tony to shift a couple of lads so he could have their table, then he goes to the bog and comes out with a drippy nose, must have a cold eh?

I hope no one thinks I'm friendly with this twat, I'd be mortified. I don't think he realises that me and Tony sort of know each other either, best keep it that way for the time being. I can see Tony feels the same way, he's playing the game, giving me big stage glares and that. I had to stop myself from giggling the first time. Right, stall for a bit of thinking time here,

'Another pint Vince?' I've grabbed his glass and I'm strid-ing off to the bar before he can answer. The problem here is that in my eyes Merry is a fucking knob of the highest order but he's also numero uno in the toon and if I piss him off too much he could order a lot of damage doing to me and mine. I've got a lot to lose here and I'll have to play it carefully.

'Mate of yours Billy?' old Tadger behind the bar almost spits the question out.

I just roll my eyes at him derisively and he smiles, getting the message, Merry is not a well liked man in most parts of this city.

'Didn't think so like,' he says, 'he's not your usual style.'

I just smile back at him saying nowt. The problem is I'm not scared of Merry or any of his hangers on. I could take any one of them in a square go or a straightener, the problems arise when five or six of the muppets turn up at your house at three in the morning. Now again, I'm not averse to making the odd home visit myself if the issue is serious enough to warrant it but I just don't want the hassle of being a fucking gangster, plastic or otherwise. If I get tangled up with that mob then people like Tadger for instance see me as one of them and I don't want that. People have respect for me because I've earned it over the years and that's something I'm not willing to throw away. It's important to me that I don't let my family down by becoming a wanker and an embarrassment. The money would have been handy but I'm doing okay now, bills paid and a bit of spare at the end of the month to put away for the old lady's retirement home. I've got a good life all round; nice house, lovely kids, sexy wife who thinks I'm great and quality of life that's the important thing.

Yeah, mind made up, need to tell that big cunt to fuck off, just do it politely. Something else has just struck me as well, Carlos never got mentioned, and surely even Merry knows that where I go Carlos Fandango follows.

'There you go Vince,' bending to put the pints down I don't notice Big Tony behind me, all of a sudden there's a shovel like hand on my shoulder.

'Where's mine you tight bastard,' he growls at me.

The fucker has actually got me lined up for a headbutt, the fence goes up automatically as I take a half step back and I look straight into those evil fucking eyes.

'He's pouring it now,' I lie, 'fucking problem?'

Merry's in between us now fussing like a big girl. Tony is either putting on one hell of a performance or the twat has a genuine problem with me, not sure I can tell myself but he's sat back down anyway.

When I get back from the bar with his soda water Merry's obviously had a word with him as he stands up and downs it in one, then as he's getting the car keys out of his pocket he looks at me and says, 'Be seeing you then,' before he fucks off.

'I told him to wait in the car,' Merry pipes up, 'this is a grown up's conversation and he couldn't behave. You and him know each other then?'

'Not really,' I say. Not strictly a lie as we're not mates or anything like that.

'Anyway,' Merry snaps back into what he thinks is business mode, 'what do you think to my proposition?'

I'm ready for this and I'm going to play it deferential, he's a big headed egotistical cunt who thinks he's a 'Goodfella' and he loves it when people bow down to him.

'The thing is Vince I'm going to have to say no,' ooh that surprised him, 'now it's nothing personal, in fact if anything it's me not you.'

'Go on,' he says, obviously pissed off.

'Well since I met our lass and had the kids I've just had no stomach for this type of thing. You know at school I could have a fight and I was up for anything but these days I just want to sit on the settee with a cup of tea and a dvd.'

He's brightened up now, he's swallowing all this shite and it's time to go super arselicker.

'You're good at this Vince, you can deal with all the shit that goes with it but I'm not sure I can and I don't want to risk what I've got now and fall flat on my face.' He's loving it, time for the clincher.

'And most of all I wouldn't want to let you down.'

I am fighting really fucking hard not to smile, the sincerity is dripping from every pore. If he thinks I'm taking the piss then me and the family'll have to move house but luckily the prick's so far up his own arse he believes everything I'm saying, now he's nodding, doing his best to look all De Niro like.

'Billy,' he says, extending his hand across the table, 'it takes a big man to admit he's not up to something, I've got to say I admire your honesty, we'll take this no further.' As he gets up I decide to ask him something that's been bugging me since the initial offer.

'What about Carlos?' I say innocently, 'Do you want me to have the conversation with him?' He turns to look at me with a smug, knowing smile on his fat, steroid freak face.

'I've already got plenty of brawn,' he says, 'I just wanted some more brain. Carlos wasn't invited.' Then with that he's off. Cheeky bastard. I can see his point but he's not exactly Jeremy fucking Paxman himself is he?

Clarty

The first round wasn't too difficult I was pounding the Spanish prick to bits. He just kept trying to dance away and cover up on the ropes but he wasn't quick enough and I was lashing into him.

I'm a bit out of breath now like but the punishment I gave him he must be well fucked. There's the bell again, now's the time to let people know I'm a man to be feared. Down in two Carlos.

Ex-pro? Boxers are fuck all.

Barry

'I thought he could fight?' one of the bouncers that came in with Clarty is shouting across the ring.

I just smile at him cos I know what's coming. In about thirty seconds time Clarty's going to be in a whole world of hurt.

Carlos

Ding. Ding.

Here we go then, the mong's actually smirking at me as he waddles that oversized frame across the ring. He thinks he's got me, oh thank you God. He throws a right, I slip it, move half a step and give him a hard jab in the nose.

'Welcome to school prick,' I shout.

The smirk has left his face and the penny's dropping, soon to be followed by the cottaging, steroid freak. He's stepping back hands in front of his face as I spray punches at him. Up against the ropes protecting his chin elbows sticking out all over the place, it's like an invitation for body shots. Don't mind if I do I think as I pound into his body, ooh there goes a rib. His face is contorted in pain and he drops his guard to cover his body, oh dear, oh dear, oh dear. Three punch combination to the face and he's got a broken nose and probably a fractured cheekbone. I could have knocked him out in a oner but there's no fun in that. He's all over the place now, doesn't know what to cover or how to do it and there's at least thirty seconds to go yet. I'm just dancing round him picking holes and hitting him hard, not enough to put him down but enough to hurt the fucker. Then he looks at me and I swear he sneers, well as much as you can when your face hurts so much you want to cry, and he says, 'I know you're fucking Sharon and I'm telling Vince.'

The look on his face tells me he thinks he's beat me the smug prick. If he's telling Merry anyway then I may as well put the cunt away, but first, maybe I'll let him know that me and Billy know a little secret about him.

'When you tell him that then make sure you mention that one of the judges at the Crown Court fucks you up the arse once or twice a week.' I shout loud enough for everyone to hear. He looks totally shocked and properly embarrassed, then he rushes me screaming he's going to kill me. I just step aside, do a shuffle and wrong foot him and then I look over to his two bouncer mates and shout.

'Can you drink steroids through a straw?'

They look at each other in puzzlement as I tap his ribs again and bring his hands away from his face. I've positioned him perfectly for my trademark right hook. As the sound of fist hitting bone echoes across the gym it's mirrored by a loud crack as his jawbone breaks away from the rest of his skull. He hits the floor a second later white and puking through pain. I just take my gloves off and walk away.

I can hear Barry laughing and then shouting over to Clarty's mates, 'You were saying lads?'

I just look at them and growl, 'So have you two got a problem with me as well?' They can't shake their heads quick enough and one of them even looks a bit faint.

I let them off the hook, even though they came here for bother, and just nod my head at the horizontal fighting champion saying, 'Get that piece of shit out of my gym.'

Now I'd best ring Billy so he knows what's happened and pre-warn him that it's going to get ugly with Merry.

Thursday

Merry

Billy Reeves must think I'm some kind of prick, he must think we're still at school. I admit the smartarse bastard used to run rings around me then but I've grown up a bit now and I didn't get to be the main man in geordieland without a bit of nous. I reckoned he was going to knock me back, the same way that I know if I want to I can just make him work for me. The thing is though if I force him then he'll be an enemy inside the camp and he's clever enough to cause havoc.

No, he's going to work for me alright, he's going to make me a lot of money as well, but I'm not going to make him. He's going to come and ask me for a job because soon he'll have nowhere else to go. He left his phone on the table when he went to get the beers in and now its mine, he probably hasn't even realised yet.

Game on.

Maxwell

Hmm this is getting a bit tricky now and my shady little friend is getting a bit greedy as well. The demands that are being made are becoming unacceptable, maybe I'll have to take steps to remove this particular problem. I'll discuss it with Merry tonight; he's good at this type of thing.

Billy

'Fucks sake where is it?' I can't find my bastard phone any-where and I'm late now to go and see this lad's dad about our Peter.

'Lisa, have you had my phone?' I'm shouting now, I never shout.

'No darling, do you want to borrow mine?'

She looks lovely as usual, always makes an effort. Strange the way we got together as well, I still don't know how I pulled her actually. I'd met her before when I was fourteen; when I done my knee playing for the school team up at Kenton. I was sprawled on the grass near the touchline cos I couldn't stand up and she wandered along with a couple of mates. They were giving me all that girly shite, 'my mate really fancies you,' that type of thing and as I couldn't go anywhere cos I couldn't move I just called their bluff and said yeah I really fancy her as well. Once they'd stopped giggling her mates fucked off and she sat down and started talking to me. We got on really well and I wasn't kidding I did fancy her, bit of a struggle mind holding my gut in for an hour. When the match was finished the rest of the lads came and got me and carried me into the minibus. She asked for my number and I had to admit we didn't have a phone in the house, god I was embarrassed, I just went red after that cos everyone was taking the piss out of me but she was dead cool and just wrote her number on a bit of paper and gave it to me. I rang her a couple of times and we got on great but she lived too far away so we just drifted away from each other but then I bumped into her again in a pub when I was twenty one.

Me, Carlos and Barry were in town down the Bigg Market one Friday night and Carlos had pulled as per usual and was flaunting her in our faces before doing off to shag her. Me and Barry were acting disinterested, but were gutted really, when I noticed across the bar, through the mass of bodies and sweat, a face I recognised. She was with a couple of mates and a few lads, one lad in particular appeared to be her boyfriend so I thought I'd just leave it and didn't try to attract her attention or nothing, but then she noticed me. She smiled at me from the other side of the room and it was like no one else was there, it's a proper cliché and I know I sound like a twat but I think I loved her from then on.

The lads who were with them went to get the drinks in and she came over to me to say hello. I couldn't believe it, she was fucking gorgeous and she was talking to me. Obviously I was dead pleased Carlos had fucked off by now, cos he'd have been smoothing right on in there and I'd have had to kill him. Anyway we were just chatting and catching up a bit, Barry seemed to be doing okay with her mate as well, when the lads came back. They didn't speak to us like just grabbed the lasses arms and started to pull them away. The lass Barry was talking to was all meek and mild and went to move off with her bloke but Lisa was having none of it, she just looked him straight in the eye and said something along the lines of, 'I'll talk to anyone I want.'

I couldn't believe what happened next, the prick only slapped her hard across the face, it was like slow motion, I was shocked. Then she stepped back and started crying, I looked at her and wanted to protect her from everyone and everything for the rest of her life. I could have just swept her up in my arms there and then and carried her off.

Instead, I stepped towards the red faced, beer breathed prick she was with and buried my forehead deep in his fucking nose. By the time the bouncers pulled me off him he was an absolute mess. I haven't been filled with rage like that since, not even when I was sticking up for Carlos. Barry said my eyes had gone and he'd never seen me like that before. Everyone sees me as the cool, calm, collected one and our Carlos as the short tempered one but that night I lost the plot. Mind you, I reckon everyone's got it in them to do it once. Anyway, her mate took her to the bog and we waited outside for her and her pal. Her, by now ex-boyfriend, had gone to hospital with his mate and I was starting to feel the aftermath of our encounter. By the time she came out I was convinced she'd think I was an animal who was no better than the future wife beater she'd started the night with. I had to wait though just in case and I'm glad I did.

When she came out she looked straight at me and walked towards me slowly. As she got to me I actually thought she was going to hit me or something but she just kissed me gently on the lips and said, and I'll never ever forget this, 'I've been waiting seven years for you Reeves. What kept you?'

We've been together ever since and have barely spent the night apart since we were married, I tell her I love her every single day and do you know what, it's true.

Wish I could find me fucking phone though.

Merry

Just had a phone call off one of the lads, Clarty's in hospital, took a right hiding last night apparently. I'd better get up there and see him, I'm not that bothered about the cunt I just want to find out the score. An attack on him is more than likely an attack on me and if anyone's playing games then they'll have to suffer - publicly. Can't find Sharon anywhere either, she'd better be here later, I'm fucking starving.

Sharon

I'm shitting myself. Still it's going to be out in the open soon, Carlos rang me last night and told me to get out and hide somewhere, so I've come to my auntie's in Berwick. I can't believe that sneaky little rat Clarty found out, I hope Carlos hurt him bad, oh god, I hope Vince doesn't kill him. I hope he doesn't kill me as well, he's always promised me that if I ever played away he'd kill the bloke in front of me and then do me afterwards.

Milo

This publisher is getting right on my nerves now, apparently putting away the inside man on a big job for five years isn't enough of a story to finish my memoirs on and he reckons what I need is a real big, gruesome story. I can see his point but opportunities are few and far between and I'm running out of time. There's a lot of violence in this town but no one significant ever gets it, just the rank and file and the criminal element.

Wonder if I could get a contract out on Ant 'n' Dec?

Merry

Clarty is in a right fucking state. Carlos Reeves has done him in goodstyle; fractured ribs, broken jaw, broken nose, severe bruising and cuts. The doctor reckoned he might have had internal bleeding as well, fucks sake, why can't the prick stay out of trouble?

I've found out the story as well, turns out Clarty went to his gym and fucking challenged him in front of his mates. What did he expect the knob? I don't like Carlos but he's no mug. I might have to let this one go. At the end of the day Carlos couldn't back down to a direct challenge like that and Clarty was a dick for trying it on with a heavyweight like him. I'd better go back in there and tell him.

Clarty

That nurse better give me some decent painkillers tonight, I don't know what's worse my jaw, ribs or fucking nose, I'm in bastard agony here. I've had plenty of time to think about things while I've been laid up though and it may just be possible to work this to my advantage. If I tell Vince about Carlos and Sharon he'll go off his nut and want Carlos killed. If Vince makes noises or even attempts to have Carlos done in then Billy will automatically go toe to toe with Vince; no question. The likelihood is that the three of them will end up dead, locked up or seriously fucked and no competition to me when I come out of hospital. Maybe I'll get Tony into the mix as well and see what happens.

Time to come clean to my dear cousin about the woman he loves, might use my own dirty little secret as well, that should be enough to send him over the edge.

Big Tony

Rumour has it that Carlos Reeves gave Clarty a proper hiding last night. He fucking deserved it as well by all accounts, going into the blokes own gym, his fucking livelihood, and calling him out. I never thought Clarty was that stupid, just goes to show. The other part of the story is the most interesting though, apparently Clarty is a shirt-lifter and he's been shagging a judge. That could look bad for Merry; people will think he's a grass. Let's face it he's never been put away for anything and he always profits when someone else goes down. Maybe I should plant that seed in a few heads as well, could be beneficial to me that.

This'll probably lead to a bit of bother for the Reeves boys and Merry will want me there. I like Billy and Carlos and I don't want to be involved against them, I'll have to decide soon when and how to make my move. Billy played it just right with me in front of Merry the other night, he thinks we don't like each other and now I sneer whenever his name is mentioned, keeps the fucking coke monster confused and that's the state I want him in.

Merry

I cannot believe what I am fucking hearing. I'm looking at Clarty all fucked up on the bed, bandaged, wired and in pain, I'm all set to be sympathetic to him and he tells me this. He's a fucking puff, worse than that, he's getting shagged up the arse off of Maxwell my business partner, I want to smack the filthy twat. He's telling me he's always been different from everyone else and it won't make a difference to us cos we're family. Fuck that, he's not getting in the showers with me at the gym any more the weirdo.

Fucking hell, he's saying Carlos shouted it before he broke his jaw last night, it'll be all round town by now. Bollocks. Now what's he saying, I can't make him out very well with that wire through his fucking skull, I think he said Carlos is shagging Sharon.

'Say that again you twat,' I growl at him.

He's making this up to cover his own stupidity in taking on Carlos, the prick wants me to sort it out for him, does he think I'm fucking stupid?

'Do you think I'm fucking stupid you fucking huckle?' I'm shouting at him. A nurse bursts in disturbed at the noise, I just scream at her, 'Fucking get out,' and she's back out the door again sharpish.

'Do you think Carlos Reeves would cross me like that? It's

just you trying to get him sorted out cos he done you.'

'No cuz,' he's almost whispering, 'ask Sharon, watch her face, I swear they're at it I've been following them.'

She has been a bit distant for a while like and it would make sense if she was having an affair. I'll let him get it off his chest while I think about it.

'Go on,' I growl at him.

It's all coming out now. He's suspected for ages so he followed her, they've been using a hotel out of town and that's why he went to see Carlos last night. If it's true, and it might not be, then I've got to give the knacker credit for taking Carlos on by himself for me. If that's the case he has gone right up in my estimation. What's he saying now?

'I did it for you cuz. I know you love her and I just wanted to warn him off but he went mental and beat the shit out of me.'

Carlos fucking Reeves shags my bird and smashes my cousin to bits. That cunt is dead. This has been coming for years, since we were kids really and if Billy gets involved then he can die as well. I shout the nurse back in and she looks all worried when she pops her head round the door.

'Sorry about earlier pet, I'm a bit emotional, make sure my cousin here gets everything he wants eh.' I slip her fifty quid and she's made up.

I look back at Clarty, the only loyal fucker to me in this city, 'I'll see you later mate, by the time you come out this'll all be sorted so don't worry about it.' He looks back at me trying to smile, all brave even though he's in loads of pain, the poor little bastard. Right, let's go and see Sharon. Then Carlos dies.

Maxwell

I've arranged to meet my blackmailer at 19.00, I'll ring Merry and get him here for 18.30 then we can have this episode put to bed, so to speak.

'Vincent; Maxwell here,' he sounds very tense.

'I've got a problem I need some help with, usual rates.' He's very non-committal, only saying yes and no, it's like he can't say anything else for fear of letting something slip.

'Yes, I need you here at 18.30, it may get messy so be prepared. Thanks, bye.' I don't know what his problem is but he'd better snap out of it, I need professionalism not working class mood swings.

Carlos

Nothing's happened yet but it's only a matter of time, I've tried to get hold of Billy all day but he's not answering his phone. I can't even get me mam to move her out of harms way, she must be out shopping or something and she refuses to have a mobile. Fucking twenty-first century, the communications age and I can't get hold of any fucker, I'd better let Barry know the score just in case.

Merry

Sharon's not at home and not answering her phone, quick check of the wardrobe and guess what, all of her clothes are gone, that answers all of my questions now. Carlos is a dead man, Billy too if he wants it and maybe even that Barry twat they hang around with. I'd best round up the posse for the lynching.

Before I get the chance though that beast Maxwell rings me, the dirty bastard who has taken advantage of my little cousin. He wants me to go round tonight and sort someone out for him, fucking right I will, might not be just the one person getting straightened out though, filthy twat.

Billy

This lad's dad is all right, I was expecting him to have a go and I even had a bat in the car, just in case, but he's ok. In fact he's a bit scared and being a bit too respectful and from what I'm hearing it's my boy who's in the wrong. They're obviously skint and apparently Peter's been taking the piss out of their boy for being a tramp so he's finally flipped and had a go and they've both got detentions. Well, I'm not having that, I fucking hate bullies and my boys aren't going to be doing that. I spent enough of my youth fighting bullies so they wouldn't have to. I'll be having words with that little wanker when I get home.

I look around their threadbare, ramshackle house and ask the bloke, Ray his name is, how long he's been on the dole. Five years he reckons, fucking soul destroying that would be. Then I ask him, carefully watching his reactions, if he actually wants a job. Fuck me he's almost angry with me, 'Of course I fucking do. So does our lass an' all. We don't want to live like this ye kna and with young Michael at school all day we've got the time now. I always get turned down though, I'm in my forties now so I'm fucked.' He's slumped back into his chair now, he looks a broken man.

'I'm not having a go Mr. Reeves,' he says, 'life's just so hard and this thing happening with your boy, well, we could do without it to be honest. I don't want any trouble with you.'

I could fucking cry, I really could. A decent family struggling against the odds and they're scared of what could happen because their son has defended himself against mine. They must see me as some kind of horrible arsehole like Merry.

Time to put things right, 'Do you know my bakery Ray?' I ask him.

'The one on the High Street? Yeah I know it, our lass's mam sometimes goes in on a Wednesday morning for us.'

'Yeah mate that's the one, well I need a delivery driver for buffets and things like that, have you got a driving licence?'

Fuck me he's perked up now, 'Yes mate it's clean as well cos I can't afford a car.'

'Right then,' I say standing up, 'I'll talk to our lass, she runs the bakery and she'll want to talk to you. Oh, has your wife ever done any shop work because Lisa mentioned someone was leaving the other day so there might be a few days a week going there as well if she fancies it?'

He's absolutely beaming now, this feels good, I'm in the wrong line of work, I should join the Red Cross or something.

'Last thing Ray, I'm assuming you haven't got a computer?' He just laughs and shrugs his shoulders as if to say yeah mate whatever.

'Well my son Peter is going to be inviting your lad round to do his home work on his pc every couple of nights from now on, just so you know.'

He is well chuffed, 'I don't know what to say Mr. Reeves,' he looks a bit embarrassed.

I'm walking out the door when I look back at him and say, 'Don't get me wrong Ray, it's not charity mate, I'll expect you to graft for your money, but I'm always prepared to help someone who'll help themselves and us working class lads have to stick together mate, if we start fucking each other over then we're all in trouble.'

With that I'm out of the door and in the car, I'm feeling good when I start it up and what happens, the radio kicks in on that poxy station again but what's on? It's only The Levellers and that one about the day being beautiful...fuck me, they're not wrong either.

Maxwell

I really must get the cleaner to start doing this, polishing my own silver is just a little bit too taxing for me these days. I don't mind doing this one though, my award from the Law Society for twenty years as a Crown Court Judge; it's a solid silver gavel, a replica of the normal one I use in court and it's very dear to me.

Bbbbrrrriiiiinnnngggggg, Bbbbrrrriiiiinnnngggggg

Who's that at the door then? It's only six so it can't be Merry he's always on time.

'Oh it's you, you're early, come in.'

'Take a seat. As you can see I was just cleaning my silver collection; drink?'

'Yes I've got some red wine in the kitchen, shan't be a mo.'

'What are you doing with that?'

'Please put the gavel down, it's of great sentimental value.'
'What are you doing, no sto...'

Merry

Oh dear, the judge doesn't look very well, looks very dead in fact I'd better ring Milo.

'Milo, problem mate; do you know where Judge Maxwell lives?'

'Well, you'd better make it your business, I'm telling you this is fucking serious.' Think I'll have a livener before he gets here as well, help me think.

Sssnniiiifffff.

Milo

I get to Maxwell's house in about ten minutes, Merry wouldn't say what the problem was but I can guess, it's all round town about his cousin and the Judge. I park the car around the corner, out of the way, and walk to the house; the front door is ajar and the hall light is on. As I walk in Merry appears at the living room door shaking his head, he's got gloves on and looks genuinely unhappy.

'What's the problem Vince?' I ask him.

He just points inside the room; Maxwell is sprawled out on the floor in an ever increasing pool of blood. On closer inspection he appears to have been simply bludgeoned to death, no finesse whatsoever; in fact it's Mr. Merry's modus operandi to a T. The wheels are turning in Merry's head as I look up to face him and he instinctively blurts out, 'It wasn't me, I just found him like that.'

A bit too quick Vincent, 'Why are you wearing gloves?' I ask curtly.

'It's cold outside,' he whispers back a befuddled expression on his face.

'You're the biggest hardest bloke in a city full of big hard blokes, you wear a T-shirt in winter and can bench press your own bodyweight yet you wear gloves cos it's a little bit cold.

Fuck off Merry, I know about your cousin, why are you wearing gloves?'

'He called me to come here and help him out with a problem. I was going to slap him about a bit and tell him to leave Clarty alone but I never killed him Mr. Milo, I swear he was like this when I got here.' He's pleading now, beads of sweat decorating his forehead.

To be honest I don't know if he killed him or not and I don't care. *'Crown Court Judge killed in own home'.* This'll be national and will easily be big enough to climax my book. My publisher will be creaming himself over this; I just need to solve it quick.

'Right,' I say snapping back into business mode, 'who else knows about this?'

Carlos

Text from our Billy, 'meet me at 63 Osborne Road Jesmond.'

A bit mysterious for him. I'll ring him first; it's probably to talk tactics about Merry. He hasn't had the chance to bollock me yet either so he'll be wanting to do that, no answer though.

Another text, cant talk, just meet me asap,' I'd best get over there, I'll try me mam again first though.

'Mam,' thank fuck she's in this time, 'where've you been? Right, sorry mam no time for that, well aye I hope you have had a nice day, but really there's no time. Look man stop talking and listen to us.' She's a fucking nightmare when she's been on the wine, been at it all day an' all by the sounds of it.

'Listen I need you to go and stay with me auntie Marjorie for a while, don't ask questions, it's important and there's not much time. Billy'll ring you later but for now I'll send Barry to get you and take you there, just pack some stuff and be ready to go, it's important mam.'

Right, ring Barry then off we go, 'Barry; Carlos; can you do us a favour mate? It's all about to hit the fan after last night, can you run me mam to Marjorie's?'

'Aye, I've got to meet Billy in Jesmond, he's just texted us now, I'll let you know what happens mate.'

'Sound. Cheers, see you later.'

Toying with the idea of ringing Sharon, fuck it, I'll just send a text 'luv u lots, c u soon,' I feel like a teenage charva now, fuck it send it anyway. Right then, quick scoot across town and see what's occurring.

Billy

I've explained the score to Lisa and she's going to see Ray and his lass about the jobs tomorrow, she wanted to talk to Peter but I think this is a man to man job. I was foaming at first but he's not a bad lad and I think guidance and encouragement is the way to go here, if he keeps it up he's getting his arse kicked but let's give the lad a chance. We're in his room surrounded by JLS and Russell Brand posters, that's a bit worrying mind, no hold on, it's alright I've just spotted a couple of Abi Titmuss and Rihanna. Good lad.

'Right son,' I say sitting down with two cups of tea, he loves a cup of tea with his old man does our Peter and I want him to be comfortable with me and not defensive.

'What's the score with you and Michael Drummond, bearing in mind before you start that I've been to see his old man and your teacher so I've got a pretty good idea anyway?' He's gone a bit red and slurps his tea, playing for time while he thinks; he's got that from me I reckon.

'Well dad,' he starts, 'to be honest, I've been having a bit of a laugh with him and he just can't take a joke; he went mental and started punching me.'

'And?' I'm looking him right in the eye now.

'Well, you told me never to let anyone do that so I had to fight back, then a teacher came and we got detention.'

Even he doesn't believe the having a laugh bit I can tell; maybe it's time he learnt a bit more about my upbringing.

'This having a laugh son, did it involve you and other lads calling him a tramp and a gyppo?'

He's looking shamefaced now, can't look at me.

'Well did it?' firmer tone of voice, pressing him.

'Yes,' he squeaks, head down, 'but it wasn't just me.'

'Oh,' I say, 'that's alright then a big gang of you calling him a tramp and making him feel like shit. That's bullying Peter, how would you like it? Answer me that son.'

'I wouldn't dad, I just went along with it, it wasn't just me,' he's snivelling a bit now and I'm melting, it wasn't meant to make him cry just make him think.

'Listen son,' I say putting an arm around him, 'drink your tea and I'll tell you a story about me and your uncle Carlos when we were about your age, then tell me what you think about bullies.'

So he cheers up a bit, pleased that his dad isn't actually bollocking him, and starts to drink his tea. I tell him the story about Merry when we were young, how he used to bully us and make us cry, how we didn't have a dad to protect us; well Carlos did but he wasn't about that often.

I tell my boy how his old man used to be reduced to a quivering wreck by this big wanker and how if he saw me then I wouldn't be his hero now. Then I tell him how Carlos and me grew up with fuck all and how our mam worked loads of hours just to put food on the table, there was no room for luxuries. We used to nick crates of empty bottles from the working men's clubs in Byker and sell them to the Asian shop down the hill just to have a bit of cash in our pockets.

I tell him how we had to have free school meals and free school uniforms and couldn't go on school trips; how Merry used to give it to us large style about this every day of our lives. Then I tell him how, in the end, with a little prodding from Grandma Val, we snapped and fought back. From that day on he left us alone and we both realised that you could never back down from a bully or you would be shit on for the rest of your life.

Then I look him in the eye again, he looks a bit shaken and I say very gently, 'So I was a tramp son, would you have picked on me as well?'

He starts to cry and just puts his head down, lesson learnt I think. I give him a big hug and he's sobbing, 'Sorry dad, I never realised, I never thought, I'm sorry, I'm sorry.'

I lift his head up again and tell him, 'All part of growing up son, it takes a bigger man to say sorry. I want you to make a friend of young Michael if you can and I'd like you to offer him around here to do his homework. Do you think you can do that?'

'I can dad and I will,' he says, 'I'm really sorry.'

'You don't have to say sorry to me son, I'm your dad, say sorry to Michael though; and do me a favour, let him think Ray, his dad, sorted this out.'

He looks puzzled, 'Why dad?'

'Because son, Ray may well have slipped down the hero ladder recently in Michael's eyes and it would be nice if he thought he could still rely on his old man don't you think?'

He's smiling back, 'No problem dad, I'll sort it out.'

'Good lad, now give us your cup while you brush your teeth.'

I've got a real sense of doing something good as he skips off to the bathroom and I head downstairs. In a way it was a bit therapeutic for me telling the boy all that, I haven't even told Lisa some of it, maybe this talking about how you feel stuff isn't a load of shite. Maybe.

Milo

In position now around the corner, timing is everything here, Reeves could see the body and do a bolt then there are no witnesses and no suspect.

Here he comes now, past the entrance to the street I'm in and is presumably stupid enough to park up outside number sixty-three. Merry's had the signal from me, he's ringing 999 to report the sounds of a violent struggle emanating from the house then he's going to fuck off out of the way. I'm going to intercept the call and let everyone know I'm in the area as soon as it hits the radio, should be enough to stop Reeves disappearing.

There it goes now, looks like I'm on. 'CI Milo, I'm in area and responding now.'

That's surprised them. 'Are you sure sir? We'll be there in three minutes.'

'No problem, I'm not afraid of getting my hands dirty, just get here quick in case it's ugly.'

Here goes, take a last look at freedom Mr. Reeves.

Merry

I've put the call in and now I'm in The Gate in the town to make sure I'm seen having a couple of pints and a laugh with the doormen. I wanted to lash Billy's phone as well, no point in tempting fate, but Milo wants it bringing round to him tomorrow for safe keeping. It's probably best; it could fuck the whole case up if that gets into the wrong hands.

Carlos

The street is quiet and dark, the type of place Freddy Kruger jumps out at you. The door's ajar at sixty-three, Billy must be inside; I push at the door and it just slides completely open without a sound. That's what I like about this area, quality of workmanship; you can tell these aren't council houses; it's a real money area. I might try and move round here one day. Even in the hall you can smell the money; big pictures going up the stairs, good quality carpet, all solid oak furniture, aye whoever lives here has done alright, probably a mate of Billy's.

For all that though there's something not quite right about this, it's too quiet, if Billy was here he'd be out to greet me by now, maybe he's in trouble and it's a setup. I'm straight back out to the car, I'm not running away and leaving Billy in the shit, just going to even the odds. Get 'The Equaliser' out of the boot, my favourite weapon, it's a rounders bat that I've customised with lead weights, makes it a lot heavier at one end and gives it a fucking evil swing. I've only ever used it a couple of times as the sight of it is normally enough to persuade people to think again.

I creep back in and suss the layout of the place. The hall stretches about twenty feet to the open kitchen door, the living room comes off the hall about ten feet along and the door is half open. Thinking quick I throw an ornament from the hall into the kitchen, as it shatters I'm behind the living room door waiting for them to come rushing out. Nothing.

Fuck it, I'm going in. I take a big breath and boot the door, rushing into the living room I scream, 'COME ON THEN YOU CUUUNTS,' and swing the bat as viciously as I can, but there's no one there. Well, there's no one alive there anyway, if you're talking corpses mind then we're in business. A stretched out body surrounded by a pool of blood is on the floor. Fucking hell Billy what have you done?

Time to go. I'm turning for the door when a hand grips my shoulder, I instinctively spin and punch; I'm not going the same way as the dead man down there. My attacker is knocked back against the doorframe holding his burst nose as four coppers burst in and jump on me. I'm on the floor looking up at the bloke thinking, well arrest him then, when he starts to speak.

'Carl Reeves I am arresting you on suspicion of murder, you do not have to say anything but if you neglect to say anything that you later rely on in court....'

Oh shit, the fucker's only a copper, looks like a high up as well, I'll be falling down the stairs tonight then. They're bagging my bat up, that'll be exhibit A now. I'm saying nowt as I'm dragged to the van but two things bother me though.

Why did Billy get me there and then fuck off but most importantly though, how did that copper know my name?

Milo

Once we get this numpty in the cells I'd better ring my publisher, he won't care what time it is when he hears this.

'Former boxing champion murders High Court Judge.'
Excellent.

Billy

Fucking brilliant day, I'm feeling really good about everything. Just stretched out on the settee, the lads are in bed, Lisa's in the bath and I'm considering a plate of toast and a cup of tea while I watch 'Shameless' when she calls me from upstairs, all husky like.

'Billy, I need help scrubbing my back.'

Toast and telly or a bath with Lisa, no competition; I'll record it.

'Just coming pet.'

'You're no good to me then.' Oh I married a comedian.

I tell you what, going by the law of averages tomorrow's obviously going to be really shit.

Friday

Carlos

I'm bang in trouble here, it's not the first time I've been locked up but it's never been for owt as serious as murder. Turns out the gadgy was a judge as well and not any judge, only the one who put little Davy away for five years. I can't understand why Billy texted us to meet him there, has he done him in? What's the fucking score?

I'm saying nowt until me brief gets here, I used me phone call ringing Lisa. Billy's phone's just switched off so I rang his home number and told his lass, she sounded shocked and said they'd be straight on it. So I'm sitting here, just me and the four walls; all grey and all depressing. Thoughts just running round and round me head. Where's Sharon? Has Merry got hold of her? If he hurts her I'll kill him; I might have to wait thirty years but I'll kill him.

Fucking hell, thirty years.

Ron

The chaps are right up for this one, have a row and slap a few mackem slags in Sunderland on match day and do their drinking in Newcastle before and after. They tried to talk me out of retirement but I've got stuff to do up there, kill a few birds with one stone; see the family, visit Tel and have a drink with Billy and Carlos the sons I never had. I never tell the geordie bleeders that but I would be proud of them both if they were mine. Billy and Lisa have a wonderful marriage and have produced two cracking nephews for me. Carlos is a top geezer, not a bad bone in his body. I'm pleased for my dead brother that Lisa turned out so well, he would have liked Billy as well, I'll tell him this weekend I think.

So then, fifteen of the Old Kent Road's finest on the bus, plenty of ale and food and off we go to the frozen North. This mob has been up here before; they're always polite and never cause trouble in their own gaff, ideal guests, the management welcome them with open arms. Personally though, I'm staying at Lisa and Billy's, the food's better.

Billy

What the fuck's going on, just had a call off Lisa, our Carlos has been nicked for murder; a fucking judge as well. Apparently he's being held at Market Street in the town and needs a brief, I'll sort that then get in to see him. Barry's just rang as well, apparently Carlos smashed fuck out of Clarty the other night and he's been shagging Merry's bird. It never rains but it fucking pours.

So, in no particular order; I've got to get him out of nick, get him off a murder charge, find out the score with Merry and if he's taking it further, get me family out of harms way and get ready for a fucking war. At the same time I've got two businesses to run, oh yeah and uncle Ron's up tonight with a platoon of Millwall boys looking for action, he'll want running to Durham nick an all to see Terry. Fuck me I'd better buy some whizz, I'm not going to be sleeping for a while. I'll ring Ron first; he'll know some good briefs.

Terry

Can't wait to see Ron this weekend and give him the good news about getting out. I haven't seen him for about six months now but he writes every couple of weeks though. Nearly twenty-five years now he's written every fortnight, the geezer's a diamond. He's staying with Billy as well. Spanish said he'd get some of Carlos's old fight programmes for me and give them to Ron to bring in, they'd be excellent to while away my last few weeks in this shithole. Two good mates, Ron and Spanish, the only two I can rely on; I'd be lost without them.

Carlos

That twat that arrested me keeps coming in and shouting the odds, he knows he can't interview me yet until my brief's present so he's just trying to soften me up. I got a couple of slaps last night on the way in as well, usual shite, a couple of them telling me I'm never getting out. I looked straight at them and said, 'That means I've got nothing to lose then doesn't it boys?'

They toned it down a bit after that. I recognised a couple of coppers from school, lads I wasn't friendly with but not unfriendly with either. They were asking me the score, 'off the record like' they said, but I know there's no such thing with coppers. Thing is I'm not really sure what happened, I know I didn't kill the judge and I don't know who did, but, I don't know that it wasn't Billy and I don't want to drop him in it so until I see him I'm saying nowt.

Ron

Just stopped at Leeds for a cuppa and a bacon sandwich and I get a call off Billy, didn't recognise the number at first and I wasn't gonner answer it. Lucky I did, he says Carlos has been nicked for murdering a judge, bleedin' hell that is a choker, he needs a brief and wants to know if I can recommend any. Told him a couple off the top of my head, won't be cheap but that's not gonner bother him where his brother's concerned. He said there's other stuff going on as well and he'll tell me when we get there. I'll have to tell the chaps that I'm unavailable this weekend, family comes first. Tell you what though, if he's got real problems then fifteen geezers who've been fighting once a week for the last twenty years and who don't give a monkeys about anybody might just come in handy.

'Boys,' I say, voice loud enough to carry but not too far across the service café, 'Billy's got a few problems that might need my attention, will you lot be okay on your own this weekend?' A couple of strange looks from some of them as they all know Billy well enough now to know there's not much he can't deal with on his own, I know that as well so things must be serious.

Billy

Got a couple of names off Ron as I was going to me mams, top rank barristers who are close enough to take the case on, he said to mention his name as well. Let's see, Irvine from Morpeth, Murray from Carlisle or some Scottish lad Donaldson from Edinburgh. Fuck it I'm in no position to be choosy, I'll just work through the list after I've spoken to me mam.

Hmm no lights on and the curtains are shut. I'm taking no chances here, I don't know what the fuck's going on but I'm not going the same way as the judge and anyone who's harmed me mam is fucking dead, no matter who they are. Got my lucky duster in my pocket, that's going straight on, quick glance up the street and I'm going in. The door's locked which is also strange, if any fucker's in there kicking off then I'd have expected them to go straight through the door. Get the keys out of my pocket and quietly unlock the door, slide in and gently close it, taking care not to click the latch. It's dead black with the curtains shut and it makes the silence almost oppressive, it reminds me of the old Hammer House of Horror films. Move through the kitchen into the dining room, adrenalin is racing through my body like Button round Brazil, I swear my heart's beating like a drum, whoever's in here has got to hear it. I'm in two minds whether to shout or not as I approach the entrance to the living room, best not, need to keep the element of surprise in case there's more than one or they're tooled up. Stand across the entrance and cannot see fuck all, fuck it, flick the light switch and take a step back.

No one here, looks like me mam left in a hurry though. I'd better ring me auntie Marj, if me mam's not here then she'll be there. I'm just going to the phone when I hear it, the creaky floorboard on the landing, someone's upstairs. Switch the light back off and silently wait at the bottom. Sounds like they're coming down.

Val

Marj is happy to let me stay for as long as I want but I need to find out what's happening to my boys. I rang both their mobiles but they're both switched off so I rang Billy's home number. When Lisa told me I broke down and cried, my Carl in a police cell, I know he didn't do it, everyone knows he's a nice lad. He didn't do it and now he could get life. I've got to see Billy and get this sorted. Marj is running me back and we'll try to track down Billy from mine, I've got Barry's number as well if I get stuck, he'll find Billy. Actually I'll ring him now, he might be able to find Billy for us getting there.

Ron

Dropped the boys off on the quayside, they know their way round well enough. To a man they said give them a ring if Billy needs any help and they'll be right there. Top geezers, can't fault them.

They're meeting up with a few of the local hooligans later so they'll be happy enough dodging round geordieland. Now I'd better go and see Lisa.

Barry

Just making my way down the stairs when the phone rings, it's so fucking dark in here I can't get it out of my pocket, I'm just nearing the bottom when I answer it.

'Hello Mrs. Reeves.'

'No I'm just at yours now, I'm looking for Billy meself.'

'Yeah, I'll wait here for you then.'

I'm putting the phone back in my pocket as I hit the bottom stair and a voice booms out of the darkness, 'Barry man, for fucks sake, what are you doing here?'

As the light goes on I see Billy two steps away from me and he's ready for action, dustered up and ready to go; the look on his face man, I'd rather take on Merry.

'Alright Bill,' I manage to squeak, 'your mam's on her way.'

Lisa

Uncle Ron managed to see the boys and say hello before they went to school, they'll be pleased about that, they love him to death. He's looking very smart, must still be eating well and looking after himself.

'What's the score then love?' he asks, those deep blue eyes trained on me. I have to tell the truth, if Carlos has got us into trouble then Ron could be the only one to get us out. I know about his past and his association with the modern day gangsters, I'm not supposed to but Billy keeps nothing from me.

'I think we're in trouble uncle Ron,' I reply, 'Carlos might have killed a judge and Billy said he'd been seeing a gangster's girlfriend as well. If it's enough to worry Billy then it's enough to worry me.' I'm starting to cry now; I really didn't want to do that and he's hugging me, telling me it'll be all right.

'No-one hurts my family gel,' he says softly, 'I made a promise to my brother before he died that I'd look after you and I made the same promise to your mum on her deathbed. Where's Billy?'

I tell him that Billy's gone to his mams and he's off up there in a taxi telling me not to worry as he goes.

<u>Billy</u>

Right then the brief's sorted and he's on his way to the nick now, I've told him what I know and he's on the case. It's that Irvine one, he was a bit snotty at first but then I mentioned I was part of the Ron Carter family and his attitude changed.

'Don't worry about money Mr. Reeves; we'll sort something out.'

I wasn't fucking worried, still, let him think I'm skint and we'll save a fortune.

Barry says me mam's on her way so I'll wait for her, I was going to give Ron a ring but Lisa's just belled me here to let me know he's on his way as well. Time for a fucking pow wow I think, heads together, bit of brainstorming and see what we come up with. Somebody'd better ring Spanish as well, he'll be fucking distraught at his boy being banged up, I'll get Barry on that.

Sharon

I can't get through on Carlos's mobile; it's constantly switched off. What's happening? Oh god I hope Vince hasn't done anything stupid, he said he'd ring me and he hasn't. What if he's had second thoughts and decided it's not worth the hassle. I can't stand this; it's a nightmare, a complete fucking nightmare.

Ron

Billy's here with that Barry kid and his mum's just turned up as well. Got a lot of time for her, a real battler, worked all her life to raise them boys and done a good job as well. Time for business. 'Barry why don't you help Val put the kettle on while I have a little chat with Bill.' He looks a bit put out at that but I stare him down and he heads for the kitchen. I want to talk about this with Billy and find out the score, who are we dealing with and how we're gonner do it? I don't want anyone I don't know one hundred percent hanging round eavesdropping.

'What's the story then Bill?' I ask him.

'Basically this Ron, Carlos was found in a house with a dead judge and apparently he attacked the arresting officer who is none other than the Chief Inspector of the Northumbria force.' He's looking really hacked off.

Something's nagging at my mind, 'Why would the Chief Inspector be the arresting officer, what on earth was he doing there?'

'I'm puzzled by that fucker an' all Ron, it doesn't seem right to me either. As well as that though the stupid twat has been shagging Vince Merry's bird behind his back and Merry has found out.'

'Bleedin' hell Bill,' I say, 'that could get naughty.' Merry's naff all in the grand scheme of things but he's got some lads behind him.

'Tell me about it,' he replies, then, almost wearily, 'there's one more thing Ron, Carlos battered Merry's cousin the other night at the gym, properly hospitalised him.'

Jesus, old Carlos don't do nothing by half does he, he's a good lad though and I ain't leaving him in the brown stuff.

'Why did he batter him Bill?' I ask him.

Billy's just shaking his head like it's all a dream.

'The prick only went to Carlos's gym and challenged him in front of everyone there. Barry was there as well, he'll tell you.'

That's a good thing anyway, 'To be fair then Carlos had no choice on that one,' Billy's shrugging.

'Aye you're right Ron, it was a legit hiding, Merry can't deny that and we'd all have done the same. There's just one more strange twist to this though, Merry's cousin is a puff and it turns out he was shagging the judge that was killed. It's like an episode of fucking EastEnders this. No offence like mate.' he adds quickly.

I just smile at him, I can see his point, this is bleedin' mental, 'Leave it aht guvnor,' I chuckle at him.

Carlos

The brief's here, Fergus Irvine from Morpeth, gets me into a private room and asks me what happened. First things first though he needs to be giving me some references before I volunteer anything.

'Where did Billy find you then?' I ask him.

He smiles, heard it all before, 'I was recommended to him by a family friend.'

'Who's that then?' I ask, still all cynical and suspicious.

'Mr. Ronald Carter, Billy quoted him as close family and that is the only reason I'm here, do you want to continue?'

'Yeah mate, just checking, you can't be too careful can you?' so I give him the story of how I got the message, found the body and then got lifted.

He just looks at me unblinking and says two words, 'Fit up.'

I've been thinking about this myself and it's obvious he's right; the question is who would do it? No way would it be Billy. Would it? Why would he?

Barry

I'm going to bell Tony first chance I get, this has got to be something to do with Merry. Carlos shags his bird and batters his cousin, got to be him. How though? He could have killed the judge, no question. How did he get Carlos there and then how could he have known the law would turn up just when he wanted them to? I don't know whether to mention to Billy that I'm working for Tony or not. He'd definitely be handy on the inside of Merry's crew and he's made it plain to me that he's disposing of the radge and taking over first chance he gets. I'll speak to Tony first then tell Billy what I know, yeah that's my best bet.

'Spanish is on his way Billy.'

Billy

Right then me and Ron are on the move, he's decided we're seeing Merry and he's calling a couple of his lads as back up once I've arranged the meet. Spanish and Barry are going to have a mooch around the area where the judge was found, see if they know anyone round there, maybe ask some questions. Me mam is under instructions to start sorting her gear out in case things don't go well with Merry, mind you, he'd have to be some sort of prick to mess with Ron Carter. Even that stupid fucker must have heard of him.

Lets find out, 'Can I borrow your phone Ron? Mine's gone missing, aye I know, tight northern bastard. I'll get another one today.'

It's ringing. Here we go. 'Vince. Billy Reeves, I think we need to have a chat.'

'Do you Billy, why's that then? Why would a busy man like me want to have a chat with you? What could this possibly be about?' The fucker's been waiting for this call I can tell, I bet he's fucking rehearsed it all morning. I'll just jump straight in with me big guns before he threatens to do something that he can't get out of, try and avoid needless bloodshed.

'Ron Carter's with me, he wants to see you as well, we need

to talk about our Carlos.' Ooh he's gone all quiet now; he wasn't expecting me to have a couple of aces in my hand as well.

'Why would Ron Carter be with you Billy?' Puzzled and frightened, nice combination.

'Have I never mentioned it before? He's Lisa's uncle, have you never met him? We've had him up here loads of times; he's always on the piss with our Carlos. Loves him to death, kna what I mean?'

'Well I'm a bit busy today,' playing for time, does he think I'm a mug?

'What too busy to see Ron when he's requested a meeting?' I'm grinning at Ron as Merry's panic increases. 'He's just here, I'll tell him you can't be arsed shall I?'

'No Billy, I'll make time,' flustered and panicking now, 'how about later on?'

'No Vince how about now,' I growl at him, 'be in The George in town in an hour.'

Click the phone shut, as Ron looks at me 'Well?'

I'm smiling back at him, 'I think once you've done your thing Ron we'll only have to worry about the murder charge, shall I tell the lads where we're going to be?'

'You do that Bill,' he says, 'and after this you can run me to see Tel, okay?'

'Nee bother Ron.' Things are looking up anyway.

Milo

I can't believe that scrote has got Irvine as his brief, he's one of the top men in the country and for Reeves to be able to afford him means he is a serious villain and deserves to go down whether he's guilty of this or not. Luckily the uniformed plebs on the scene were all a bit young and naïve. As I dragged Reeves' bat through the congealing blood a couple of them looked at me strangely but I gave them the 'scum must not win' speech and how we sometimes had to help justice against the red tape of cosseted politicians, they fell for that and gave the bastard a couple of extra kicks as he went into the van.

I'm interviewing him myself along with one of our dimmer

detectives. The story is that I'm helping young Duncan gain experience, he's not long up from London and has a reputation as being a bit dense, when really I'm obliged to have a partner in there and I don't want anybody too bright. At the very worst Reeves just has to be inside when my book comes out, however, look at the evidence against him: present at scene of crime, brandishing a weapon that is covered in victim's blood, reacts violently when challenged by police officer and the piece de resistance, which I only remembered ten minutes ago, he threatened Maxwell with violence in front of witnesses not long ago. When his mate got that five years for the warehouse job he had to be thrown out of court and was distinctly heard making violent threats at the much esteemed and sadly missed Mr. Maxwell. Oh yes, we have definitely got a case, and if, in five or ten years time it is deemed a miscarriage of justice has occurred, well who cares? I'll be long gone just like numerous corrupt officers before me, I think the Americans call this a win-win situation.

'Are you ready then Detective Duncan?' Stern and authoritarian, this young man needs to know who's in charge from the off, no getting clever and playing detective.

'Yes sir, let's 'ave 'im.' Dense and indeed cockney, I can tell that from one sentence, exactly what I wanted.

'Okay then let's show this scum that killing judges just doesn't happen, not in my town.'

Merry

Sssnnniiiffff, Sssnnniiifff

Fucking Ron Carter, Billy Reeves is related to Ron fucking Carter. Jesus Christ. Why has no one ever mentioned this? For fucks sake the amount of eyes and ears I've got in this town and nobody knew that. I'm going to have to play this very, very carefully. Can't turn up too mob handed cos it'll turn into a war and then I'll die. Can't turn up on my own cos they might already know what happened with Carlos and Maxwell and then I'll die. I'll be doing well just to stay alive today. I tell you what though, if Carlos gets away with the murder charge then he can fucking have Sharon, she's not worth going up against Ron Carter for, no woman is.

Right, I'll take Tony, Fat Kev and a couple of others; I'll spread a few bodies round the bar as well in case it goes off.

Sssnnniiifff, Sssnnniiifff.

Now let's get the story straight. I found out from Clarty that Carlos had been shagging Sharon, got home ready to ask her but she'd left, I thought she'd fucked off with Carlos and spent the night looking for her. I also want to have a word with Carlos about giving Clarty a hiding, that's only natural; you'd all do the same. Obviously, I'm as shocked as everyone when I heard that Carlos had killed a judge, it's not like him is it? That sounds truthful enough, keep repeating it and stick to it and I might get through this. Jesus, Ron fucking Carter. I can't let the boys see I'm scared or I'm finished but at the same time though I can't come across all cocky or disrespectful or I'm dead.

Fuck, fuck, fuck fuck fuck. Right then, I'd better round them up and get moving, it's going to be a long day.

Sssnnniiifff.

<u>Val</u>

My Carl arrested for murder, it's not true, I'm his mother and I of all people know it's not. He's not capable of it and I know it wasn't him. I just know it. There must be some sort of evidence to prove it wasn't him. Billy says Ron put him on to a top solicitor so he'll surely be able to sort it out. Spanish is taking Barry to have a poke around down there; he's as upset as me. He's basically a good man Spanish, I've still got feelings for him, they never went away. Thinking back it's sad that we ever split up really; he's always been a good father, even to Billy, just a crap husband.

I hope between them they can sort this thing out. I just know it wasn't my boy that killed that judge. The other stuff as well, stealing that woman off the bullyboy and chinning his cousin.

Billy thinks it might get rough but I don't care about that, as long as Carl is happy then I'm happy and if she's worth it and good enough for my baby son then I'm right behind him.

Spanish

Bizzies all over the fucking street down here, they've sealed the house off and they're just looking us up and down as we loiter at the top end. I reckon I know a woman a couple of doors down from the judge's house, as I recall she was single so no husband to upset if I knock, might be worth a word. 'Come on Barry, I've had an idea.'

Milo

The scrote's not saying anything, his brief's obviously prepared him well. He's just sticking to his original story that he saw the door open and went in.

'Why did you have a baseball bat then?' Cool as a cucumber, look at him.

'I thought there may be violent burglars in there, you never know. Obviously given the new police priorities these days I thought you lot would be out harassing motorists or serial rubbish bin offenders and I didn't want to face a gang of junkies on my own.' The wanker's smiling at me as if to say this is a piece of piss.

'How do you explain the fact that your bat has the murder victim's blood on it?' Get out of that one boxer boy.

'Well,' he replies, looking at the tape recorder and grinning, 'I could tell the truth and say that you made sure you dragged it through the pool of blood while your muppets were beating shit out of me or I could just say that it must have been thrown over there accidentally during the struggle. You choose which you prefer Chief Inspector.'

Cocky fucker isn't he; time to play the joker. I stand up and walk behind him then approach him silently to about two steps behind his back. Before he has time to adjust I scream into his ear, 'SO HOW DO YOU EXPLAIN THREATENING JUDGE MAXWELL IN COURT, IN FRONT OF DOZENS OF

WITNESSES WHEN HE JAILED YOUR FRIEND?'

That did it; he jumped a foot in the fucking air then. His brief is glaring at him and Mr. Reeves is suddenly a lot humbler.

'No comment.'

Ron

Billy's got us in this bar in the centre of Newcastle, I've got the Bushwhackers and a few of their geordie counterparts spread around the place, there's just me and Bill waiting for this Merry slag. I knew he'd get here early and do the same thing so we spiked his guns a bit; he'll be paranoid about who's with us in the bar and who isn't. He'll know we've watched everyone come in as well so we'll know who's with him. Billy's looking tense, I know he's dealt with this slag before and he's wary of the consequences to the family but I'm gonner deal with that. It must be hard as well knowing your brother's inside being charged with murder, a naffin' judge as well, that'll be at least thirty years. Let Irvine sort that out we need to concentrate on this thing now.

Here he comes, I've never met him but I can already tell it's him. Big red-faced steroid freak was Billy's description, yep that'll be him.

Billy

Here's the prick now, body language giving him away already, he's shitting it. Full of coke as well judging by his nose and eyes. He takes a seat facing us; Fat Kev and Big Tony flanking him. Kev's trying to smile at me but I blank him, let's keep this formal. I make the introductions and Merry falls over himself to shake Ron's hand, I thought he was going to kiss his ring for a minute the sad cunt.

Ron starts the spiel, 'Do you know who I am Mr. Merry?' He asks all polite and quietly spoken. Merry just says, 'Yes Mr. Carter,' like when he was a kid at school in front of the head.

'Good. Then you'll understand that I'm not a man to be

messed about. I need to know a few things and to straighten a few things out. Firstly, I have no intention of taking over or interfering in any of your ventures in Newcastle, I'm strictly a London boy where business is concerned. Are we clear on that?'

'Yes,' says Merry nodding his head.

'Okay then,' continues Ron, 'I want to know what you intend to do about Carlos Reeves seeing your girlfriend behind your back and please be honest with me Mr. Merry, I know when people are lying.'

I can see the wheels turning in Merry's head, he starts to speak, stops and then starts again.

'Basically Mr. Carter I want to smash his skull in for taking the piss. After that, he can have the slag.'

Ron holds his hands up stopping Merry in his tracks.

'Mr. Merry I understand your views on that and so,' he says turning to me, 'does Billy.' He turns back to Merry and continues, 'When Carlos gets out of prison you have my word that the two of you will have a straightener, after which, win or lose this issue is sorted. Do you agree to this?'

Merry's got no choice, he's just nodding, 'Yeah, no problem.' I'd back Carlos against that arsehole though, he'll fucking eat him. You ought to be careful what you wish for Vincent.

Ron moves to the next item on the 'fuck off Merry' agenda. 'Also Vince, can I call you Vince?' he moves on without waiting for an answer making Merry look two foot small. 'Also Vince, there is the matter of your cousin challenging Carlos in his own gym, in front of his friends and, even worse, paying customers. Now I do not think, and I'm sure you'll agree with me here, that Carlos did anything wrong by giving your cousin a severe beating; I'd have done the same. What do you think?'

Merry can't argue this one, he just sits there shaking his head and spluttering out 'N-n-no Ron, understandable in the circumstances. It's the least that could have been expected.'

Ron smiles in supposed understanding, 'Nice to see we think the same on that one Vince. Now to my final and most important point. As you know Carlos got nicked for murder last night, now no one knows for sure if he did it but let's face it, the chances of that are minimal to say the least.'

Merry just starts nodding again, 'Aye Ron, bit of a shock that like.'

'Well,' replies Ron, moving his face right into Merry's across the table and staring straight at him; cold, dead, unblinking eyes boring right into his soul, thin lips stretched across barely covered teeth, hardly moving as he growls, 'that's my point. Someone has obviously stitched him up. Would you know anything about that sonny?'

I'm looking straight at Merry, ready to go over the table and beat him to death if there's any sign at all of nervousness. Anything that could be considered a tell; sweat on the forehead, scratching the nose while he talks or even a failure to hold eye contact with Ron, but there's nothing, he's either a good actor or he genuinely knows nothing. Cool as fuck he just says, 'Honestly Ron, I'm as surprised as you.'

Ron sits back and relaxes, so does Merry thinking the interview's over, then Ron springs across the table and grabs him by the throat, pushing those mad cockney eyes right into Merry's face. Fat Kev and Big Tony don't know what to do as they're grabbed by a couple of hefty old school hooligans and the rest of Merry's men are picked off across the bar and blocked by a combination of Gremlins and Bushwhackers. The local boozers and the all day stag parties know the score and just move away from the scene without spilling a drop or seeing a thing.

Merry's protesting, 'I don't know anything about it Ron, I don't.'

Ron just growls at him, 'If I ever find out that you do or if any harm comes to any of the Reeves family other than at the straightener then you die. Do you fucking understand me you overblown bag of wind and piss?'

Merry looks like he's gonna cry and just whines, 'Aye Ron, but it's all sorted now isn't it, there's no need for this. It's all sorted, just a straightener when he comes out that's it.'

Ron sits back down, straightens his tie and says to Merry, 'Good, I'm glad we had this chat.' He drains his drink and says, 'I've got to go now, nice to meet you,' and extends his hand.

Merry just shakes it, half fearful it's going to be the start of a hiding. Then Ron gives me the nod and we're out of the bar and off to Durham nick leaving steroid boy with the shakes and a bad case of diarrohea. I tell you what, he's the closest thing I have to a father-in-law and I'd class us as good mates but Ron Carter scares the fuck out of me.

Carlos

The brief went fucking mad with me in the interview room after that Milo had gone, wanting to know why I hadn't told him about the thing at court. The truth was I'd forgot, I didn't even realise it was the same judge. Milo went on and on about how I planned to do him in for jailing my mate but I just kept saying no comment. The other copper looked at me a bit strange when I mentioned Milo dragging my bat through the blood, it was like he didn't know this was a fit up. He was writing stuff down after that but I couldn't read it once fucking numbnuts started screaming in my ears. I could well be in the shit now though because of this shouting at the judge thing. Irvine reckons there's no chance of bail and I'll definitely get charged in the next twenty-four hours, then it'll be off to Durham on remand. Might see Davy in there, bound to be someone I know, thing is there's bound to be some fucker in there Merry knows as well.

It's not like I've just got one thing to worry about is it. I wonder what Sharon's doing, I bet she doesn't even know, everyone'll be going out of their mind about me and all I can do is stare at the walls in this little grey cell.

Fuck.

Terry

Ron's looking good, I haven't seen him for six months and he's looking well, middle age suits him. He's says he's got Billy outside with him but they wouldn't let him in, shame that I'd like to meet the lad. Still won't be long now anyway. I've given Ron the news and he is fucking well chuffed.

'I'll sort you a job out straight away Tel. Legit if you need one for the probation officer and a little bit of afters on the side mate, no probs,' he says, winking.

'That's the thing Ron,' I say, 'I was thinking of staying out of London and trying my luck up here. Spanish says I can stay with him for as long as I need.'

He looks thoughtful at that, 'Under normal circumstances Tel that'd be a great idea, Billy and Carlos would sort you out somewhere I'm sure but these ain't normal times mate. Things changed yesterday, bleedin' rapidly and took us all by surprise.'

What's he on about, 'What do you mean Ron?'

'It's young Carlos,' he says, 'in no particular order; he's been servicing the local gangster's bird and got caught, beat seven bells out of the aforementioned gangster's favourite cousin and last but definitely not least he got nicked at the scene of a murder yesterday. Not any old murder either, oh no, only a bleedin' judge.'

I slump back in my seat, 'Fucking hell Ron, how's he getting out of all that then?'

Ron leans forward and drops his voice a couple of levels, almost whispering, 'I've sorted the local boy out, he's been promised a straightener when Carlos gets out and I gave Billy a couple of decent briefs to pick from. Thing is Tel if you stay up here and it kicks off then you're gonna get dragged into it mate and you'll be straight back inside.'

I can see his point but Spanish ain't missed a visit to me since the mid-eighties and Carlos and Billy have sent bits of stuff into me over the years that have helped get me through this. Spanish'll be in bits over this, Carlos is his pride and joy; I'll have to stay.

'I'll have to be here for Spanish Ron, next to you he's my best mate in the world.'

He's looking thoughtful again, 'I respect that Tel I know he's been a good mate to you. What I'll do then is put you on a retainer up here. You can be my eyes and ears and if this palaver starts to get out of hand then I'll know that Billy's got a bit of back up and I'll feel better knowing that there's a bit more protection for Lisa and the kids. Okay with that mate?'

'More than okay Ron, I've heard so much about those geezers over the years they feel like my own family anyway. I'll do whatever's necessary to help mate.'

Time's up, we shake hands and he's ready to go when he stops and turns to me. Looks like there's a glint of a tear in his eye and he says, 'Next time I see you mate we can have a drink, I've missed you, you big ponce.'

Then he smiles and he's off.

It's starting to sink in; I'm going to be out soon. Carlos though, he's looking at thirty years, my fucking heart's going out to him.

Sharon

I still can't get through, what the fuck's going on? My stupid auntie keeps going on and on, 'If he loved you he'd have at least called by now, he'd have been here by now, he'd have made time to do it.'

She's got half a point but this isn't a normal situation, he could easily be in hospital or something, I don't even know Billy's number to ring him and find out. I can't stand not knowing what's happening. She's doing my head in as well, 'You had a good life with Vince, he gave you everything, you should have stayed with him', yes but he's a prick who beats people up for fun and I fucking despise him.

If he hasn't called by tomorrow I'm going back, whatever the danger. I have to know what's happened.

Monday

Terry

I can't fucking believe it; I was ready to do a few more weeks. All set for the mind games the screws play. 'Your parole's been revoked, we'll keep you in here' that type of thing. I remember them winding young Richie up before he got out, he'd done fifteen and was due to get out in a weeks time. For the whole week they were winding him up about this and that. 'We'll plant some gear in your cell, we'll say you attacked a screw and then beat the shit out of you to 'restrain' you' all that bollocks. The poor geezer was on tenterhooks, he'd waited that long to get out and he genuinely thought they were going to take it away from him. In the end he was that tense and wound up that he landed one on some taff during an argument in association and they added another month onto him for that, bunch of wankers.

So anyway, I'm ready for all that; cool as a cucumber. Nothing they say will get to me or surprise me. I'm ready for breakfast, looking forward to a bit of tea and toast when all of a sudden they come and tell me 'Pack your gear Briggs you're leaving.' At first I thought they were on a wind up, then, when I realised they were being serious about me leaving the nick I thought they were putting me closer to London in preparation for my release. I had to say to them 'Look, I'm staying in the North East for a bit when I get out, I don't need to be moved to another prison.' And then...it was fucking beautiful chap it really was...the screw Hall, the alright one he says 'No Terry, you're leaving us today, for good hopefully, get your gear together and you'll be out of here in half an hour.'

I just slumped on the bed. After twenty-five years of prison, nearly half my fucking life, I was finally getting out. I could have a pint, go to a football match, go on holiday, fucking hell I could get some skirt. It just wasn't sinking in and I was sure some twat would come along in a minute shouting about it all being a mistake, so I tried to busy myself a bit by sorting out my meagre possessions and hurrying the process along.

I had a big stash of Mars Bars and some tobacco so I gave Psycho Bates a shout along the landing and bought Spanish's mate little Dave some protection. I also mentioned that a very good friend of mine, Carlos Reeves, might be arriving here soon and it'd be nice if he didn't get any aggravation. Batesy was choked that I was giving him all this and promised faithfully that he'd look after the boys. After that it was all systems go to the exit door. Word had got round quickly and there was a queue of bodies shaking my hand on the way out. A lot of the lads I'd coached in the gym were gutted to see me go as they were doing well at the boxing but obviously pleased for me at the same time.

Into the office to process my details and that bit was just a blur of signing forms and trading insults with the screws. Sign this; see you next time; no you won't you northern monkey; aye we will Briggs you're scum; all that type of shit. Then, into the minibus to the station, a travel warrant to Newcastle pressed into my hand and I was on the outside.

Sitting back on the minibus seat I'm just trying to take it all in. The other lads on the bus are full of it, like excited school kids on a trip, bouncing up and down, singing and all that, but me, I'm just thinking ahead and back all at the same time. I've never been to Newcastle, nearly twenty-five years in the North East and I've never been there. I haven't got a mobile phone either; apparently they're all the rage these days. I'll ring Spanish from a phone box when I get there. What is it they say up here? Howay the lad, fucking right chap, I'm out.

I'm out.

Billy

Lisa's got a lot on at the bakery today and the lads are off school, fucking teacher-training day my arse, they'll all be on the piss if they're anything like my owld teachers. I've decided to take them up the coast like we used to when we were kids and, on a whim, I've invited Spanish and me mam, take their minds off Carlos a bit. So, we're diving round the arcades, Kenny and Peter getting all aggressive on the air hockey just like we used to and me mam telling me not to bollock them cos they're just lads being lads. The sun's out and the wind's dropped, the beach looks pretty empty and the sky's a real proper blue colour. Little clusters of families and pensioners wandering along the front having a break from the usual shite and getting some clean air into their lungs. It's turning into a bit of a family day out and I wish Carlos was here, he'd be spoiling the little fuckers rotten, he always does. We stop and look at the owld Spanish City site, it's shut now, a decrepit looking owld fairground that was tiny anyway. When I was a kid though it was fucking magical, me and Carlos had some great days here with his owld fella when me mam was working and couldn't look after us. He'd always kid on it was named after him and we'd kid on we believed it.

We decide to stop for a cup of tea and a cake just off the seafront and the two lads are just running round the place they're that excited. Me mam just looks at me laughing and says, 'Déjà vu there son, they even look a bit like you two.' She's right mind, Peter's a bit more serious, reserved even and Kenny, well, he's a hyperactive chatterbox.

'Aye,' I say all straight faced, 'the owlder kid's always the best looking as well have you noticed?' She just clouts me round the back of the head, her and Spanish sitting next to each other and having a laugh together. Then, when the boys are starting to get out of hand and crashing into people and that, I decide enough's enough and I'm getting up to give them the message when me mam beats us to it and takes them for a candy floss.

That leaves me and Spanish sitting at our table watching them through the window. He's a shell at the minute without Carlos, I know how he feels like, I miss the good looking bastard something chronic and I know I can't do thirty years without him. Mind you I think we all feel like that.

'Do you remember when I used to bring you boys down here?' he says staring at the kids through the window.

'Aye,' I say, 'some of me happiest childhood memories them were mate, me, you and our Carl and the way you used to let us get away with murder. I remember you used to stick a fiver in me hand and just let us get on with it in the arcades while you had a pint. Then it would always be fish and chips on the front and into the fair after that. You would always pay us on any ride we wanted, as many times as we liked and at least one of us, if not both, would always puke our dinner back up on the grass outside the gates,' I say, chuckling at the thought of it.

I'm away on a trip back in time here, set adrift on memory bliss alright, that's me right now.

'I remember it always being sunny and busy, always a great smell of chips and toffee apples mixed, everyone laughing and joking. Because it was so far on the bus it seemed like you were travelling miles from Newcastle, it was the closest we came to being on holiday anyway. A right good day out it was for me and wor kid, made a change from Byker. Do you know what the best bit was though Spanish?' I ask him.

He's looking at me now, 'What was that son?'

'For them days when you brought us down here, it was like I had a dad for the day. When we were little lads back in the seventies we were a bit of a novelty on the estate me and Carl. It was bad enough for him having to explain why his mam and dad weren't married but I didn't even know who mine was and everyone thought it was worth commenting on and that's hard work when you're not even ten. The thing was mate you never ever treated me any different to him and, even at that age, I noticed that. I was made to feel different enough at school so when we had our days out it was like being normal and I could take my guard down and just be my age. I never said thank you for that mate, I just want you to know that I appreciated it then and I still do now. I don't care who my dad really is, as far as I'm concerned you're it and you're granddad to my kids as well, full stop mate. I just wanted you to know.'

I've rambled on a bit now and he's quiet, then he turns to look at me, away from the window and there's a tear in his eye and he just says, 'Thanks son,' and it's a nice moment. We sit quiet for a bit watching the lads run me mam ragged round the candy floss stall then he turns to me and says, 'Do you remember that time I'd went for a pint and left you two in the arcade and you had a bit of a set to with them little Scottish twats over Carlos?'

I'm thinking about it and I can just about remember it, not totally but just about.

'Vaguely,' I reply smiling at him.

'Well,' he says, 'I came out of the pub that day to put a bet on and I heard the noise of fighting and I knew it would be one of you two. When I stuck my head in the arcade you were battering this jock lad for calling Carlos a half caste, him and his mate had made him cry when your back was turned so you did the both of them.' I do remember that now, I still give Carlos stick about it.

'You might remember that I didn't turn up for about another fifteen minutes after you'd had that fight with them lads. Well that's because their dad was on his way over to clout you when I got there. He was saying to their mother about slapping the little geordie bastard and his dago mate, how if you had a proper dad you wouldn't be wandering wild round arcades and bullying kids from respectable families.'

I'm gobsmacked, I remember seeing a mad looking Scottish bloke with the two boys but I can't remember him having a go at me. 'I remember their dad but I can't remember him trying to dig me.' I say to Spanish.

'That's because I headed him off and took him round the back and fucking leathered him Billy. That's the day when I made you my other son, I was proud of you that day and I have been ever since, whoever your dad is Billy he's a mug for giving you up. I was happy to try and fill the gap for you son and I always will be.'

Fucking hell, I've got to drink my tea before I start crying, I haven't cried since I was ten years owld but I'm close now. I think Spanish is the same so we just gulp our tea and talk about football a bit until me mam comes back with fucking Ronnie and Reggie. Then we go for a wander along the beach kicking a ball about. I hope the lads enjoyed it today cos we're going be doing this a lot more often that's for sure.

Milo

Now that is a turn up for the books, I would never have thought in a million years that the old homo had kids, well one kid to be specific. I know he was dallying with girls when he was at college and he got friendly with a waitress in the canteen there but a kid? No woman in the seventies would have brought up a kid single handed if she could possibly avoid it. It makes me think though that in fitting up Carlos Reeves I may be closer to the truth than I thought, I mean it was a quick decision as time was against Mr. Merry and myself but it may well prove to have been the result of a very good instinctive hunch.

Oh yes, this will make things very interesting for the investigation; let's see what Mr. Irvine makes of this. The murdered man's will has amongst its beneficiaries the chief suspect's brother, namely one William Reeves. He's going to inherit one million, three hundred thousand pounds while his brother goes to prison for it.

Carlos

I can't believe it, Billy's dad was the fucking judge. He's left him loads of money as well. That Milo wanker reckons that puts me bang in the frame, he reckons I've either done it to gain the money for the family or Billy's done it and used me as an alibi. He's decided either way I'm involved and he's putting me away. That other one, Duncan or something, just keeps scribbling stuff down and saying nowt, nods whenever Milo needs him to.

My brief's just arguing coincidence with him but fuck me what a coincidence. My brother has just made nearly one and a half large because someone died, someone I allegedly had a grudge against and I'm found next to his body with a baseball bat. Cause of death - bludgeoned to fuck with a blunt instrument. And why was I there? Because my brother texted me to meet him there. I can't work this one out at all; I hope it is fucking coincidence.

Terry

Newcastle Central Station. It's like a big old Victorian type station, big airy platforms and glass arched roofs and loads of hum and noise about it. Fucking brilliant. Find a phone box and give Spanish a ring, get myself sorted and then celebrate re-joining the civilised world. I don't know what to do first, drink or shag? Maybe I'll ring Spanish first and sort my digs out, get my bearings. There's a phone box and I've bought a paper with my rehabilitation allowance so I've got some change. It's all over the nationals as well as the locals about that judge, fucking gutted for Carlos.

Bloody hell these phone boxes have changed. The Internet? In a phone box? I only want to talk to my mate for fucks sake.

'Spanish, yeh mate yeh. I'm out. Yeh I know I wasn't either, just surprised me this morning. That offer still stand? Okay mate no probs, there's a pub on the station I'll be in there. See you in an hour.'

Couple of cards in the box offering various services that I may make use of in the very near future but for the time being I've got an hour to kill while Spanish makes his way back from a family outing down the seaside.

Lovely. Time for a pint then.

Barry

I need to see Billy I think, I've had a word with Tony and he doesn't mind if I tell Bill I'm working for him. The thing is Tony's obviously planning a takeover and knows that Billy and Merry didn't get on anyway before all this shite kicked off, never mind now. Tony has told me to tell Billy he'd like a meet, to their mutual benefit, that type of thing.

I'm not meant to know Tony's eyeing up Merry's empire but it's fucking obvious, he's undercutting Merry's dealers with his own, me included, and sorting them out the prime spots in the clubs in town. He's got his own loyal little squad of bouncers within Merry's organisation and he's ready to go, it just needed something to spark it off and now he's got it.

Billy Reeves carries respect in this town and Merry doesn't, end of story. Merry's constantly slapping people around, been doing it for years, goes back to when he was a kid so if Billy or his mental cockney uncle do him in then no one's going to give a fuck. Same for Clarty, he's just a snidey little wanker who's traded on his cousin's rep for years. He's been quick to hand out slappings to people when Merry's been there to watch his back, the whole town laughed when Carlos gave him a hiding and Tony knows this so he's getting on the winning side now. I just need to keep an eye out for Billy from the inside. Tony's okay but he's been around for years and he's no mug, if it came to Billy disappearing for him to get what he wanted then he wouldn't think twice about it.

I'll give Billy a bell shortly see if he fancies a pint and a chat, see what's happening with Carlos as well.

Billy

There's two coppers standing in front of me, in my own house, in front of my wife and children and I cannot believe what they are saying. They're only asking me down to the station to 'assist with their enquiries' I'm not having that, not one bit of it, I stare straight at the copper who's asked the question, 'Are you arresting me?'

The copper doesn't really want to know I can tell, he blushes, he's fucking younger than me as well and the woman one with him, what if I kicked off, what would they do? It's no wonder judges get murdered if this is the best we can do, what do the government spend all of the fucking tax money on? The Lord Chancellor's wallpaper? Two jags for Deputy Prime Ministers? Secret bin coppers? Oh no, I remember, it all goes on massively overpaid spin doctors leaving a couple of quid to pay for some 'community street wardens,' still, it gives the local youth some spitting practice.

I ask him again, 'Are you arresting me?' I'm not going to kick off cos I'm not stupid and I know that that's what they want. My voice is low, controlled and threatening, my eyes boring holes in the cunt's head. The woman copper breaks the silence; the other one's bottle has gone completely, 'Mr. Reeves in light of new evidence we just want to ask you some questions.'

'Well ask me here then,' I say, 'I'll put the kettle on.'

They're shaking their heads and saying it has to be down the station so I just say, 'No then.' That's it, the cuffs come out and the spiel starts from the, by now highly dangerous as he's shitting it, male copper.

'Mr. Reeves, I am arresting you on suspicion of murder. You do not have to say anything.' He's pulling out a truncheon as well as he speaks, so I stop him dead.

'I'll come with you son,' I say, holding my wrists out for the cuffs, 'just try and calm down a bit will you, you're in my house and in front of my family.'

The woman copper is looking daggers at him and he's all apologetic now, just doing me job mate and all that, can't blame the bloke really I scare meself sometimes. I look over to Lisa, she's veering between being worried for me and apoplectic with rage for bringing this to the house in front of the boys, I'll probably be safer in a cell tonight anyway. I just smile at her and say, 'Darling this'll be a misunderstanding, I've done nowt. Will you give that brief a ring, his card's in my wallet.' Then looking at my boys who are about to watch their hero carted off without a fight I say, ' Remember lads, this is what happens when you don't help the police, learn from it eh?' Peter's looking serious and Kenny looks like he's going to cry but I give them a wink and the lady copper stops the young lad putting the cuffs on, good of her that like, things like that stick in kids heads.

Then I'm in the car and we're off to Market Street.

Wonder what the fuck this is about.

<u>Spanish</u>

Terry's just sitting quietly in the corner of the bar reading his paper and sipping a pint, sipping it? The longest I've ever done in one go was eighteen months and I was fucking gulping them down two at a time when I came out. It's hard to believe, looking at him sitting there, that he was Ron Carter's right hand man down the smoke in the seventies. He's such a confident, assured bloke that he doesn't need to puff his chest out or strut round the place, he knows who he is, how he looks and what he can do, to him there's no need to throw his weight around because he's not into that competitive shit, it's a nice change to see someone like that these days. Tell you what though, I heard Merry shit himself when confronted with Ron at The George, he'll be paranoid as fuck when he hears Terry Briggs is in town and staying with me. He'll be fucking convinced Ron has left him up here, no chance of the prick doing anything too stupid now.

It's good to see the big lad out though, I've done a lot of reminiscing today and I'm enjoying it. Those things Billy said about me being his dad, well, I could have cried, I just wish I'd treated Val better, maybe I can make it up to her some time. First things first though, I need to steer someone who's just landed into the twenty-first century through the minefield of the modern city. When he went away punk was just on the way out, lager was a woman's drink and Doctor Who was the most cutting edge thing on the three channels that passed for television in this country. Now we've got hundreds of channels full of transsexuals swearing, a computer in every house, lager louts and fucking alcopops.

'Tel,' I shout across the bar making a drinking motion with my hand, he's straight up on his feet, fucking beaming he is, nodding and giving me the thumbs up. As I get to the bar it hits me, we've been mates for twenty years and I've never bought him a pint, I don't even know what he drinks. I just get lagers in; fuck it, after twenty-five years inside he'll drink anything. He's still beaming when I get to the table and jumps up again to shake my hand.

'Welcome back to the real world mate,' I say, 'there's a few things have changed so don't be scared to ask me about anything.'

He jumps straight in with, 'When the fuck did beer go up to three quid a pint?' he laughs and then says, 'Jesus Span, if that's inflation how much does a whore cost?'

I just piss myself laughing, he's right, what price progress? I'd better get him a job sorted fast.

Barry

Just called round for Billy and got a shock as Lisa said that the bizzies had took him away on suspicion of murder. What the fuck is going on? I asked her if she needed anything but she said she was alright, told me to keep it quiet as the brief reckoned Billy would be out in the morning.

Then, I get back here to the flat and fucking Sharon, Merry public enemy number one, is waiting on my doorstep in fucking tears. Not sure what to do so I invite her in and make her a cup of tea, then she just asks me where Carlos is and why won't he answer his phone. She doesn't know, oh fuck, she's already in tears and now I've got to tell her what's happened, she'll be hysterical. All I need now is for Merry to burst through the door and accuse me of shagging her as well.

Clarty

I'll be out of here soon. Vince has told me what's going on and I'm surprised that fucking idiot has managed to engineer such a result out of this. Well, not that surprised, in a moment of weakness he mentioned his contact on the other side of the law, a Chief Inspector no less, that explains who the bloke he's been meeting over the years is then. He swore to me he didn't kill the old man either, like it means fuck all to me, he was just a shag and a payday; I don't love everyone I fuck.

He told me about Ron Carter as well, seems he's connected with the Reeves boys. He's fucking shitting himself about some washed up old cockney gangster, I told him those blokes are only hard in the books they write about each other down there, don't worry about him. He went mad then, made me promise him not to do anything about Carlos, and said the plan was to have a straightener when he came out of nick. He smiled at that and wouldn't say why, just said it was best I didn't know, the fucker's obviously not coming out if Vince is in with the Chief Inspector, mind you I think Vince has had his day now, maybe it's time I took more of a direct role in things.

I'll be out of this hospital soon; we'll see what happens then.

Terry

Spanish has got a nice little gaff, got my own room and a view of the river. Couple of decent pubs close by and not too far from Val Reeves, he says he likes to be close by in case she needs anything. He's gonna introduce me tomorrow, I'm gonna meet Billy and his family as well, I've heard a lot about them and I'm looking forward to it. First things first though, I've got a twenty-five year old itch that needs scratching and Spanish is gonna drop me off at a place he knows. 'Can I borrow some aftershave mate?' I don't need to make an effort for these girls but I want to, for me, it's been a long time and I intend to enjoy every second of this.

Irvine

Just got off the phone to Ron Carter and he is adamant that Billy Reeves would not have stitched his own brother up but I'll have to take Ron's word for that as I don't know the bloke. Got to go in and see him now, got a call off his wife earlier, Ron's niece, apparently he's been arrested as well due to the 'new' evidence. I've had a word with the desk sergeant and they won't be holding him long as they're just trying to see if there's any connection between Billy Reeves getting the money from the will and his brother Carl being there. As his appointed solicitor I get to see him without witnesses present so it's about time I unravelled a bit of this.

I motion the guard to leave the cell, Billy's not going to attack his own brief is he and I don't want anyone hearing what we discuss. He stands up to greet me as I approach, it's the first time I've met him and he's an impressive looking chap, must be about sixteen or seventeen stone, six foot tall and shaven head. Looks like your archetypal bouncer who's gone to seed a bit, not quite fully fit if you like, Carlos is obviously the sportsman.

I'm just about to say hello when he speaks first, 'Why am I here?' I just look back at him a little confused, 'Didn't they read you your rights Mr. Reeves?'

'Yes,' he replies, 'but they just quoted new evidence coming to light and as I've never been anywhere near the house concerned I can't see what that would be.'

Fucking hell he doesn't know. He doesn't know that his dad is the dead man and now I've got to tell him. I've seen some bluffers and chancers in my time, occupational hazard in this line of work you might say, but I can tell at first glance Billy Reeves is not one of them.

'You'd better sit down then Billy,' I say, 'this might come as a bit of a shock.'

He sits down on his bench, back against the wall, shoulders hunched forward just looking up at me.

'The dead man left his only child a substantial amount of money in his will, a very substantial amount in fact, one million, three hundred and fifty thousand pounds to be exact.'

'What's that got to do with me?' he says, realisation slowly turning his face pale as he mouths the words and thinks about what it is I'm saying.

'I'm sorry to be the one who has to break this to you Billy and I'm sorry it's had to happen in a place like this. The dead man, Judge Maxwell, is, was, your father.'

I'm seriously thinking of calling the guard back in as Billy digests this information, clenching and unclenching his fists. Then, his face changes from council estate wide boy to one of utter sadness and disappointment. He leans back against the wall, closes his eyes and moans softly to himself. This takes a couple of seconds and suddenly the mask snaps back into place and Billy becomes businesslike once again.

'What's the score with Carlos?' he asks

'He was found at the scene with a baseball bat, he attacked the arresting officer and on later investigation was found to have threatened the judge, in his courtroom in front of witnesses, not long ago. The judge wasn't killed with a baseball bat, I've found that out through a few contacts at the forensic department but the arresting officer, Chief Inspector Milo, made sure he dragged the bat through the victim's blood and this has muddied the waters somewhat.'

Billy looks thoughtful, 'Why was he there in the first place and why would a Chief Inspector be there first as arresting officer?'

'Officially, he saw an open door and went in there to help, unofficially, you texted him to meet him there. As far as Chief Inspector Milo goes I wouldn't trust him as far as I could throw him, something smells there.'

He's shaking his head, 'My phone went missing the night before it happened, I had it in the pub when I went to meet Merry - wanker.' Then he's looking straight at me again, 'You've got eyes and ears all over the place I'd imagine,' he says. I nod my head silently and he continues, 'Any chance you could find out if there's any connection at all between a bloke called Vince Merry and our beloved Chief Inspector?'

I can see where he's going, I've heard of Vince Merry and the whole of Newcastle now knows that Carlos took his girlfriend and damaged his cousin, revenge would definitely be on the agenda there.

'Leave it with me Billy,' I say, 'they want you for questioning in a bit but just keep telling them that you know nothing about the murder and you've only just found out about Judge Maxwell being your father.'

A look of pain flashes across his face then it's gone and determination sets in once again.

'And Billy,' I say, 'I'm sorry.'

'Not to worry mate,' he replies smiling, 'at least I can afford your fees now.'

Spanish

Dropped Terry off at the whorehouse, he said he'd get a taxi back as he might be a while, I'll fucking bet. Thought I'd drop in at Vals for a cup of tea and she's in bits as Billy's been nicked now as well. Lisa's been up with the kids to see her and they've both had a good cry about it; their worlds are falling apart. Val's still inconsolable now, she just keeps saying over and over, 'It wasn't meant to be like this,' and I'm just trying to lift her spirits a bit.

'They'll be all right Val, the bizzies haven't got nothing on Billy have they, he wasn't even there.'

She just looks at me, broken, and says, 'You know how they'll link him Spanish, you always knew.'

She's right, I put it out of my head for all those years but I knew that Maxwell cunt was Billy's dad; I turned up after him and tried to look after the lad. That wanker rejected him before he was even born, his own boy, probably just as well though, the queer, sick twat might have warped his mind.

'Val,' I say softly, 'it means nothing, how many enemies must a judge have? Anyone could have done it.' She's crying softly, 'That's what I thought would happen, that's what the police should think isn't it?'

'Don't worry,' I say, 'Billy'll be out soon, you'll see.'

She brightens up at my confidence, and I am confident about that, looks at me again and says, 'Do you think the money will have any bearing on it?'

I'm looking back at her now confused, 'What money?'

'Well he'll have his son in his will won't he?'

Fucking hell I never thought of that, he'll be minted as well I bet, that's a motive and a half that is.

Carlos

Just spoke to the brief and he says Billy's in the next cell. The poor sod's just found out who his dad is, I'm gutted for him and want to smash this fucking wall down to be with my brother when he needs me. He told me Billy had his phone nicked the night before it happened when he was meeting with Merry about something. Doesn't take Spender to work out that Newcastle's top gangster, who hasn't had so much as a parking ticket for the last ten years despite selling more gear and beating up more blokes than a Colombian drugs baron, has got a link to the thin blue line. Cunt.

Irvine's told me that Billy'll be getting out in the morning as it was obvious in the interview that he didn't have a clue the judge was his dad. Even Milo couldn't pin it to him, he reckons that Duncan one was very interested in Billy though, something not right about that bloke either. Anyway, before he went he arranged for the night duty sergeant to leave our hatches down and ignore our chatter, fair play to the copper I say. So let's make the most of it, it's going to be a long night for Big Bro so lets see if I can help.

'Hoo chunky...'

Terry

Spanish has dropped me off at the house and I'm sitting here having a drink while the brass in charge gets me a selection together, she'd better hurry up I'm poking my own fucking eyes out here. One thing's for sure this won't take long, well not the first time anyway.

There's a big, daft, loud geezer in the kitchen talking to one of the gels, he must be coked up or something, full of himself. He's talking louder and louder like he wants people to hear, big headed bastard, another plastic gangster, he'd have lasted two minutes in my day. Fuck him anyway here's the skirt. No models among them but plenty of pretty looking honest to goodness pros, just what I want. There's one about thirty, big tits and a filthy laugh, fucking ideal. I'm about to choose her when a name comes out of the kitchen that stops me in my tracks, I put my cock on hold for five minutes and play it cool, I say I'll have another drink while I'm choosing and then I sit back and listen to the geezer.

Billy

Carlos is shouting me from the next cell, he'll get us fucked off the bizzies if they catch him, mind you when you're facing a murder charge I suppose a bollocking off another copper's not the end of the world is it? The hatch is down on my cell door so I don't even have to shout, it looks deliberate so I'm wondering if it's part of what is definitely a fit up.

'Alreet charv,' I say back, a bit cautious, 'is your hatch down?'

'Aye,' he says, 'the brief sorted it, he's alright him like. How you doing?'

'Alright I think, still trying to take in what's happened, have you heard me news?'

'I have Bill, I have. I'm sorry it had to be a dick like him but he's not your dad really is he, he was never there. The fucker doesn't have any rights or claim on you now, dead or not.'

He's right. 'You're right Carl, I was just saying to Spanish today that I considered him me dad above all else even if he did spawn a numpty like you.'

'Ha ha, do you remember that time we first ever took acid, in that club. Lucky the owld fella was around that night eh?'

Fuck me do I remember that. I'm eighteen and he's seventeen, we're in Manhattans and we're bored, down to our last tenners and it's only eleven bells so I said fuck it let's get some drugs and see what happens. I saw this owlder kid I knew from Byker and we were on our way, we didn't even know what was going to happen, we just sat there for a bit and then started giggling.

Once we'd really started tripping we had to get out of the club sharpish, habit took over and we walked back to Byker and headed for a Chinese. We're sitting in there mumbling shite to each other and giggling when this bloke comes running in and demands money. The Chinese bloke tells him to fuck off, as you would, and the bloke runs back out to his mate's car, which then screeches off. Next thing I know the fucker's back, he could have been gone an hour or thirty seconds for all I knew the state we were in. Then he just tries to throw a brick through the Chinese window, his mate's telling us to move but we were too far gone by then. We watched this in slow motion like in a film as we were sitting by the window, the brick glistened and shone from the streetlights as it arced onto the window and then the window just slowly bent in but didn't shatter. I was transfixed, it was beautiful. Then the coppers turned up and we just pissed ourselves laughing at them, they realised we were on something and couldn't really be arsed to nick us, so they just took us home, or thought they did. The owld lady would have went mental, so, being the clever one I somehow managed to give the law Spanish's address and he kidded on we lived there. Then the poor bastard spent all night talking us down and making sure we didn't freak out, above and beyond the call of duty from him that was.

'Aye, I remember that all right, lucky we moved onto amphetamines and off that shite eh?'

And that's it we're off for the night keeping each other's spirits up with former glories and both of us ignoring the fact that at least one of us is probably going to prison for thirty years. Fuck it, worry about that in morning.

Merry

I'm talking too much, I know I am, but fuck it, I'm Vince Merry and who would go against me in this town. 'I'M VINCE MERRY, THAT'S ME VINCE FUCKING MERRY ha ha.'

Chop another line up and I'm telling her about it all, 'Carlos fucking Reeves Joanne, shagging Sharon behind me back and then giving Clarty a hiding, not on. Well I've sorted that twat, sorted him properly, he's inside now Joanne, he's inside and he's never coming out. My mate says he's putting him away for life and when he's inside properly, a couple of years down the line I'm having him done in. Ron Carter can fuck off then, he'll think it's a prison fight but before Carlos dies, before the blade goes into his heart he'll be told. You should never have fucked with Vince Merry - NO ONE FUCKS WITH VINCE MERRY.'

I'm snorting it down two lines at a time, fucking top gear this is mind, I'll have to talk to Tony about that, he got it for us. Joanne's asking what I'll do now Sharon's gone and I look at her. She never fucked us about, never kicked off about us getting her pregnant and never tried to claim owt off us, she even grafts for her money.

'You're a proper lass Joanne, you've never tried to shaft us like the rest of them, I should have stuck with you. The bairn as well, young Dennis, I should have looked after you both a lot more.'

She's smiling and kissing us, aye we'll be upstairs in a minute I'm getting a Charlie horn now and she's getting it but there's just one more thing I've got to say, the chemicals are just forcing everything in me brain out through me mouth.

'Billy Reeves as well, if he goes down for this, I'm killing him as well. That prick's always thought he's better than me. He dies as well.'

Then she's leading us through the living room past this big older gadgy who's taking his pick of the whores, I just manage an, 'Alright mate?' as I go past and he gives me a nod, can't say I know him like.

Billy

Me and Carlos had a great chat before he fell asleep then the wankers threw me out just after half four, anything to avoid giving me a breakfast the stingy twats.

'We may need you for further questioning so don't leave the country Mr. Reeves.' That's it, no lift or nowt, won't ring a taxi for us and I'm out in the drizzle just a t-shirt and jeans on. I didn't bring me phone cos I left in such a hurry from the house. Looks like it's a long walk to the taxi office.

There's a taxi now, 'Whoah ye fucker,' bastard, went straight past, fucking typical, looked like there was someone in it mind and I can't blame him for not sharing. I could be anybody. I could be the type of psycho who bludgeons judges to death or anything. It's not the end of the world anyway walking; it'll give us time to think. Now Merry and the copper, have they killed the judge? I know Carlos didn't and I know I didn't. Fucking tricky one this is, I need to work it out though and then deal with it. The question is how?

Terry

Jesus that was tasty, I picked well there. I didn't fuck about, gave her the story straight away and told her there was about twenty-five years of come stored up there and she went to work. We did it three times in the end, in between plenty of petting, fondling and generally getting to know a woman's body again. She just said as soon as I'd told her, 'Take your time mate, we've got all night for two hundred and fifty quid.' So I did.

Now that's out of the way though I need to get back to the flat and think on what I heard. I ain't impressed with Mr. Merry one bit, no class at all. Now I know what he's done and what he plans to do I need to call Ron. I'm not telling Spanish just yet cos I think he'll get a gun and do it himself and that won't help Carlos or Billy.

This taxi driver's not fucking about either, just nearly knocked some geezer down over there, a pisshead in just a t-shirt trying to wave him down in the middle of the road.

A t-shirt in this weather!? Fucking geordies.

Tuesday

Billy

Lisa let me lie in this morning, I could hear her getting the kids off to school then she brought me some tea and toast up with the papers. I should get nicked more often if this is what happens. This fucking judge thing is all over the nationals now as well, the tabloids will pick up on him being on the other bus an' all shortly and it'll fucking explode. I'm surprised the local hacks haven't jumped on that one yet mind. When it happens though all the tabloid scum'll be up here sniffing about and then it'll come out about me getting his cash in the will. The journos will fucking love that, the sleazy wankers, I can see them getting excited about it now, the judge's bastard son and his brother the murderer. Fucking hell. I've got a couple of reporter mates if it does start to head that way like, maybe I can deflect it a bit onto Clarty and Merry, hint at the copper as well. Do it Blair style with a bit of spin.

A shadow falls across me as I'm just deciding to get out of bed and I look up. Lisa's standing at the door of the bedroom wearing a tarty copper's uniform and saying, 'So then William Reeves to sum up, I find you guilty of being a big, fat, sexy bastard and I sentence you to a quickie with your wife. Assume the position.'

'I hope there's no batteries in that truncheon,' I laugh as she jumps on me and we roll around the bed, 'and less of the fat, I'm just well built.'

She just says, 'If you're getting thirty years inside then I'm getting as much as I can now so come here and do your husbandly duty.' Fucking hell I expected a bollocking off her at best, I wonder what she'll be like when I tell her about the money, should be fun finding out anyway.

Milo

Absolutely magnificent, the tabloids are covering this Maxwell thing extensively, my publisher is creaming himself and my retirement fund is looking good. Just as well. I've made a bit over the years through Merry but that's pretty much been pissed up a wall and blown on a succession of tarts, hookers and poor quality drugs; again supplied by the versatile Mr. Merry. I need this lump of cash from the book quite badly in order to have a comfortable end to my life; I'll travel, eat and drink well and obviously fuck whores in every country I inhabit. Superb.

My agent is booking me onto a lot of the morning talk shows as well; the tabloids have managed to outrage the country in the way only they can. Mr and Mrs 'I believe everything I read' Joe Public are just bursting to get their ill informed views across via Trisha and Jeremy Kyle and I'll be there to stoke their fears. Not forgetting to mention of course that I'm retiring soon and that I can reveal a lot more in my autobiography than I can on the telly. Remember folks, '*Don't. Do. The. Crime...*' available at all good bookshops and most bad ones, only £16.99. Ha ha the gullible bastards.

Merry was chuffed when I told him we'd pulled Billy Reeves in last night, does him some sort of favour that apparently. I wasn't doing it for him though; we had to question him really, if only for appearances sake. Once the money was left to him it gave a motive even though I know it wasn't him. I knew he wouldn't be there long and I knew we didn't have enough to charge him. It all adds to the intrigue though doesn't it, gay judge killed by only son's local celebrity brother. What will the redtops make of that when they get hold of it I wonder? '*Fudge nudging Judge Grudge,*' ha ha, what about '*Gay Judge takes a sore one from behind,*' no not as good or '*Boxer gives homo Judge one in and out of the ring*' ha ha ha ha.

I'm having some extra bacon I think; bugger it I'll go in late today.

Merry

Fucking head's banging today. I went overboard with the Charlie and the beer last night, shagged the arse off Joanne, don't know how she ended up here afterwards though. Got a phone call off Milo this morning as well, fucking early one and all by the way I was still half out of it, I got the message loud and clear though. They nicked Billy Reeves last night as an accomplice to the murder, new evidence and all that. Wouldn't tell me what it was, says it's more than his job's worth and that he can't make any waves this close to retirement. Still must have been something meaty to nick him for.

'Do you want sauce on your sausage sarnies pet?' she's shouting from the kitchen.

'Aye, plenty red sauce Jo.'

Why's she still here? Who's looking after my, her, kid?

'Where's young Dennis Joanne?'

'He'll be off to school now, he's used to being by himself it doesn't bother him. I got him a Playstation Three and a DVD player last Christmas so he's happy enough.'

Aye, suppose so, he is fifteen now. Big fucker from what I've seen of him as well, takes after his dad.

'How does he get on at school?'

'Well,' she says, plonking a plate of sausage sarnies down and a cup of tea. Belter. 'He's been accused of bullying a few times and he's been suspended for it but it never comes to nothing.'

'Mmph what about,' it's fucking hard to chew, breathe and talk at the same time, 'his schoolwork?' I gasp at her spitting sausage about the table.

'He's in the bottom sets for everything,' she says, 'he reckons he's going to join the army anyway, you don't need brains for that do you?'

I can feel an idea forming in my mind here, 'He's a handy fucker then? Fighting and that I mean?'

'I don't think he's lost any yet, so his mates tell me anyway,' she says slurping her tea, no sandwiches though, a pro's only got a limited shelf life and she doesn't want to hurt her earning potential.

'I'm going to the gym later on,' I say, 'what time does he finish school?'

I can see a bit of father and son bonding going on here and maybe a career opportunity for my boy.

Clarty

I'm getting out today all healed up and ready to go. Take it easy for a bit the doctor said but fuck that, I haven't been training for a week; I'll need to get straight back into that before I turn to mush and fat. I've been thinking about things as well, it'll be all round town by now that I'm queer so I'm going to get a lot of stick. I think it's time I started asserting myself, not the way I did at Carlos's gym that was fucking stupid, no, use my head instead of my fists for a while. Vince said if he did anything to the Reeves family outside of the straightener then he was a dead man and if Vince becomes a dead man then a gap appears at the top of the food chain, a gap just waiting to be filled by my good self. Vince thinks that me and Big Tony are the only ones he can trust; I'll have to change that, don't want him trusting anyone but me from now on. Oh yes, I've got some work to do when I get out of here.

Got to wait a couple of hours yet for the doctor to discharge me. Speaking of filling gaps that porter over there has been coming onto me all week. Might as well take it while it's on offer.

'Excuse me. Yes you, porter boy, I think I need a hand to get to the toilet,' aha weedy, submissive and grateful, just how I like them.

Billy

She is absolutely fucking astounded by that news, one point three mill is a lot of money and even taking into account the inheritance tax I'll be left with about seven hundred and fifty large. It'll easily buy me mam a house down the coast and make the rest of us a lot more comfortable. I'll need to talk to Carlos about winding up the drink and tabs thing, I'm not giving the law any more reasons to chase us. We can keep the bakery on and he's got his gym, maybe look at something else, taxi firm or something.

Lisa asked us a valid one just after I told her.

'I know this sounds like a stupid question because it's a lot of money but are you sure you want to keep it? The bloke was a bastard, treated your mother and you like shit and left you all in poverty for years. I would understand if you didn't want to.'

I had actually thought about that myself while I was locked up, once Carlos had drifted off to sleep and it was just me and my thoughts. He's getting used to prison life already, me, I kept expecting a big sex case to burst in any minute and try to use me as his girlfriend so I kept my fucking eyes open. I thought about the money and whether I should accept it or give it to charity. We're not well off but we're comfortable so I could live without it but me mam worked hard all her fucking life and what's she got to show for it though? A council house in Byker surrounded by foreign gyppos and local charvas. There was no question about it really, my dad could have been Saddam Hussein for all I care, I'm still taking his fucking money and buying me mam a house in Tynemouth.

I just looked back at her, the woman I love with all my heart and said, 'No I don't want anything to do with the prick but I am keeping it,' and she understood.

Spanish

Terry's still sleeping; he must have got his money's worth last night, I don't think he came in until well into the early hours. Fuck it after twenty-five years away I'd have turned my cock into corned beef through pure shagging as well. I'll nip over in a bit and see if Billy's out yet, find out what the score is and then I'll check Val's all right. She was a bit strange last night might need to talk to somebody.

Ron

The newspapers are full of this bleedin' judge nonsense, just saying that an unnamed local man is being held for questioning up there. Irvine rang me this morning to let me know that Billy was taken away last night and then let out again; apparently the judge is only his naffin' dad and he's left him a load of cash, well over a million. A nice touch for Lisa and him but it's only gonner bring more trouble, the filth have got about three different motives now and it's looking black for Carlos. The thing is though Irvine reckons it's a stitch up, he's been talking to a couple of the local coppers off the record and they reckon Carlos just wouldn't do it. He mentioned another one in particular, a detective called Duncan, said he was a London boy and he was going to have a word with him on the quiet, thinks he recognises him from somewhere.

I'll ring Billy later and check he's okay, no trouble with that Merry slag or anything, and then I'll bell Terry and see how he's finding life in chilly geordieland.

Terry

First night of freedom in twenty-five years and I spent it screwing followed by a massive kip, I must have went out like a light when I finally got back. No bells or whistles and I can stay in bed as long as I want. What a good night though, blew me wad in more ways than one. Spanish must have went out so I'll get up and have a cup of tea and wait for him to come back, he's taking me to meet Billy and Lisa later. Then tomorrow I've got to meet my probation officer and look for a job, or pretend to at least.

He's left a paper for me as well, top geezer, plenty of milk in the fridge and biscuits in the cupboard, I might as well make a pot and read the paper cover to cover. Now that's a luxury I wasn't allowed inside, the authorities used to cut out all the news that they thought would be relevant to us, worried we might get unruly or riot. Having said that the bastards used to cut the football out as well for a laugh sometimes, which just made us worse.

Looking at some of these stories in here it seems that a lot has changed in two and a half decades. For instance criminal gangs aged twelve and thirteen terrorising people, can't you just give the little bleeders or their dads a slap? A bloke was locked up for defending his young son in his own garden against two lads what had jumped the wall and were nicking his shoes. What the fuck is that all about, am I still in the right country? A kid gets half a million compensation for falling through a warehouse roof he shouldn't have fucking been on in the first place. Eh? It's all to do with human rights apparently, something the government brought in on the orders of our European guvnors. Wonder if I can sue for distress at being punished for a crime I was guilty of, probably happen any day now that one.

Ah but look at this speaking of our European cousins again, it looks like some things never change. Our elected leaders dipping their noses in the trough on a jolly across Europe at our expense, officially a fact finding tour, cementing diplomatic relations and building trade links for the benefit of the country, unofficially they're probably screwing, drinking and living it up on the taxpayer. Granted I haven't paid any tax for a while but if I had, I'd be fucking livid.

Billy

Lisa's having a couple of hours off from the shop and we're heading up to me mams. Spanish'll be up there with Terry and I'm looking forward to meeting him cos I've heard a lot about him and he's staying with Spanish for the time being. I've got a package for him from Ron as well that I need to make sure he gets. I'd better tell me mam about me biological father as well, the cunt'll never be me dad though, end of. Just tell her that I know who he is now and how he's left me a load of cash. I hope she doesn't get too upset about me keeping it and using it to buy her a place out of Byker but at the end of the day a chance like this won't come along again.

Lisa's talking to me about something but I'm not really listening. For once I've brought a disk for the car and I've got The Jam on the cd player. We're driving past my old school and they're singing something about teachers who said I'd be nothing, aye you wankers how wrong were you? I own a small business, two if you count the other stuff, I've got a nice house, two lovely kids, a wife I'd die for and three quarters of a million English pounds coming my way. So fuck you. I won.

I can still remember the shite they used to give me, 'You're stupid Reeves, you'll always work for someone else Reeves, ever thought of joining the army Reeves I would if I was you, bright but lazy Reeves, you'll never amount to anything Reeves.'

Some of them were all right, the weirdy, beardy, lefty ones who wanted you to talk about stuff and that but in the main they were all just a pain in the arse.

What they didn't know was that even at that age I had an entrepreneurial spirit. When I was about thirteen it became fashionable down south to wear a label known as '*Boy - London*', proper load of shite it was but it was trendy so they were all on it, then some bright spark up here came up with '*Lad - Newcastle*', playing on the traditional disdain of anything cockney, and started knocking out snides of this '*Boy*' thing. Can't claim it was me who thought of it but it was me who banged them out round school and made three quid a go on caps & t-shirts, I probably made as much as the teachers some weeks, it beat doing a fucking paper round anyway.

If they'd spoke to me properly then I'd have done much better when I was there, I've got a thirst for knowledge me like, if they hadn't just assumed I was a stereotypical little bastard from a council estate then I might not have just switched off when it came to learning and exams. Mind you, as much as I disliked it at the time, you could say it made me the person I am today. I've fought for everything I've ever had and don't owe anyone anything. Maybe I should thank them?

Yeah the old place looks almost gothic as we're driving past, all dark and menacing in the rain. I get a shiver down my spine just looking at it. Fucking glad my kids don't go there mind.

The Modfather's chanting about a thousand men in uniform now, fucking seems like it at the minute an' all and they all seem to be after me and Carlos.

Fuck, my mind's working overtime here.

What if Merry has contacts inside the prison service as well?

Shite.

Merry

I think Billy may well have to think again about coming to work for me. It's about time I started throwing my weight around again and told people what they're doing instead of asking them. He won't cause me any problems now, his brother's going down and isn't coming out, not that he knows that yet like, and that leaves him spreading himself thin trying to look after his mam and his own family. He might well take some advice and realise he needs me for protection up here, if he's in my crew then his family's protected, simple as that. I know he's got Ron Carter and I know I got a scare when he pulled him out of the woodwork but at the end of the day he's down in London. I've had time to think about things now and the man's in his mid-fifties, the up and coming young tearaways won't respect him anyway, they'll see him as yesterday's bloke. The new young firms up here know me and are scared of what I can do to them, they won't give a fuck about Ron Carter. I'll need to go and see him and talk about it, he'll either see sense and work for me or he'll have to go, I can't afford to have him outside the tent pissing in. I'm not allowing him to say no to me again, I'm number one in the town and people need to fucking remember that round here.

Barry

Sleeping on the bastard settee has fucked my back; being a gentleman I gave Sharon my bed, she was in a right state when I told her where Carlos was, sobbing and moaning like she was in pain. I told her it was all a load of shite and he'd be out soon but she was properly gutted.

'It's Vince,' she was saying, over and over again, 'it's got to be, he hates me and Carlos now, I don't know how he did it but it's got to be him.'

'I don't know how he could have done it Sharon,' I was saying back to her, 'I agree he would have done it if he could, straight away just to get you both back, but how could a dick like him have managed to get someone fitted up for murder?'

She was fucking adamant it was him though and had me believing it in the end. Eventually, in the early hours of the morning when we couldn't think about it any more we went to bed.

Now, after sleeping in and fucking my body on the settee it's late morning. I'm putting the kettle on and seeing if there's anything in the cupboards for breakfast, only white bread, toast it is. She's obviously still asleep the lazy cow, I'll give her a knock before I make her any toast in case she doesn't like it or something.

'Sharon,' no answer, 'Sharon, are you getting up?' still no answer; cautiously open the door in case she's getting up quietly, I wouldn't mind seeing her stark bollock naked but I wouldn't fancy the clout I'd get off Carlos.

Fucks sakes, where's she gone? The bed's been slept in but she's nowhere to be seen, fucking women. Bollocks to her, I'll have me toast and then try and catch up with Billy, I still need to talk to him about Tony.

Clarty

Taxi just dropped me off, think I'll have a bath and think about how to proceed, I'll have to check in with Vince at some point today but that can wait. That porter might have some bruises to explain to his boyfriend when he gets home from work tonight, I could tell he liked it rough just by looking at him. He was desperate for me to take his number and give him a ring next time I'm available, shouldn't think I'll bother.

Terry

'Ron, Tel here, got a bit of info for ya.'

'What's that Tel?' He's all ears.

'I bumped into that Merry geezer last night and heard him shouting the odds about Carlos and Billy.'

'Oh yeh, did he know who you was?'

Likes to weigh up the situation does Ron, likes to know every glance, every word and every tone of voice, how it was said, when it was said and, most importantly, what wasn't said.

'No mate, I was just another punter to him. Anyway, he basically said that he'd sorted Carlos for screwing his bird and doing his cousin, reckoned once he was put away properly that he was having him bumped off. Said no-one fucks with him.'

'He definitely said that did he?'

'Yeh mate he was ranting away to one of the whores, full of drugs I think, tosser wouldn't shut up.'

'Anything else he came out with?'

'Yeh mate, this was nasty as well, he said if Billy got sent down for it he was doing him too, said he'd never liked him and he was having it if he got the chance.'

'Right Tel, got that. Anything else I need to know?'

'That's about it mate, like I said he was with a whore and she was trying to get him upstairs while he went on about being the man and nobody fucking with him. The slag seems to think if you shout it loud enough that makes it true.'

'Okay mate,' he sounds a bit thoughtful now, 'do me a favour will you and let Billy know all this when you meet him. Tell him you've told me and I don't want him to do anything hasty until I ring him.'

'Alright Ron, I'm seeing him later. How's things?'

'Okay Tel, things is okay. How's life on the outside?'

'I've done the necessary mate, sorted me bollocks out and now I'm ready to go to work again, just tell me what you want doing about this Merry ponce and it'll be done.'

He's laughing now, 'Bleedin' hell mate, you must have blew her head off when you come. I'll ring you about Merry, just keep your eyes and ears open for the next few days okay?'

'No probs Ron, I'll speak to you later. See you mate.'

Merry

I'll go to his bakers shop and see him, must remember to say that I tried to ring him but got unobtainable, don't want him realising that it's me that nicked his phone. He shouldn't have been able to talk to Carlos yet anyway so he shouldn't know about the text message. No point in taking chances though, I'll just play dumb on the phone thing with him.

Must give Clarty a ring later as well, he was getting out today, probably at home having a rest the poor little fucker. I won't forget what he did for me though, nearly got hisself killed off that dago prick and all on my account, that's loyalty that is. Family loyalty can't be bought or sold, it's there forever. I'm starting to have a few doubts about Big Tony though, that gear the twat got me last night wasn't my usual and it definitely wasn't the stuff I sell in the club. My stuff's not that good, I know that for a fact. So where did that cunt get that from? Obviously another supplier and obviously not one of mine. Now why would he do that? I might have to keep a close eye on him from now on, could be a job for Clarty, someone I trust.

Anyway, jump into the Shogun and get down to the bakery and see the boy Reeves, I'm going to make him an offer he can't refuse ha ha.

Sharon

Careful to avoid the dog shit and chewing gum I stroll down Bloxham Street, this is where Joanne Merrick lives. Vince thinks I don't know about her but I do, I've known for years that he's got a bird he sees now and then and I also know he had a kid to her before I came on the scene. I knew but I didn't care and still don't but I am going to see her, if anyone knows anything that could help my Carlos out of nick she will.

This street's a nightmare; gardens with rusting cars and old mattresses in them, a group of scruffy kids running barefoot round the street in the puddles that are left, glue bags and gas cans dotted around the kerbs and graffiti everywhere. What a fucking disaster zone, Comic Relief want to think about coming here now and then. I know which house it is and I bang on the door, no answer so I bang harder then it flies open, a teenage lad, white faced and spotty with a fat gut stares out at me, 'Yeah?' It grunts, obviously a chip off the old Merry block. There's an overwhelming smell of biscuits and toast coming from the house and there's a cat perched on a kitchen counter eating from a tin, I can feel the bile rising in my chest.

'Is your mother in?'

'No,' he says, 'she's at work.'

'In the daytime? I know what she does for a living son, don't worry I'm not a social worker.' I try to push past him to get into the house but he easily blocks me and throws me back into the garden.

'Fuck off out my house you crazy bitch,' he shouts clenching his fists.

I realise I'm not getting in so I shout loud enough for her to hear wherever she's hiding, 'Tell her Sharon came round, I want to talk about Vince. It's important.'

He comes out of the house now, probably the first time he's seen sunlight in days and chases me down the garden path to the gate, 'I told you she's not here, now FUCK OFF.'

I leave quickly, still avoiding the dog shit, keeping my head down.

Big Tony

Barry hasn't got back to me yet about Billy, he'll meet me though and I reckon he'll be happy to help when I tell him what I know. Billy's no threat to me once I take over cos he's not bothered about shit like that. I'll be able to concentrate on running the firm properly and expanding, make some links with other mobs round the country and do some sensible business, none of this smacking out little boys in nightclubs like Merry.

Billy's cockney mate, that Ron Carter, proper face he is, could well be a lucrative contact if I play it right with him, especially if I've helped out the Reeves boys. Merry's a fucking idiot, I can take him now on my own if I want but if I'm seen to be doing Carlos and Billy a favour at the same time it can only be good for me, might get messy but I'm too clever for that thick prick Vince Merry. I'll give Barry until tomorrow then I'll ring him again.

<u>Spanish</u>

We're all here at Vals, I wanted her to meet Terry so he'd be a face she recognised if owt ever happened and I wasn't around. He's a capable man, into his fifties now but more than able to sort out some of these lads half his age. Billy turned up earlier with Lisa and Val cheered up knowing he was out of nick. I think those two have got a bit to talk about though. Terry reckons he needs to talk to me and Billy anyway about something that happened in the brothel last night but we'll have a cup of tea with the ladies first and then get down to business.

Young Barry's just turned up an' all, says he wants a word with Billy as well, there's a bit of a queue forming here, the poor bugger's head must be spinning.

<u>Val</u>

I was so pleased to see Billy turn up with Lisa that I almost cried, he smiled at me as well so I knew he wasn't angry about his father and when I was making the tea he came out and had a quiet word with me in the kitchen. Lisa knew what he was doing, she always does, she can read him like a book. I said sorry to him that I picked such a bastard to be his dad and he told me not to worry about it and that he wasn't bothered.

Nothing bothers him, ever, not outwardly anyway. I worry though sometimes that he's hard all the way through, I think he's got a soft centre but it would be nice to see it sometimes. Then he told me that he'd been left over a million by that thing, he reckoned after inheritance tax he would get about seven hundred and fifty thousand. Him and Lisa are going to buy me a house down the coast as soon as the money comes through and will pay all the bills, I couldn't speak and I did cry this time, the tea took a while to get made. I'm so proud of both my sons; I know if the roles were reversed that Carl would have done the same. I just hope we can get him out of prison and put all of this behind us, then it'll all have been worth it.

Barry

There's a houseful at Vals, I'm having to wait to speak to Billy as Terry the cockney gadgy has got him at the minute, that looks like a serious conversation mind. Spanish speaks well of Terry and apparently he's a mate of cockney Rons so he'll be a handy bloke to have on your side I'd think.

I'll have to mention that Sharon's turned up at mine as well, just in case, wonder what she's up to?

Billy

This is the first time I've ever met this Terry Briggs bloke, Spanish reckons he's a good lad and Ron and him were best mates for years, still are, one of the few people Ron really trusts so he must be okay. First things first, we've went into the dining room out of the way and I handed him the envelope Ron gave me for him. He wasn't expecting it I don't think which again sums the bloke up really.

'Leave it out Billy, there's ten grand in here I can't have that,' he's flabbergasted.

'Ron said it was for you Tel,' I say, he seems genuinely shocked that Ron's sorted him out.

'But I wasn't on a job, it was my own stupid fault and I deserved all of what I got, Ron's not obliged to look after me,' he says again, still amazed at the large clump of cash in his hand.

'I don't think it was a case of him being obliged to help you out mate,' I say, 'you're his best mate from way back and I know he was gutted when you went down, I think he wanted to give you something to start off with. Enjoy it Tel that's what it's for.'

He is properly grateful and that tells me everything I need to know about him.

'Now what's this you've got to tell me?' I ask him.

'I was in a whorehouse last night,' he starts, 'and I bumped into your mate Mr. Merry.'

Oh that's a turn up for the books Merry's paying for it since

Carlos nicked his bird, sad prick.

'Oh yeah,' I say, 'and what did he have to say for himself?'

'Well Billy he don't know me from Adam so I just sat and listened, he was full of drugs I think cos he just ranted and raved.'

'What sort of thing was he saying then Tel?' I'm interested in this cos Merry, for all his faults, isn't known as a loose lips and I'm convinced he's behind the murder so if he's dropped his guard then we could find out something useful.

'He said that he'd taken care of Carlos and once he went behind bars properly he'd take care of him for good, he said he'd have him stabbed Billy.'

The fat, steroid addled cunt I knew it was him, I just don't know how. He won't kill my brother though not if I fucking kill him first. I'm feeling the temper rise in my body but I control it, keep it down and glance into the living room, Lisa's looking at me questioningly and mouthing 'alright?' at me. I just nod and give her a wink and she's happy. Then Terry gets my attention once again as he says, 'And Billy, I'm sorry to have to tell you this but you need to know. He said if you get in his way then he's gonner kill you as well.'

I look back at Lisa sharing a joke with me mam, the two of them cackling away, they've got on well since they first met them two. I think of my boys trying to get through life without a dad and my chest feels like it's going to fucking explode my heart is beating that fast. I'm going to have to deal with this arsehole and I know what it's going to entail.

Terry puts his hand on my shoulder, 'Billy, I've already told Ron and he said hang fire on anything and give him a ring. Would you do that?'

It's a sensible idea, 'Yeah Tel, thanks for telling me all that mate I appreciate it.'

'No problem Billy,' he says, 'old Miguel in there, he's talked about you two for the last twenty years to me, I consider your family mine and when it goes off I'm there if you need me.'

'Cheers Tel,' I say, the bloke's just got out after half his life behind bars and he's offering to put himself at risk of going back there just for me and Carlos.

Andy Rivers

No way, I couldn't be responsible for putting him back there, I'll manage without him.

Barry

I've finally managed to get Billy on his own to tell him about Big Tony and he's looking thoughtful.

'Just run that by me one more time Barry,' he says.

I have to take a deep breath, I'm not proud of flogging pills and that in clubs but it's a living.

'I'm working for Big Tony flogging gear round the clubs for him and he gives me a percentage of what I sell. I collect the gear from his around teatime and weigh him in the next day. He's got quite a few blokes doing this and they're all in Merry's clubs, we undercut Merry's dealers and the bouncers that are on Tony's side send the punters to us rather than the other ones. He's told me he wants to talk to you about his plans for the future and what he knows that could help you.'

'What are his plans for the future?' Billy, poker faced as usual.

'He's going to take over the town and dispose of Merry and his hangers on one way or another.' First time I've said that out loud, I have to look behind me to check there's no one there.

'Arrange it then Barry, somewhere neutral. I want you there watching my back as well.'

'Sound. I'll ring him in a bit.'

Then as I turn to go back into the living room a massive shadow blots out the glass panel on the kitchen door and there's a knock. As Billy answers the door I nearly shit myself.

It's Merry.

Merry

Billy looks a bit surprised at me turning up at his mams, that's good, it just reminds him that I know where she lives. Ever polite he invites me in, there's a house full so I don't hang about just tell him that I'd like a word in private at some point

181

tonight. While he's humming and haahing I have a look round the room: smile at his Mam and Lisa, they aren't smiling back, fucked if I know why but I don't care; Spanish, give him a nod, cunt ignores me and looks at the telly; some bloke I vaguely recognise, don't know where from though and that Barry fucker's flitting about in the dining room.

'Why don't we just have a chat in the garden now Vince,' he says a bit aggressively for my liking, caught me unawares as well that did like I thought he'd try and avoid me. The bloke I don't recognise all that well is getting up looking at Billy. He's a biggish gadgy but he's getting on.

'You're not invited mate,' I say to him.

The cheeky fucker just looks me up and down and says, 'I don't take orders from you geordie boy.'

The twat's a cockney, he's obviously here on Ron Carter's behalf which changes things a little bit.

'I just want to talk to Billy about a bit of business,' I reply, 'private business.'

Billy's holding his palm up to the bloke, 'It's alright Tel,' he says, 'I'll be okay I've known Vince here for years.'

Ha, the prick suspects nothing. We head off outside, the cockney fucker watching us through the window, I'm sure I know him from somewhere.

'What you after then Vince?' he says spinning round a bit quick as we step into the garden.

'Billy,' I start, my prepared speech melting away in my brain. I'm tapping my pocket subconsciously, fuck me I could do with a line or two now. 'Your family's in trouble and your brother's going down for a long time from what I'm hearing. You need me, I could keep trouble from your door. I'm a big player in this town and I want you working for me.'

He just looks straight at me and says, 'Where did you hear Carlos was going down for a long time then Vince?'

Fuck, said too much again, 'It's all round town Billy, I've heard it a couple of times, can't remember where.'

He's just staring at me and I have to look away, can't hold his glare. When I look back he's moved position and eaten up the space between us, his face is right in mine, our noses touching. I can hear the back door opening as he spits at me, 'I will never work for you Merry, get that into your head. Now fuck off and leave me and my family alone.'

I grab his throat and he fucking nuts me, Billy Reeves fucking nuts me, me Vince Merry. That's it he dies here and now. Then there's a body between us, it's that cockney, he just pushes Billy gently away and says to me, 'Mr. Merry, I'm here as an associate of Ronald Carter, I believe you two have met. If you don't wish to meet him again I'd suggest you go home and forget about any ideas of hassling the Reeves family any further. Do you understand?'

I look at Billy; he's ready for it no two ways about it. I can't do it though. Ron Carter will kill me; his boy here would probably do it now if I gave him enough provocation. I'll leave it, go home and think about it.

I just nod at the cockney and at Billy and try and inject a bit of humour as I'm going, 'That's a no then Bill?' I smile.

Barry and Spanish struggle to hold him back as I go; at least I had the last word.

Joanne

Dennis thinks I should tell Vince that Sharon's been round. They got on well at the gym and Vince said he wants to see more of him and try being a bit more of a dad, so yeah I will tell him. I'll make some stuff up as well to really make him mad at her and get him to fuck her off properly, then me, him and Dennis could be a proper family. Yeah that's what I'll do.

Clarty

I've come round to Vinces to check in and it's obvious he's proper foaming about something. He's caning the charlie fucking goodstyle, there's scattered wraps everywhere and empty cans and the fucking stereo's blasting some old rock shit as well. I turn it down to deafening and get myself a can, I don't bother with the gear; it makes you paranoid that shit.

'You alright cuz?' I say.

He just snaps back, 'I can't trust any fucker. They're all out to get me. Fucking Tony's at it now and Sharon's been seen in town bad mouthing me.'

'Oh yeah,' I say, opportunity knocking in my mind.

'The twat's selling his own gear in the clubs,' he shouts, absolutely outraged, 'a couple of my dealers have mentioned now that there's rivals in the clubs and they seem to be helped by the fucking doorstaff. I can't trust any bastard.'

Oh yes opportunity knocks alright, 'You know you can trust me Vince,' I say quietly and meekly, 'we're family and I proved that last week.'

'You're right,' he says, tears in his drug addled eyes, the chemical shit fucking up his thought processes. He's fell for it hook line and sinker 'Do you fancy doing a job for me?'

'Anything you want mate.' I say, looking enthusiastic.

He wants Tony keeping an eye on, wants to know who his dealers are. Then he tells me what occurred today with Billy Reeves and the other bloke. Seems Mr. Carter has a bit of clout after all, maybe I can kill a number of birds with one stone.

Definitely worth a try.

Wed-
nesday

Irvine

I've worked out who Detective Inspector Duncan actually is now, it took a few phone calls and some favours were called in but I got there in the end. This has some implications for all parties in this affair so I need to start spreading the news to the people concerned.

I'll let Ron know first, then I need to see Billy, after that I'm letting Mr. Duncan know that I know who he is. We can move this thing forward to a satisfactory conclusion now I feel. Time to go and see Carlos and lift his spirits a bit.

Big Tony

I love being here at the gym when I need to think. I'm meeting Billy tomorrow and I need to outline my plans to him and see what he thinks but first I need to think about how to present it to him. On the face of it he's going to have to trust me a lot and we don't know each other that well.

'Put another ten kilo on that bar Rob.'

I have to pump some iron while I run this round my head. Clarty's here as well, that's about the third time I've seen him today. He's getting loads of stick off the boys, giving him 'Hello sailor' and all that, he's not losing his rag though just smiles at them, I thought he'd have swung at one of them by now but he hasn't. Must have learnt his lesson not to fuck with the big boys, the prick needs to realise he's out of his league sometimes.

Spanish

Terry's worried about Merry, he thinks he'll do something to Billy, his reasoning is that by nutting him Billy has undermined him and he'll lose face. He's worried that Billy will take it to him as well, just snap knowing that Merry's going to have his little brother killed. If Billy goes to see him and do him in, well he could end up inside or worse. Merry can fight these days by all accounts and he's got a lot of backup. Tel's already rung Ron about what happened at Vals last night, he's giving Billy a bell I think.

I've arranged for Tel to see Carlos's gym this morning and meet owld Dave, loves his boxing does Tel. He did a bit of coaching inside and he'll happily help Dave out if he's struggling while Carlos is away.

Clarty

I've had to come down the gym and get all the shite out of the way; they're all giving it to me goodstyle about being gay but fuck them. I'm just grinning and letting them take the piss out of me, inside I want to beat shit out of them but I'm keeping a lid on it, use the head not the fists; I've learnt that one through bitter experience. I'm down here keeping an eye on Tony as well in case he gets up to anything incriminating, doesn't matter if he does or doesn't anyway though, I'll still be telling Vince he's up to no good so I don't really have to keep tabs on him that much.

Time to start my plan I think, it's got to begin sometime and now's as good as any, think I'll use some of these pricks that've been taking the piss as well.

'Daz, round up Walshy, Bucky and Nee Neck in half an hour, I need to have a word with you about a job for Vince. I'll see you all in the bar over the road.'

That's shut the wankers up, they must have forgot I'm still Vince's cousin gay or not. I thought about using Fat Kev as well but he's still reasonably close to Vince and I don't want this getting back to him until it's too late. The rest won't like what I tell them they're doing either but they'll think they don't have a choice.

Merry

Clarty's on the case with Tony, he'll let me know the score with the big twat then we can decide what to do with him, he's becoming a liability I think and once Clarty confirms it then

I'll have to decide how best to deal with him. Joanne's been round as well this morning; she had a visit from Sharon yesterday. The bitch has been in hiding since I found out about her and the dago but she surfaced at Joanne's yesterday shouting the odds about me. Joanne said she was shouting in the street how I had a little dick and was shite in bed, she reckoned she was screaming about me not being able to get a hard on without Viagra and that all the steroids had rotted my balls. Bitch, I only used the Viagra for a laugh, nowt else. Anyway, Joanne says young Dennis gave her a slap for me so that's a little taster for her, when I get hold of her she's getting more than a fucking slap.

<u>Billy</u>

I haven't slept a fucking wink; kept expecting Merry to turn up at daft o' clock in the morning with a posse of his finest, muscle bound, empty-headed freaks. I've been pacing the living room all night with my bat and duster close to hand, Lisa doesn't know but I've also got a collection of blades in the cupboard under the stairs and as soon as she went to bed I had the biggest two out and in my waistband. Now it's mid-morning, my head's throbbing and I'm tired. The kids are away to school and Lisa's gone to the bakery, I'm going to need to sort this out one way or another, I can't live like this for the rest of my life. I need to ring Ron as well I think, maybe suggest that Lisa and the boys take a little holiday down the smoke, go and watch Millwall lose with their favourite cockney granddad.

The last time I was in a situation like this was, ironically enough, to do with Merry as well, when I was about to start senior school. He'd had a go at Carlos and me, as usual, on the way back from the baths one morning in the summer holidays and we'd battered him, I think this had shocked him a bit cos he normally terrorised us and was used to us giving in and just taking it. As I remember me mam had made me fight him, a sort of face your fears type of thing, Carlos had followed my lead and between us we'd won. He was making a bit of a rep for himself then and couldn't take the humiliation of being routed by two littler lads so he put it round the estate that he'd be seeing me without my brother when I started at the big school. Outwardly I was cool about it but inside I was shitting myself, as the days counted down to going back to school I was getting worse and struggling to sleep. I used to get the shakes thinking about it and what he'd do to me. I think Carlos must have told Spanish in the end cos he had a little chat with me one day about what to do.

On the first day I was ready for the fucker, I didn't even wait for him to find me. I marched straight up to the fat prick in the playground with a couple of my new mates. They were petrified of him and his crew cos they'd heard he ran the school but they were interested in seeing what I was gonna do. A few second and third years wandered over to watch, they hated Merry as well cos he was a bully and a prick. As I got to him his mob casually half turned to face me, feigning disinterest but half scared really, no one had ever had the bottle to front them or their leader before and they weren't used to it.

I just said, 'Here I am then Merry, I hear you've been looking for me.'

He just laughed and took a step forward saying, 'You're a cocky cunt Reeves. You've got bottle, I'll give you that, but you're very stupid as well.'

As he drew his fist back to punch me I pulled a little penknife out of my pocket and stabbed him in the leg, just like that. The shock and horror on his face was brilliant, his mates absolutely shit themselves. I just said, 'Any of you grass me up and you're next.' Then I walked over to the fence round the playground where Spanish was waiting and he took the knife off me and jumped back into his car with his pals saying, 'Any more bother son, let me know,' and that was it.

Merry never bothered me again and Carlos got safe passage through school as well after that and between us we got enough confidence to do something with our lives. Like I said to Spanish, I've always considered him my dad and he's always been there when I've needed him and fair play to the bloke but I don't think he can get me out of this one, this is going to be me and me alone I reckon.

I need to ring Ron later and then I'll have to talk to Lisa, if anything happened to her because of me I don't know what I'd do. I'm meeting Tony tomorrow as well maybe he'll know something useful. There might still be a way out of this.

Carlos

I've been charged, remanded, and sent to a proper nick now, Durham. The big grey walls seem to rise up and block out the sky as we get close to it. The van's bumping around a bit as we approach the gates of my new home, it might not be for the next thirty years but it'll be a couple of months at least. The bizzies opposed me getting bail on the grounds that I'm dangerous and short tempered and the judge, who obviously knew Maxwell, agreed with them and so here I am. My brief, Irvine, seems quite chirpy today though, it didn't bother him that I got remanded, he just said keep my head down and he'll have it sorted soon, said he couldn't go into it but not everything was as it seemed and not to worry. Easy for him to say, he's driving a Porsche back to his fucking multi-million pound house and his undoubtedly gorgeous, model fucking wife. Me, I'm making do with two wanks a day and prison food. No comparison really, no wonder he's fucking chirpy.

I wish I could see Sharon, once I can have visitors I'll have to send an order through to Billy for her, 'til then it's just me and my overactive imagination. Not so good for when it's night-time and you're thinking of all the things your enemies are up to but handy when you've got a hard on and only a prison toilet for company.

Clarty

Oh they're not happy about that, not happy at all. They were right up for it until I told them who they'd be messing with then their arses fell out of their trousers. Quite happy to terrorise some innocent immigrant or refugee, intimidate a normal person or bully a lone housewife but, when it comes to someone like Billy Reeves who will fight them all day, four onto one if necessary, then they shit themselves.

'What's the matter boys,' I taunt them, 'does the puff have to do it on his own? Haven't you got the bollocks?'

'It's not that Clarty,' moans Daz, he's a proper bodybuilder him; loves the oil and the preening, convinced he's got the biggest arms in the world, 'none of us have got a problem with Billy or his family, he's done nowt to us.'

I cut him dead by putting my hand over his whining mouth, 'He's done nowt to you personally but he has to Vince, you all take Vince's money and now he wants a job doing, if you want to leave his employment then just say, but you don't pick and choose your jobs for him. Incidentally, if you aren't with us on this then you're against us so you'd better choose quick.'

That's done it, they're scared of Billy Reeves but they're more scared of Vince so the job's on. I tell them where to go and what to do, I won't be with them as I've got another job tonight, then tomorrow I can sit back and watch the fallout envelope everybody leaving me clear to take centre stage.

Terry

This gym is fucking brilliant, exactly as I'd want a boxing gym if I could have my own. We'd come in the door where you could see a couple of rooms at the bottom of some stairs and that was it, Spanish said it was the toilet and a basement room that old Dave sometimes slept in if he was here late. I'm a bit disappointed at this point but then, as we get to the top of the stairs, I see it properly.

It's a proper old school, spit and sawdust joint. The smell of stale sweat hangs in the air alongside the heavy bags, solid, bare floorboards worn smooth with thousands of shuffles and steps over the years. Skipping ropes and medicine balls dotted around the place looking worn and well used. Pictures of various fighters all over the walls, big one of Carlos on the back wall, looking down the length of the room. The ring's sitting in pride of place in the middle of the room, it's at odds with the rest of the gym, the white canvas is pristine and contrasting sharply with the faded grey walls, the corner posts deeply coloured against the brilliance of the ring floor and the ropes pulled tight, encompassing it all and giving it an artist's straight lines. Tracey Emin could churn out her shit for a thousand years and still not get near anything as beautiful or moving as this.

There's a few young geezers scattered around the place, a couple in particular looking sharp and powerful as they pound the uppercut bag in turn in one corner of the room. Spanish introduces me to old Dave, the man who trained Carlos from a young age and nearly made him the British Light Heavyweight champ. I've got nothing but respect for the old boy and make sure I tell him when I'm shaking his hand.

'Spanish tells me you've done a bit of coaching Terry,' he says.

'Yeh,' I say, 'just in prison though guv.' Where's this going?

'Coaching's coaching,' he says, 'no matter where you do it. I need a bit of help in here while Carlos is away. It'd look good with your probation officer and we could make it official and put you on the books as a part-timer and I'll pay you a bit more cash in hand. What do you say? We can look at it again when the big lad gets out.'

I'm fucking well chuffed at that; I'd have done it for nothing. I don't need the money just gainful employment so this is ideal.

'I'd love to mate,' I say, shaking his hand again, 'fucking love to Dave, thanks very much.'

'Can you be down here for ten tomorrow morning?'

'Yeh guv, seeing the probation officer today, I'll tell her and she'll cream herself. Job done.'

'Okay then you two stay as long as you like and look around, familiarise yourself with the place, I've got to do some work with the two lads over there now and I'll probably be here a while. If I don't see you leave I'll see you tomorrow Terry.'

'Yeh mate cheers, can't wait.'

He shuffles over to the two tasty looking lads and starts some pad work with 'em, I watch for a minute. They must be about sixteen or seventeen but they're good, quick and powerful, throwing bombs every time. I'm looking forward to working here already. I turn back to Spanish, 'I can't thank you enough buddy I really can't. You've looked after me, introduced me to the family and even got me a job I'm gonna love.'

He just smiles back at me, 'Nee problem Terry, you're one of my best mates.'

I'm deadly serious now. 'I mean it Spanish, you've went well beyond what a mate would do and I really appreciate it. Even if Ron and Billy weren't related I would still get involved and help out any way I could with the aggravation that's been going on. You're all like family to me now.'

He just shrugs and pats me on the back saying, 'It's nee bother mate honestly, do you fancy a pint later on?'

'Deffo, where we going?'

'Stags Head bonny lad,' he says, 'my old local when I lived with Val, it's all of ten yards from her house so we can see if she fancies one as well if you want.'

'Sounds good mate,' I say, 'I'll see you after I've seen my probation officer.'

Get that out of the way then a couple of pints with Spanish, I like it up here.

Ron

Irvine's sussed out that Duncan copper, turns out he's one of the filth who investigate other filth, the lowest of the low in their eyes. Normally I'd have naff all to do with any copper if possible, I only bother with 'em when there's business to be done but this one could hold Carlos's liberty in his sweaty little trotters. The way to do this is find out who he's after and what he wants then give it to him in return for Carlos suddenly not facing prosecution after all. I've got Irvine on it, he's discreet and it doesn't look suspect if a brief talks to a pig.

I had Terry on the blower earlier as well cos that cheeky ponce Merry turned up at Val's house last night looking for Billy. Unfortunately for him he turned up not long after Billy had found out his plan to top both Carlos and him; apparently Billy dropped the nut on him and was ready for action until

Tel stepped in. It's lucky Billy and the rest were there really though, who knows what the wanker might have done if it was Val who'd answered the door.

Looks like Mr. Merry is going to have to be stopped now whatever. I've got half a plan but it'll need delicate handling and I'll need to know what's happening up there at all times. I'll ring Billy and talk to him first, get his thoughts on it and then I might need to go up there myself and direct operations.

Carlos

That's me processed then and in my cell now, I saw little Davy on the way in, he gave me the thumbs up, at least there's some fucker I know in here. I was sort of hoping Terry Briggs would be here cos me dad's always on about them being pals but he's just been let out apparently. Fucking typical. Mind you, some other bloke came up to us earlier, said his name was Bates and he was a good mate of Terry's. He reckoned he'd put the word out that I was under his protection and if I want anything just ask. He fucking looked the part as well man, tattoos every-where: *'cut here'* round his neck, *'love and hate'* on the knuck-les; proper skinhead as well with scars all over his face and arms. I just said cheers mate then fucked off into me cell out of the way.

Lock up now anyway, I've somehow got a cell of me own but I don't know how long that'll last, might well be something to do with uncle Ron though.

Clarty

I clocked Tony in a huddle with that Barry one earlier, the two of them had a pint in The Northumberland Arms at dinner-time. That's official then, proof that Tony's at it, Barry boy is a known scallywag and part time dealer, looks like he's went part time on the scallywagging and full time on the dealing.

This is exactly what Vince needs to know and I'm the man to tell him. He's in the kitchen in the minute on the pretence of making us a cup of tea, the loud sniffing sounds are obviously because he's got a bit of a cold, the twat's losing it and can't see a way past Ron Carter. If he stopped sticking that shit up his nose for a couple of minutes he could think about it properly. Still, he's too far gone now anyway and just needs putting out of his misery I think, well I'm the man for that particular job.

'Cheers Vince,' at least he remembered to actually bring the tea in with him.

'So,' he says, looking as businesslike as you can with snot water forming on your nostrils, 'what's the score with Tony?'

I tell him what I saw and embellish it a bit, how matey they were, how I'm sure I heard Tony say that Vince was a prick, that type of thing. He is fuming, I can tell, he wants to go and do the big fella now.

'No Vince hold on,' he's staring at me as if to say who the fuck do you think you are, well the prick'll never find out cos he'll probably be dead when I take over. 'Listen, I've got an idea of how we can dispose of all of them,' holding my hands up to him palm out, submissive like.

'Let's hear it then,' he growls, sitting back down.

Val

That's got all the shopping done, the cleaning's finished and now I can sit down and relax for the rest of the day. Michael was trying to get me out for a drink with him and that Terry later but I can't be bothered. Inspector Frost's on tonight so I'll put a bottle of wine in the fridge and have a bath.

I'm still worried about Billy and Carl but Michael reckons it's all being sorted and there'll be no more hassle. I hope so, it would kill me if Carl went to prison for a murder he didn't even do.

Big Tony

Merry's just rang me out of the blue, said we have to go for a drive to discuss a plan he's got. He's coming to get me in half an hour.

I'm not convinced I like this, I've seen Clarty everywhere today as well. Best stay alert on this trip.

Merry

I've got to hand it to the little faggot, that's not a bad plan at all. Billy now has to be removed and so does Tony, this'll take care of that and it might just be enough to satisfy Ron Carter that nothing dodgy went on. If it's not and he comes for me, well, I'll be ready and waiting for the cockney cunt.

Carlos is getting it as well, I've got a man in Durham who's prepared to do him for me and he's serving a long-term sentence anyway so the risk is fuck all to him. Fat Kev's outside in the car, Tony was a bit nervous sounding when I told him we were going for a drive into the country and he should be the snidey, fucking Judas, but not today. He's getting it soon but at the moment I need him to help me with Billy Reeves, then, when he's helped me do that wanker, he disappears as well.

Clarty

He went for it the big, daft, cokeheaded knob. Him and Fat Kev are taking Tony to discuss Billy's burial site and while they're away I'll sort myself out for my own little mission later on tonight. I'll give Bucky a quick ring and check that the four lads are ready for what they have to do and then it's all systems go. The best result today though was Vince knowing that nutter in Durham who'll do Carlos in and he's having it done the same time as Billy gets it; they're both being told that their brother just died as well when they're getting topped.

Maybe, when this is over, the people in this town will realise not to fuck with me. They'll have to when I'm running the whole show.

Fat Kev

Vince has told me there's a plot to get rid of him and asked if

I'm still with him and I told him straight away, 'I've always been loyal to you Vince and I was there from the start when we were kids.'

That was enough for him; he knows he can trust me. Then he told me that we had to kill Billy Reeves. I think he wanted to see my reaction but I surprised him a bit, 'I've got no problem with that at all,' I told him, 'I've never liked him.'

He wouldn't tell me all the plan, just that it was going to be him, Big Tony and me, we're gonna bring Billy to the place we're at now and do it here. Tony and Vince must have been thinking about it on the way up here cos the atmosphere was a bit tense in the car. I just kept quiet but when we get closer to doing it I might ask him if I can pull the trigger. I'll make Billy beg for his life and then blow his bastard head off.

Merry

This place is fucking ideal, a quiet little village graveyard twenty miles north of Newcastle with a wood running from the back of the fence, the church at the front and open fields either side, only one road into the place as well. Now it's time to bring Tony into the game.

'What do you think then Tony?' I ask him, all friendly.

'As churches go Vince it's lovely. Why are we here?'

I swear that twat is getting cockier by the day and it's all I can do to hold myself back. Instead I look around like an actor in a murder mystery, all dramatic like, and say, 'This is where we're going to do Billy Reeves.' As I say it I snap my gaze back onto him and he never flickers, he is definitely a professional, be a shame to top him really.

'Why we doing that then Vince?' he's asking, genuinely confused I think.

'Because Tony, he has challenged me one too many times, he has physically assaulted me, and his brother, who is also getting it by the way, battered my cousin and shagged my bird.'

That should put him straight, no he's going to ask another question.

'What about Ron Carter though Vince, he'll kill us all?'

Fat Kev paled a little bit there as well. I'll have to take control of this situation, nip their fear in the bud and make them believe in me, Vince Merry, gangster number one.

'Ron Carter won't realise it's a hit, he might suspect it but won't be able to prove it. Then when he makes his move on what he thinks instead of what he can prove, well, then I can turn it into a North/South turf war and tell all the other local crime families and the bizzies that this cockney cunt wants to take over geordieland. He can't beat us all Tony and he'll realise that and stop trying.'

He looks quite impressed with that does Tony, Fat Kev does as well but he's a footsoldier and doesn't matter anyway. Tony looks up at me again.

'What's the plan for Billy then?' he asks smiling. Looks like the boys have bought into this one with a minimum of fuss, I should go into politics.

Spanish

Terry can't believe how expensive beer is these days so I told him to go back to the smoke for the weekend, he'd find out what fucking expensive was then. Val didn't fancy a drink so it's just me, him and a scattering of the locals. I've kicked his arse at pool a couple of times and we're just chatting about stuff now. His probation officer was well impressed with him getting a job so soon and stuck it straight on his file, eager to integrate into society she wrote, daft cow. You'd think at do-gooder school someone would tell these dicks about us council estate lads but no they fall for the same shit week in, week out. I remember telling one twenty years ago that I came from a broken home and that was why I stole as I'd never had anything in my life. She was so sorry for me that she recommended rehabilitation rather than prison and I was shagging her for six months.

The barmaid thinks Terry's great, when he went to the bog she said he looked like a painter, very sensitive hands apparently. I didn't think it was my place to tell her those hands had not so sensitively done someone in twenty-five years ago, still ignorance is bliss eh? He's giving her a bit of chat and she's asking him if he's ever painted and holding his hands up to look at them and I'm just taking the piss out of them both while he blushes, when there's a crashing sound outside.

'Aye aye,' I say leaving the lovebirds to it to look out of the window, 'sounds like a pagga.'

There's four big blokes out there all hoodied up and they're putting Val's windows in, she's at the back door screaming at them and they're moving towards her.

'TERRY,' I shout, 'BOTHER,' and I'm out the door and racing into the cunts.

I smack the first one and he's not expecting it so he goes down, the other three turn my way and start laughing, 'Come on then granddad let's see you take on the big boys.'

I just start swinging and I catch one of the pricks good but the other two have grabbed me, there's one clouting me in the back and the other's got his hands on my throat and I'm in trouble now. Val's screaming and lights are coming on behind net curtains in the other houses.

I'm just starting to struggle for air when the pressure is released and I fall forward, Terry is standing over one of them glass in hand slashing him repeatedly across the face. The one I belted first is just coming to so I run over and boot him clean in the nose and spread the fucker all over the street.

The other two are backing off, it's a fair fight now and they're not that interested any more but too late, they're fucking having it. They're blowing hard by now as well, all them steroids make you look big but they don't do fuck all else for you, all wind and piss these cunts. Terry runs at them and nuts the biggest one while his mate just freezes, Tel, all maximum aggression, still has the glass in his hand and sticks it straight in his face, he just goes down squealing like a girl. I look back at Val and she's sobbing at the back door in her dressing gown, 'It's my own fault,' she's saying.

Well I'm not having that, I go over and comfort her, 'It's not Val,' I say, 'these bastards have been sent by one man and one man only, it's nothing to do with you.'

I look over and Terry's going mad on the spineless pricks, booting their already prostrate bodies into next week. In the distance the sound of sirens, I need to think quick as Terry's on probation.

'Tel,' I shout, 'bizzies. Do one back to the flat and I'll ring you to come back when it's all clear.' He calms down quickly and fucks off giving me the thumbs up. I make sure all of the neighbours are clear on the story about four good Samaritans giving these radgies a kicking and then doing off, they're happy with that one. As the bizzies pull up I catch the bar-maid's eye at the door of the pub, she's been around the block and she's well used to casual violence after closing time but even she looks shocked at the carnage Terry caused. I just put my finger to my lips and she nods and goes back into the pub.

Clarty

No one about? Good. Nice and dark as well but it won't be in five minutes. I can hear the sirens in the distance at the other end of Byker, sounds like the lads are on the job so it leaves me a bit of time to do this. I burst the lock with my crowbar, the wood splinters and I'm in. Carlos never bothered putting an alarm in here thinking no one would ever do his place, wrong dago I'm fucking doing it. I pull the door closed breathing silently, I don't want any fucker getting nosey, then I'm up the stairs and into the gym itself, splashing petrol from the can I've brought all round the place. I make sure the ring gets a good splash and I pull down the big picture of Carlos at the end of the room, I spit on that and then cover it in petrol, that fucker'll burn first.

My heart's pounding but I've done it and I'm ready to go, just leaving a trail of petrol down the stairs to throw a match at when there's a noise behind me. I spin round quick in the dark just as a shape comes towards me. It's the old man.

He's shouting, 'I know who you are, get out you bastard, get out.'

Well if he knows who I am then he's got to go, he's got a bat in his hand but I just boot him in the bollocks and he drops it.

I can't believe the cheeky old get tried to take me on, does everyone think I'm fuck all, DO THEY? I'm hitting him and hitting him over the head with the now empty can, there's claret everywhere and I'm shouting, 'DO YOU THINK I'M FUCK ALL AS WELL? DO YOU?' Fuck it calm down.

Right, time to think, need to get out, we've made a bit of noise. I strike the match and look at the old man by the light of the flame. He must be about sixty or seventy, probably trained loads of lads over the years, kept them out of trouble and gave them a better path to follow, bloke like that should be taking it easy now at his time of life. If I was a better person I'd spare him but I'm not so fuck him; he's in my way so he dies, simple as that.

I drop the match onto the petrol trail, there's a whoosh and it races upstairs, I get out just in time. Allowing myself a quick look at my handiwork I can see the fire is taking hold quickly and starting to rage upstairs, and I can hear myself shouting, 'HAVE THAT YOU DAGO PRICK.'

Turning to leave I almost bump into two teenage lads I vaguely recognise coming out of the shadows, they look straight at me with hard man stares and I stare back at them until they say sorry then I'm offski.

Everyone bows to me now.

Ron

The phone's ringing and it's late, I was just going to bed. I never get phone calls at this time of night unless it's trouble. The display says Billy. It must be trouble.

'Evening Bill, what's up?' I'm concerned straight away, Billy is a very courteous person and he wouldn't ring at this time without a good reason.

'Ron, I'm really sorry to ring you this late but I need a favour,' he sounds a bit flustered, not like him at all.

'Anything mate, you know that,' I mean it as well, 'I meant to ring you earlier but you know how it is.'

'I need to get Lisa, the boys and me mam out of town for a bit while I sort some shit out. Can they stay at yours, bit of a holiday in the nation's capital and all that?'

'Of course they can Bill you don't even need to ask,' like I said he's courteous, 'what's happened?'

'It's Merry,' he says, 'the wanker's had four blokes put me mam's windows in, it's lucky Spanish and Terry were about or she would have got hurt.'

So Mr. Merry has decided to try his luck has he, 'Did Spanish and Terry see 'em off then?'

He laughs at that calming down a bit now, 'Yeah, two in hospital with slashed up faces and the other two have got broken jaws, fractured ribs and shattered noses. Terry doesn't fuck about does he?'

'Nah,' I say laughing as well, 'he's a tough old boy. When can I expect everyone then?'

'I'm putting them on the first train in the morning, there was another thing as well Ron.'

'What's that Bill?'

'Someone, no prizes for guessing on who's instructions, burnt Carlos's gym down and owld Dave was in there. He burnt to death the poor old sod.'

'That's a step up from windows Bill, looks like Merry's upping the stakes. What you gonna do?' I'm asking him because I think I'm going to have to get involved and at the end of the day I can be there in four hours; it's not the other side of the world.

'I'm seeing a couple of people tomorrow about that Ron,' he replies, 'I've got a meet with a man on the inside of his crew. My idea at the minute is to try and avoid any more deaths mate. I'm gonna challenge the arsehole to a one on one to clear all grudges on either side. Then I'm gonna hammer the prick so badly he'll never be able to think about me or my family again without shivering.'

I can see Billy's thinking, he's an honourable man and he'll do this the right way but I know that Merry won't.

'He'll double-cross you Bill,' I say, 'I guarantee he won't be on his own when you get there.'

'I know that Ron,' he says, 'but the bloke I'm meeting wants to take over from him and is high up in his gang, he's been undercutting Merry for months. He's the one who'll be there. I'm gonna sort out the finer details tomorrow with him, I'll let you know what's said.'

'Okay Bill you do that but just ask yourself when you're dealing with this bloke, how much can you trust him?'

'I'll be careful mate, ring me tomorrow when the family arrive and I'll let you know the score.'

'Okay Bill, see you later.'

I'd better prepare the guest rooms then I'll need to make some phone calls. I had an interesting one myself today from Mr. Bates in Durham nick about a job he's been given to do by the aforementioned Mr. Merry. There's no way he'll let Billy walk away from a straightener with him. I'll need to sleep on this and be ready to act when it's necessary.

Big Tony

That was a strange one today, I could have swore he was on to me. I was ready for the kick off but it was like he was my best mate at times. Mind you, he takes that much fucking charlie combined with the steroids that his mood swings are all over the place, I can't tell if he's happy or not most of the time. He pulled the two old gravediggers over to one side and told them he wanted a grave digging on the edge of the cemetery and an old headstone or something putting on it so it looked legit. Much as I dislike the prick I've got to say that's not a bad idea to blatantly put the grave where everyone can see it and they probably won't even look for it. The old chaps were a bit hesitant at first until he offered them a grand apiece then they were up for it.

Then he told me to go and get the car with Fat Kev and he said something else to them, I was bit paranoid and asked him what it was, he just grinned and said he was making them realise that now they're in this far, if they were to back out they'd end up in another grave. Then he laughed like a fucking pantomime villain. Too many drugs that bloke does man.

I'm seeing Billy tomorrow but I won't mention this until I know what his plan is.

Milo

I've just had a call from the station; things are intensifying between Merry and the Reeves family. The mother's windows were smashed and the gym burnt down, worse for Merry though, there was someone in the gym and he died, that makes it murder. The desk has taken an anonymous call about someone seen at the scene of the fire, exact same description as Merry's rent boy cousin, I'll have to ring him, then I'm going to have to distance myself from the idiot before he jeopardises everything.

DI Duncan

Had a very interesting chat with Mr. Irvine today, I knew he'd clocked me from day one but I'm a little surprised it took him this long to work out who I am and why I'm here though. He's going to put a couple of questions to Billy Reeves for me and I'll take it from there. I know Carl Reeves didn't kill the judge, I also know his bat wasn't the murder weapon and that Mr. Milo only made it seem that way. The question is why? And how do I make a connection between Milo and his partner in many crimes, one Mr. Vincent Merry.

Thursday

Irvine

Had a very productive chat with DI Duncan yesterday, I know which way the wind is blowing now and it's looking good for Carlos. He wanted me to ask Billy if he could help with a couple of things, off the record obviously, which may get Carlos out sooner rather than later. I'll give him a buzz now.

'Billy, Irvine here. How are you?' He sounds tired, 'Sorry it's early.'

'Not to worry I'm up anyway. I've had better weeks though Mr. Irvine, what about yourself?'

'Fine Billy, fine. Listen, I've got some news for you, do you remember DI Duncan the one who sat in on your interview with Milo?'

'Yeah mate vaguely, he didn't fucking say a lot.'

'That's the one, well, between you and me, he is an undercover police officer with the Internal Investigations Squad. They're looking very closely at Mr. Milo as it is believed he has been doing business with gangland types in Newcastle for many years.'

'Fuck me, it's about time they realised Merry was too stupid to have planned his own way up the ladder,' he growls.

'Quite,' I say, 'anyway, DI Duncan does not think that Carlos killed Judge Maxwell, he thinks that he has been set up as the fall guy for Vince Merry. He also has bits and bobs of evidence on Milo but just needs something to tie him in with the murder, any scrap of information may help, anything at all.'

'Weeell,' he says slowly thinking aloud, 'I can only think of one off the top of my head and that's my phone.'

'What do you mean Billy, I don't quite follow?'

'Carlos took a text off my phone telling him to go to the house did he not?'

'Yes he did,' I reply, 'and I made him keep it in case it ever became useful.' I'd better not mention that I thought it would become useful against Billy himself when I thought he was stitching up his brother, my client after all, for the murder of the judge.

'So,' he continues, 'if Merry or the copper are stupid enough to have kept the phone anywhere it might be worth paying them a visit and having a look. It's a bit of a long shot like but it's all I can think of.'

He's right it is a slim chance but it's better than nothing, 'I'll pass it on to him right away Billy, it's worth a try. I'll speak to you soon.'

Barry

Thank fuck I managed to persuade Sharon to piss off back to Berwick until this is sorted out. I told her Carlos would send her a visiting order as soon as he could and she broke down in tears. I couldn't understand why she was still crying and I had to tell her to pull herself together, she's been acting like a spoilt child over the last few days. The bloke's looking at thirty years and it was all about her know what I mean?

Then she told me why she was so upset. The amount of shagging that jammy fucker has done over the years it was inevitable he'd get caught in the end. I spared Carlos the nightmare of upsetting her and having to ask her if it was his kid by doing it myself. She just told me she hadn't slept with Merry for nearly four months and Carlos and her had been at it like rabbits. She said she'll happily take a DNA test though to prove it if he wants cos she loves Carlos and knows it's his. It was a bit of a bombshell to be honest but then it's his problem not mine. My problem was to get her out of the way sharpish so I just used it to convince her it was safer for her and the baby to get out of harms way and when Carlos came back they could have a shot at the family thing. She was happy with that so I ran her up to Berwick, early doors like.

Got back about half an hour ago and was sorting myself out for Billy's meeting with Tony when I got a call from Muzza. He said that the gym was torched last night and owld Dave was in it and he died. Hammy and him saw who did it, they said it was the musclebound knob that Carlos battered that night. They know he's Merry's cousin so they didn't set about him as they're not stupid but they did make an anonymous call to the law and gave him to them on a plate. Before all that though I got a call off Spanish telling me that Val's windows got put through last night by four of Merry's doormen, unfortunately for them cockney Terry and Spanish were in The Stags and came out and battered the fuckers. Terry went to town on the pricks apparently. Good lad.

If I know about all this then Billy will as well, I tried to ring him before I set off for Berwick with Sharon but his lass answered his mobile and said he was driving them to the station and couldn't talk. He told her to tell me he'd see me as arranged. So all the way up there I'm thinking. Has Tony set up a trap here? Is Billy next on the list and have I been used all along to draw him into it? No time for fucking about I'm meant to be there in an hour. I'm ringing Spanish back.

'Span, it's Barry.'

'Hello again kidda, you alright? Has Sharon gone now?'

'Yeah mate sound, she's away back up there, took her myself. Anyway what are you and Terry up to now?'

'Not much mate we've just watched the glazier put Val's new windows in and now we're going home.'

'Right, do you fancy watching mine and Billy's backs when we meet one of Merry's crew?'

'No probs mate where and when?'

'An hours time in The Northumberland Arms keep it low key though Span, I don't want Billy to know you're there either.'

'We'll be there mate, any way you want to play it.'

'Okay, see you in a bit.'

Right then, get the biggest knife from the kitchen and put it in my coat. Here we go.

Clarty

Busy night last night so I've had a long lie in this morning. Just fancy a bit of breakfast now. Paperboy's not been yet, lazy little twat. I'll ring Vince in a minute and play it dumb about last night's goings on, that's if he knows yet like. Kettle's on, radio's playing some pop idol bollocks for ten year olds and the sun's shining. Can't see a fucking thing in the street, no one about and nothing moving at all, strange really, there's normally people bustling about now and people gardening and that, but no, nothing.

Toast's done and I'm whistling that crap tune to myself while I butter it, it's not the end of the world I suppose when your only worry in life is how you're going to get a shite song out of your head. I'm pouring the tea when I hear the door crashing in and the realisation of why no one was about hits me hard.

Very. Fucking. Hard.

Then I'm cowering on my knees with guns pointed at me and being shouted and screamed at.

'ON THE FLOOR NOW, HANDS WHERE I CAN SEE THEM.'

The kettle's on the floor and my cup is smashed to pieces. While they're cuffing me and tearing my house to bits all I can think is fuck me, I'm glad it's the law and not Billy Reeves.

Milo

Merry was shocked when I gave him the news about his cousin torching the gym. He was even more shocked when I told him smashing Billy's mother's windows was a stupid thing to do, he was adamant it was nothing to do with him and he didn't even know about it. I told him though, Billy Reeves won't believe that and he'll be wanting to talk to you. Merry's cousin's in the shit now as well, they're charging him with murder as we speak and he's looking at a long, long time in prison. A gay bodybuilder; he'll be currency inside, passed from inmate to inmate to pay off debts and favours. Poor bastard, not as poor as the bloke he killed though. I had to tell Merry that was it as far as our partnership goes, our association ends now. I'm retiring very soon, the book is nearly ready to go and my pension lies in its hands. I can't afford for any corruption smears or worse to taint the zero tolerance solution to crime that I'm selling.

So, in the absence of any viable alternatives or evidence to the contrary I'll be advising the Crown Prosecution Service to go ahead and prosecute Carl Reeves for the murder of Judge Maxwell. Detective Inspector Duncan has been no help at all during this case and I'll be pointing that out to his commanding officer as well, he's simply followed me everywhere, nodding and taking notes, which, quite conveniently, is just what I wanted really.

Big Tony

Billy's just arrived with Barry in tow, good; I was starting to get a bit nervous sitting here on my own. I've got the beers in already and I've took the liberty of ordering a couple of sandwiches in case they're hungry. I deliberately chose this table; it's round a corner from the door so you can't see us just by casually sticking your head in but if you want to see who's sitting here then we can see you so no unpleasant surprises in store.

I give them a nod, first at Billy then at Barry. Billy does not look happy at all and is the first to speak before he even sits down, 'Who put me mam's windows in Tony?' He growls at me.

'Fucking news to me Bill.' I reply, a bit disturbed by his tone of voice. He needs to realise that I'm not the enemy here. Barry's on the corner scanning the room with his hand behind his back, there's hardly any fucker in here anyway. Does he think it's a set up?

Billy's not letting up either, 'And Carlos's gym, who torched that? Owld Dave burnt to death in there last night.' He's nearly spitting the words out and is stood up against his chair.

'Whoah kidda,' I say back, 'fucking calm down man. Firstly I know fuck all about it and secondly we're here to discuss getting rid of Merry. I'm not with him Billy I'm against him.'

If he moves towards me I'm primed to burst out of the chair and panel him. He ponders what I said for a second and then just instantly calms down and snaps into professional mode again.

Finally sitting down and picking up his pint he says,

'What's the score then Tony?'

I'm a bit flustered myself now so I take a drink and give myself a couple of seconds, 'I don't know how much Barry has told you Billy but what I'm about to say should convince you of my honest intentions. I could get killed for saying this in public but here goes. I intend to take over from Merry as the main man in this town; at the end of the day he's a prick and a bully. I've already started slowly strangling his drugs business by putting my own dealers in place and I've also recruited a hard-core of his doormen, blokes I've known for ten and twenty years who presently work for him but hate the arsehole.'

Billy looks impressed that I've done this much and managed to keep it secret.

'What do you want from me then?' He says simply.

I was waiting for him to ask this, 'In all honesty Billy, nothing. I could take the prick out myself now but that would cause a war between his lads and mine. No one would win and no money would be made as the normal punters would keep out of town and out of the way. If you're the one who gives him a hiding though, a real fucking good one, then when I take over there's no war as everyone respects you in this town and everyone knows you've got a genuine grievance against Merry.'

He's looking straight at me, 'So I batter him and you then make sure, in your capacity as top boy, that it ends there and my mother keeps her windows in future.'

I smile at him, I like Billy. 'More or less,' I say, 'you'll have to give him the type of hiding that makes him think twice about going anywhere near you or yours again though, think you can manage that Bill?'

He smiles back at me like a shark circling a surfer, 'After what that cunt's been up to, you might have to stop me killing him Tony.'

'Right then,' I say, 'now we just have to decide how to get you and him in the same place with none of his boys about.'

'Easy one that Tony,' he jumps in, 'I want a straightener with him over me mam's windows and Carlos's gym and I also want it to take into account the grudge over Carlos and Sharon and the hiding Carlos gave Clarty. Tell him I'll square it with

Ron Carter and it's all systems go. I want it tomorrow night under Byker Bridge at the bottom of Shields Road.'

Fuck me he doesn't mess about, 'Right then,' I say, 'I'll see him and arrange it, I'll set it up with him so it's just me and him there. He'll double-cross you with me and obviously I'll just let you get on with it.'

He seems okay with that and stands to go. It's gone well so I offer him my hand, he just stares straight at me and takes a step forward as he shakes it saying quietly but firmly, 'Tony I trust you but if you let me down or try to stitch me up then, like Merry, there'll be nowhere I won't find you. Do you understand that?'

I wasn't expecting that and can only stammer a reply; the menace behind that stare is spine chilling. Then they're gone leaving me to work out how to sell Merry a straightener to end all straighteners.

Clarty

Fucking shitting it here like. I'm in an interview room with a uniformed copper who's talking about twenty odd years for murder, it wasn't murder for fucks sake I was just torching the place. All right I knew he was there but he attacked me, if he hadn't he'd have got out. I can't spend the best part of my life inside.

Another copper enters the room, a stern looking one in a suit, must be CID.

'Good afternoon my name is DI Duncan and I want to talk to you about your future,' he says.

What the fuck's he on about, future? I'm panicking now and I can't see a way out of it. 'What about my future?' I manage to say.

'Well,' he says, sitting back in his chair, 'you don't appear to have much of one do you Mr. Clark. It's a well known fact that you have a grudge against Carlos Reeves, there's evidence of petrol all over your clothes which you very helpfully left in the washing machine and there are two independent witnesses who put you at the scene.'

Those two fucking kids, if I get out of here they're dead the little bastards. And why didn't I just torch the clothes as well, fucks sakes. Then the reality hits me. I'm going down for murder.

'He wasn't meant to die was he. I was just torching the place to get back at Carlos, no one was meant to die.' I'm close to tears here, why didn't the old bastard just leave it alone? He had to push me; everyone always has to push me.

'So then Mr. Clark, for the benefit of the tape,' he's all cool, calm and collected the smug prick, loving this, 'you're admitting you set fire to the Byker Boxing Club?'

Before I can stop myself I'm shouting back at him in his face, 'Yes, he wouldn't leave me alone so I hit him and left him there. Everyone treats me like shite and I'm sick of it,' then I slump back into my chair. That's me fucked then.

He's nearly creaming himself now, quickest clear up of a murder in history this must be. 'Oh so you knew he was in there as well. Looks like that's that then boys.' He gets up and I'm starting to sob, the injustice of it all finally getting to me.

'It's not fair, I can't go to prison for twenty-five years, it's not fair. I'll do anything you want, I can't go down for that long, I'll tell you anything you want to know.'

He's at the door looking at me with a mixture of contempt and disgust when, as if it suddenly strikes him, he turns to me saying, 'Maybe there is something you could help me with.'

Then he goes out of the door and leaves me confused and sobbing alone in the room.

Barry

Billy gave me a lift home, nice of him but that radio needs fixing. We had the windows down and we're driving past a load of little honeys; skimpy tops, miniskirts, that type of thing and what happens? The poodle haired DJ on that poxy station plays that eighties rock shite The Final fucking Countdown. I couldn't get me head down and the window up quick enough. Billy just laughed and said it was apt. I love the bloke to death but I don't fucking understand him sometimes me.

Big Tony

Shit. Billy was in and out of the bar that fast and took me so much by surprise with his attitude that I forgot to tell him about Merry's plan to do him in. I'll ring Barry now, that's the ideal way to convince him that I'm on the level and not some kind of double agent.

'Barry, sorry, just remembered something, listen carefully, you need to tell Billy about this. Merry plans on taking him up to a cemetery just outside the village of Cragstone north of the toon, he's had a fresh grave dug in the actual graveyard and has even got a bogus headstone ready, he plans on topping him there with me in tow to help. It shouldn't get that far anyway but it's just extra information for you to use if you need to.'

He's sounds like he's writing it down, I can hear him repeating it to himself, then finally, 'Okay mate.'

'Right, see you later.' Now I just need to get Merry to agree to the straightener.

Duncan

I've got this no-mark already so no need to turn up the pressure. Just going to try one more thing to satisfy my own curiosity and then I'm making my move.

'Chief Inspector Milo, sorry to bother you sir it's DI Duncan.'

Snappy as fuck, 'What do you want Duncan I'm a busy man?'

'Of course sir I know that, it's just we've got a prisoner downstairs and we're charging him for the arson attack on the gym in Byker as well as the murder of the old chap in there and he's claiming he knows you.'

Stunned silence on the end of the line, then, 'I'll be right down.'

I go back into the interview room and the prisoner is just sitting staring into space, eyes red with self-pitying tears. I fucking hate people like this, if you can't handle the consequences then don't do the deed, it's that simple.

'Listen, there's a copper coming in here in a minute and I want to know if you know him and how, don't tell me until he's gone though and we'll maybe look at changing this to manslaughter.'

He just looks at me and then the door bursts open and Milo strides in, his face betraying his fury while his voice tries to appear calm and placid. He takes a look at Clark and turns to me saying, 'There must be some mistake Duncan I've never seen him before in my life.' He's looking straight at me challengingly so I put my head down, subservient, don't let him know yet that he's in the deepest of shit. Then, thinking he's made his point he sweeps back out slamming the door.

I turn back to Clark, 'Well?'

He just nods and says, 'My cousin Vince Merry meets him every fortnight in the multi-storey car park at Eldon Square.'

Gotcha.

Merry

I can't believe that stupid twat Clarty got hisself nicked for torching Carlos's place. I had this all under control, he didn't need to do that. Well, he's on his own now I'm not getting involved in it, I've got problems of my own to deal with. Big Tony's just rang me, he's had contact with Billy Reeves, yeh I bet he fucking has, apparently he is fuming about the gym and his mam's windows. He reckons Billy wants a one off straightener to cover all of the bad blood between us and that Ron Carter has agreed. My first thought was to tell him to fuck off, I run this town not fucking Ron Carter and the gym and the windows were fuck all to do with me anyway. Then, after taking a minute to think properly about it, I realised I was cutting my nose off to spite my face. This is the opportunity I needed. I can do both of the cunts here, the hole in the ground is ready and waiting and I can ring the old boys to be there to fill it in on an hours notice if I need to.

So, it's on, tomorrow night under Byker Bridge at the Shields Road end. I told Tony that he'd be there with me and we'd be giving Billy a hiding together, then taking him for one last trip to the country. I said that he'd never got on any school trips as a boy cos he was a tramp so it would be nice for him to see a bit of England's green and pleasant land before he dies.

Tony had a little chuckle at that, playing along with me the devious fucker. What's really gonna happen is that Tony's going to side with Billy when we get there, I'm not meant to know that but what Tony doesn't know is that Fat Kev will be parked round the corner with a nice big fuck off gun that he's just dying to use.

Spanish

Nothing happened in that meeting between Billy and the big bloke, Tony I think his name is, he's been around for donkeys years anyway. We sat round the corner of the bar ready for it if there was any noise but it seemed okay. I spoke to Barry later on and he told me that Tony had put him in the picture about a plan Merry has to top Billy. Apparently there's a village cemetery with a hole dug and a headstone waiting for him, Barry doesn't reckon it'll get that far anyway as Billy and Tony have planned what's gonna happen. I asked him what the plan was but he was stood too far away from them at the corner of the room to hear. Hope he's right though, I'll tell Terry anyway, just in case.

Me and Tel are going along to the gym as well, burnt to the fucking ground and owld Dave dead. The bizzies have nicked someone already, no one knows who yet but I hope the bastard gets a proper fucking hiding in nick though.

Fat Kev

Vince has told me it's on for tomorrow night and he's also told me there's a change of plan, Tony's been making moves behind his back to take over so he dies as well. Suits me I've never liked that big bastard either. Vince reckons he's been selling gear on the quiet and trying to get a hold on the clubs and he says that he's double-crossing him with Billy as well.

The plan is that Vince takes Tony with him and they both do Billy in, Vince knows that Tony will help Billy out though and that's where I come in, just me and an equaliser.

You've had this coming for years Billy Reeves, I still remember you slapping me round the red pitch after the Whitley Bay thing you wanker. I aim the pistol at my living room wall mouthing the word, BOOM. And the time you chinned me in the yard at school in front of the whole fifth year before I left school for good just because I'd blasted the ball at Carlos's face in the gym and made him cry. BOOM. I try it gangster rappa style, side on, in front of the mirror, looks good, suits me. When this is done Vince is going to need a trusted lieutenant and I'm the man. With Clarty inside and Tony dead that leaves his oldest friend as the only person he can trust. It'll be Vince and me against the world.

Ron

It's lovely seeing the boys running round my house and making a bit of noise, it's been too quiet here for far too long, the house needed a bit of life, has done for years. Val and Lisa are on edge, they know Billy's going to be fighting and they know who with. Billy tells Lisa everything, that's one of the many things I like about him he's honest. I know she's putting on a brave face for the kids but she's scared about what's going to happen to him I can tell.

Knowing Billy they'll have had a long talk last night about each and every eventuality and how Lisa should deal with it, from him killing Merry with his bare hands and walking away through to Merry killing him. He wouldn't have flinched from discussing his own violent death with his wife because he's a real man and his only priority is his family's safety and well being. I can't speak highly enough of the geezer and there isn't much I wouldn't do for him. Lisa's snapping at the boys now and telling 'em to calm down but they're all right just high spirits. I bought a playstation thing for 'em this morning on my way to the station so I send 'em upstairs to play on that while I talk to Lisa and Val.

'He'll be alright gels, I promise.' They're both tearful now the boys are out of the room.

'How can you know that though Ron?' Val's worried, one son banged up for life and the other possibly about to lose his.

'Billy can fight Val, he'll bite Merry's head off.' That is true; in a fair fight Billy would destroy the oversized steroid freak.

'If he's that confident then why did we have to come down here out of the way then?' Lisa this time, she just wants to know everything'll be all right, I can't guarantee it but I'm fairly sure it will be.

'You both know Billy,' I reply, 'he's careful about everything and he won't take any chances with you lot, the people he loves. On the offchance something does go wrong, and that's a very slim chance, then he'll know you're out of harms way and that will comfort him won't it?'

'Aye, I suppose so,' Val says sadly, 'at least if he's not worrying about us he can concentrate on punching that fat bastards lights out.'

'That's the spirit ladies,' I cut in quickly before the gloom descends again, 'now where shall we go tonight, I'm taking you out for a meal?'

I'll give 'em a treat and show 'em a proper city; somewhere you're allowed to wear a coat.

Terry

As soon as Spanish told me about Merry's plan I made sure it got back to Ron, always best to be on the safe side. Absolutely fucking gutted about the gym, old Dave as well. No doubting this was Merry's handiwork either, that mug has definitely got it coming. We're at the gym now and it's a fucking mess, the fire brigade put it out as best they could but there was petrol everywhere apparently and it burnt quick.

There's a couple of young lads here as well, the two teenage boys from the other day and we're all trying to salvage some bits for Carlos. All his trophies are gone, melted. The pictures of him with some of the best fighters in Britain all burnt; Chris Eubank, face twisted in a half sneer, Nigel Benn, only his chin left, Frank Bruno, big smile, nuffink else. All very depressing. Then, like a miracle, a picture untouched buried underneath some debris. Carlos with Ali in the States when he was training for a fight over there; Ali, looking old and frail even then, but still with that twinkle in his eye, Carlos, apparently for once in his life, keeping his mouth shut and being all quiet and respectful. I give the picture to Spanish, he looks at it and smiles, knowing Carlos would appreciate it, then he shows the two lads and they gather round it smiling as well, the all time greatest with a snotty nosed kid from Byker. That's more encouragement to the people round here than any fucking work initiative or new deal.

Old Dave didn't have no family either by all accounts so we'll be sorting out his funeral. I know Spanish ain't got much dough and Carlos ain't in a position to get to his money at the moment so I'm happy to spring for it, after all the bloke offered me a job two minutes after meeting me. He spent his life taking hooligans, no hopers and wild boys like Carlos and turning 'em into disciplined men, gave them self respect. He's done more good for society than a hundred plastic policemen ever could and he didn't fucking deserve this.

'I hope I get the chance to bump into the cunt that did this.' I say quietly, more to myself than anyone else. Spanish looks up at me and then at the two lads and replies, 'They saw the fucker running away Tel, it was Clarty Clark, Merry's cousin. He's been nicked for it as well.'

'Well I hope the mug ends up sharing a cell with Carlos then,' I say and the other three burst out laughing at the thought of it, I join in, it would be fucking carnage in there. Me and Spanish have to go to the undertakers now to sort out the arrangements for Dave, the police haven't released his body yet but it won't be long if they've nicked someone. Before we go I take one last look at the half intact building, the bottom floor which was a recording studio or something is untouched but the top is levelled and this gym which has been here for about half a century is gone. Just loose bricks and rubble mark the spot where Byker produced a great fighter. It's a sad, sad waste and it breaks my fucking heart.

Milo

Got a bit of a scare today when Duncan rang me I must say. I nearly broke my neck getting down the stairs to that interview room. I only vaguely recognised the ponce who was putting my name up. I have seen him before but I've never spoken to him, even so I was careful not to let anything show on my face, Duncan's dim but you can't be too careful. I'm relaxed now though, had a bath, had a Chinese delivered and opened a bottle of wine. All this shit will be history soon and I'll be cruising round the world as the royalty cheques pile up. Lovely.

There's a knock at the door. For God's sake who's calling at this time of night, if it's a local politician come to lie to me then I shall not be a happy bunny.

'Oh Duncan, what do you want?'

'Can I come in sir? It's about the Maxwell case, I've had some new evidence come to light.'

'Well yes if you must,' what's he got the two uniformed plebs with him for, 'what's with these two?' I ask.

'Oh just on our way to another house, we were passing so I thought I'd drop in and bring this to your attention.'

Ah, the perils of having an utter spanner as a sidekick on an investigation, I'm required to do all of the thinking all of the time. Still, he has at least served the purpose of making everything look above board without asking any awkward questions.

'What's this evidence then Duncan?' The cheeky bastard has got his phone out now and is ignoring me. 'I said, what's this new evidence then?'

'Shan't be a minute sir,' he says, pushing a couple of buttons. There's a muffled, tinny sound coming from somewhere and Duncan is looking at me strangely. I look at the two uniformed numpties and they just look as baffled as me. When I look back at Duncan he's staring at me with a big grin on his face.

'Shall we find out where that sound is coming from Mr. Milo?' He asks. I'm forced to correct him before we proceed, 'That's Chief Inspector Milo detective, and don't forget it.'

Then that strange smile again and he just says, 'For now.'

He's moving across the room to my welsh dresser and then starts pulling the drawers out until the sound gets louder, shit, it's the phone Merry gave me for safe keeping.

'Fools Gold, nice one,' he says looking at the phone and then at me, 'it suits you really.'

'Chief Inspector Milo, I am arresting you on suspicion of the murder of Judge Bernard Maxwell, you do not have to say anything when questioned but anything you do say may be later given in evidence. Do you have anything to say?'

The uniforms grab me firmly from behind and I am so shocked I cannot do anything but splutter out, 'It wasn't me, it was Merry.' I'm dragged out to the waiting van, treated like a common criminal, no respect or consideration for my position. It appears that my retirement is now closer than I thought.

Ron

I've brought the family to a lovely little Italian place that I eat at regularly, there's not much point in cooking for one really so I eat out a lot. I'm well known here though, actually I'm well known in most places in London, so we get the best table in the house. There's a couple of bottles of plonk on the table, the girls are loosening up a bit and the atmosphere's lifting, then the phone rings and they all freeze again, looking at me. The display reads 'Bates' so I take it outside, excusing myself I say to them, 'It's alright, it's nuffink to do with Billy,' and they relax again.

'Mr. Bates, good evening. What's happening?'

'Evening Ron, it's all sorted, Carlos is being moved now and the story is going round that I've done him in and am being put in solitary.'

'Excellent, where's he being put?'

'They're taking him to a police station in Newcastle and holding him there out of the way, let the rumour mill work overtime.'

'Good work Batesy, money to the usual place is it?'

'You know the guvnor Ron, he don't like to be seen in contact with you but he'll take your dough.'

'You're ain't wrong there mate, that's another one I've bought a gaff for over the years. Anyway, well done mate I'll speak to you soon.'

Then I'm back in the restaurant smiling and enjoying myself. Things are starting to come together.

Merry

I'm staying round at Joanne's tonight, officially it's so I can spend some time with her and the boy but really it's just in case Billy or Tony try anything. They're doing my head in already though so I've escaped to the bathroom and am having a few crafty lines. I've locked my house up and left a couple of lights on then fucked off. I wouldn't expect Billy to do owt sneaky but I would Tony, he's a dirty snidey bastard and I can't wait to plug him, I've got more respect for Billy than him. I've known Billy most of my life and I still won't really give a fuck when I do him, Fat Kev's been nagging me to let him do it and I might but I've never killed anyone before and I'm definitely doing one of them.

Ooouegh ya cunt, that's cut with fucking bleach or something. Once Tony's gone I'll have to muscle in on his supplier, his toot's far better than mine. Sniiifffff, that's better. Yeah I've known the fat boy most of my life as well, he's always hung round with me and backed me up when I needed it, not that I've ever needed it much, I've only ever lost two fights and they were both with Billy Reeves. The first one was when him and his brother jumped me years ago, the two of them had been to the baths or something and just attacked me as I came round the corner, for no reason at all. Then the second time was a couple of weeks later, Billy had just started at Benfield and I'd put it round I was going to do him when his brother wasn't around, the cheeky fucker walked straight up to me in front of all my mates and stabbed me in the leg. I admit I'd bullied them a bit when they were young but nothing too bad. I was foaming about him making me look a twat in front of the lads and I was going to cut him up bad after that. Fat Kev was urging me on as well but his brother's dad got hold of me after school that day and told me if I ever bothered them again he'd kill me. Spanish was a handy fucker in them days so I let it go. Maybe I should kill him as well? Yeah, I only ever lost two fights, if you could even call the second one a fight and Billy Reeves has been involved both times, looks like it'll be third time lucky for me then.

Had the call from Durham as well, the Carlos thing is done and Psycho's in solitary for it. His timing's out like, I wanted it doing tomorrow night when Billy gets it, but it's probably more difficult in prison. At least he died thinking his brother was getting it anyway. I'll keep it to myself for now though, while Billy thinks it's a normal straightener then he'll keep to the rules, once he knows Carlos is dead then all bets are off.

Looking forward to telling him just before I make him beg for his life though.

Snniiiif.

Milo

I'm in deep shit now I know I am. Dipshit Duncan the dense DI has just revealed his true identity; he's actually part of Internal Investigations. The fact that they've even noticed me means I'm fucked, never mind actually catching me for something. My only option is to spill my guts about everything and hope for leniency, they might want to avoid the bad publicity and just retire me early.

'So Mr. Milo, why don't you start with the murder of Judge Maxwell and your part in it and then later on we'll go over your criminal association with one Vincent Merry, going back all the way to the late eighties I believe.'

They've got me fucked here, oh well, nothing for it but the truth.

'I received a call from Vince Merry on the night of the murder asking me to come to Maxwell's house...'

'For the benefit of the tape could you please state the address Mr. Milo.'

He is loving this the sadistic bastard, emphasising the mister part as well and pointing out that I'm immediately and forthwith, before any trial or anything, not a copper any more.

'Sixty-three Osbourne Road, Jesmond.'

'Thank you, please proceed.'

'As I was saying, I received a call from Mr. Merry asking me to come over to Maxwell's house urgently as there was a problem, he wouldn't say what. When I got there the judge was obviously dead, lying bludgeoned to death in a pool of blood. There was no obvious murder weapon at the scene.'

He's looking smug the wanker.

'Go on.'

'I questioned Merry as I immediately suspected him of committing the crime, he was wearing gloves and had a motive as he had just found out his cousin was having a gay affair with Maxwell.'

'And you were satisfied with Mr. Merry's answers were you?'

'At the time I was but with the benefit of hindsight I now realise that he was in fact using me to get back at Carlos Reeves and gain revenge over him for a grudge they have.'

'And how did he do that?'

'He had acquired Billy Reeves' mobile phone and used it to send a text message to Carlos Reeves requesting him to attend the house soon as possible, he deliberately left it vague so Carlos would assume the worst. The plan was for Merry to then go to a bar in the city centre and be as vocal and visual as possible to provide an alibi, should he need one, and he would then ring in an anonymous tip about a violent incident at the house which I would happen to be passing just as Carlos entered.'

'And the baseball bat Mr. Reeves was carrying?'

'Pure good fortune on our part.'

'Is there anything else you'd like to add to this statement Mr. Milo?'

'Only that I have served this community for over thirty years now and have always done my best. I wish this to be taken into consideration as well as the fact that we all know what will happen to me in prison. I am quite willing to take early retirement without a pension if necessary to avoid that.'

He just looks at me blankly, giving nothing away.

'I'm sure you would Mr. Milo, I'm sure you would.'

With that he's gone and I'm taken back to my cell. A long sleepless night beckons.

Carlos

I don't know what the fuck's going on here, I'm ready for the night when my cell door opens and a couple of screws tiptoe in. 'Get your gear Reeves and make it quiet and quick.'

Now I'm not happy about this at all, not after the conversation I had earlier with that Batesy fucker. He comes up to me on the landing and whispers, 'I'm gonner push you into your cell shouting and screaming, let me do it then smack me in the mouth, I'll fly back out and it'll look like we've got a grudge. You'll find out why later.'

I didn't even have time to think about it when the cunt started screaming at me, 'I'M GOING TO FUCKING KILL YOU, YOU DAGO CANT. YOU THINK YOU'RE SOMEBODY. I'M THE FACKINGMANINTHISNICKYOUCANT.'

Then he steams into me and shoves me back into the cell so I just fucking hooked him in the jaw and burst his lip. Two screws came running over and dragged him away and he was still kicking and screaming he was going to fucking kill me. Everyone in the block was looking at me and whispering and a couple headed straight for the phones. I pulled little Davy and asked him what the score was and he just looked really, really pissed off.

'It's all round the prison Carlos, I've been trying to find you to tell you. That nutter Bates has been contracted to do you in by Merry.'

Fucking great that was, I was on edge all fucking day and I didn't have any credit left on my phonecard to ring anyone. Now these two screws are bundling me off somewhere else and spraying some fake red shit all over the cell. What the fuck is happening here?

Duncan

I've had Carlos Reeves brought to the Market Street nick in the centre of town, he'll be released tomorrow morning and all charges dropped. I contacted the governor of Durham where he was on remand and he seemed to think Carlos was in danger of being 'hit' and had put in motion a plan to remove him from harms way. He'll be a free man tomorrow anyway and Mr. Merry will be locked up at Her Majesty's pleasure - for a long time.

Mr. Milo on the other hand is a different matter entirely. If I had my way he'd be locked up as well, it's scum like him that destroy the reputation and morale of the police force. I can take an ordinary criminal but one of your own, working against you from the inside, hanging's too good for him. Office politics being what it is though, the chances are he'll retire quietly to protect us from any unsavoury publicity; his book will have to go as well. Still it's not my decision to make, given his senior status this will probably come from the top.

Big Friday

<u>Billy</u>

Up early this morning, I couldn't sleep at all; far too much going round me head. I'm a bit out of shape and it's just a little bit too late to start training for a fight I'm having later on tonight so I decided to go for a long walk. Before I met Lisa and when I was on the dole I used to go on massive walks just to fill my day, it always helped me think as well, so I got me trainers on and headed out the door. I've walked about three miles already up the Fosseway from Walkergate to Byker and now I'm heading over Byker Bridge and it's still dark, I wasn't even thinking about where I was going, just turned corners absent-mindedly and found meself heading into town. I know things could go wrong tonight and I need to consider everything. I spent last night writing letters to Lisa, Peter, Kenny and me mam just in case. They need to know how much I love them and how much they changed my life for the better in their own different ways. It's sad that I can't say these things to the people who matter but that's just the way I am, maybe I'll try harder after this.

I wander past Ozzy's on the bridge, fuck me this place brings back memories. Carlos, Barry and me got our first tattoos here a few years back, Barry and Carlos were seventeen and I was eighteen, quite old for a first one round here really. We went on a Thursday night and thought we were the dog's bollocks, me and Carlos got these Union Jack bulldog things and Barry got this bulldogs head with a bow tie and a flatcap. We gave him that much stick about it that he got it covered over a few years later. I remember going home and keeping quiet about it, we were all brave in the shop though,

'Aye man, I'll just tell her, what can she do once it's on. I do what I want me.' All that type of thing. Then when we got home, fucking nowt. Ha ha.

We kept it a secret for about three days and in the end it was Barry that grassed us up. He rang for us on the Saturday morning to see if we were going to the match and had a bit of a chat with me mam, finishing the conversation with, 'What did you make of their tattoos then Val?'

She was like a fucking exocet missile up them stairs to get us both. Ha ha typical of him mind, we used to have a saying about him, me and wor kid, 'The less Barry knows, the less the bizzies know.'

I'm thinking about that and grinning to meself as I come past the Warner Brothers place, it was a picture house but it's shut now. Ironic really as this was the place that did for the old Apollo on Shields Road, the first of the big multi-screen jobs to hit the toon and now it's been superceded by The Gate. It's true what they say like about what goes around comes around.

Anyway they used to have a big board outside about twenty foot in the air that told you what was on and without fail every Friday and Saturday night we'd be pissed up or pilled up and climbing the thing to rearrange the letters. Every bus going into town from the east end of Newcastle has to go past it so everyone knew that C A R L O S   S U K S   C O K S and that B A R R Y   F U X   L A D Z. We got chased off the law every now and then but they never caught us. We had to stop it once they'd been round me mams to have a word with me though.

I woke up with a thumping head one Saturday morning to find two bizzies downstairs, me mam with a face like thunder and Carlos pissing himself laughing. It turns out I'd decided to tell the world how great I was the previous night and the whole of Newcastle knew that B I L L Y   R E E V E S   I S   N O 1.

Aye, well it was good while it lasted.

I'm into town now and walking past Market Street bizzie station, the main one in town, this street round the station gets properly mobbed up on a match day, bizzies and hoolies alike all watching and waiting. It makes me think of our Carl, I miss him badly and I worry about him as well, what if he's being bullied in the nick or even worse what if Merry's got a couple of boys in there. I could do with him tonight, I don't rate Merry as a fighter or as a man but I'd still like a bit more back up. Cars and buses have started going past me belching smoke into the air, quick check of the watch, it's only half seven and I've walked at least eight miles. Fuck it I'm going for breakfast, I've earned it and I'm going to read the paper and forget about everything for half an hour. After that I'm getting the bus home, locking the house up, switching me phone off and preparing properly for Merry the fat, drug addled, steroid head piece of shit. No distractions, no sentiment.

Carlos

Proper fucking result. All charges dropped, 'Sorry for the inconvenience Mr. Reeves.' They even gave me a breakfast and a lift home. I was back in the flat for half eight. Typical Newcastle morning like, cold, drizzly and windy, it was fucking great. A one minute conversation changed the course of me whole fucking life, from thirty years inside to going to the match on Saturday, just like that. I just stood on the steps of Market Street gulping in the air and laughing, people probably thought I was a fucking junkie or something but I didn't give a monkeys. Then the bizzies put me in the car and brought me home. I rang Sharon on the way but she was asleep so I left a message with her auntie to give us a buzz. I can't get Billy on the phone to tell him either, he's probably asleep as well the lazy fat get; I'll pop round later.

First things first, I'll see me mam and set her mind at rest then nip down to the gym and check Dave's okay, sort out the bills and that sort of thing. Give Barry a bell and then, assuming fat boy's out of bed, I'll visit my favourite sister-in-law and nephews, give them all the good news. Carlos Reeves is back.

Duncan

Hmm, Mr. Merry appears to have gone to ground. We ransacked his house last night and I've had men there all through the night in case he comes back but he's disappeared into thin air. I had the uniforms check a number of his known associates and it seems four of them were put in hospital the other night by an unknown gang of assailants whilst in the process of smashing someone's windows. Good, that'll teach the wankers. Two of them in particular sustained some savage injuries from a broken glass, the like of which I've only seen pictures of once before and that was a few years back, before my time really. His other close colleagues Messrs Milo and Clark are both behind bars and their houses have been checked, so where is he?

Fat Kev

Today's the day. I couldn't sleep last night for thinking about it. Vince told me I could definitely do one of them, probably Billy cos he's really fucked off with Tony and he'll want to do that cunt himself. I've had the gun under my pillow all night; I half hoped some tosser would break in so I could blow their fucking head off.

I've got to play it cool today though Vince says, do everything as normal; go to the gym, do me shopping, just be boring and don't attract attention. Most importantly though, say fuck all, he doesn't know who he can trust and who he can't. He can trust me, he knows that.

Ron

The gels are keyed up and tense this morning, it's obvious why. Billy rang earlier and spoke to 'em, and then he spoke to me. He's switching his phone off to psyche himself up, he's explained this to me before. He needs to hate, he needs to become furious and believe that the bloke he's about to fight is the most evil, horrible bastard in the world and he can't do that when he's talking to the people he loves. I understand it totally.

Anyway, this should cheer 'em all up, I got a call off Irvine earlier and all charges are dropped against Carlos. He's out. If nothing else I'll point out to Val and Lisa that Merry's got no chance against the two of 'em. I'll feel better as well, I don't like the thought of Billy relying on a bloke I don't know, this Tony character may be okay but he may not, you never know. I'd better go and tell 'em the good news about Carlos and find out their plans for today, I've got a bit of business on later so it may have to be takeaway for them tonight.

Carlos

No fucker about at me mams. It's all locked up and there's something not quite right about the front of the house either, I don't know if it's the bricks or the windows, they just look too clean, you kna what I mean? Billy's phone's still switched off and he's not answering the home one, it just goes to that annoying fucking American woman on the answering machine. For fucks sake.

'Puff, switch ya phone on man, that's the whole point of a fucking mobile.'

Shit, I shouldn't have swore on his home phone, he'll go mad if the lads hear it. Fuck it, it's done now, at least I'll get a reaction. Might as well go down the gym and see Dave.

Sharon

Carlos is out. I can't believe it. Oh god I've missed him so much. Me auntie has just told us he rang earlier when I was in bed. I wonder if Barry's told him yet? I wonder if he knows?

I should tell him face to face really but it has to come from me and if he doesn't know yet he will as soon as he bumps into Barry. I'll have to ring him and tell him now. I'm so nervous, excited but nervous. What if I've got him all wrong and he runs a mile when he hears about the baby? What if he only found it exciting when he knew it was dangerous? I'm too scared to ring him he might tell me to fuck off. Oh god I'm going to have to do it now.

'Carlos.'

'Alright babe, how are you?' He sounds cheerful he mustn't know yet.

'I'm fine, it's just so nice to hear your voice again, I've been so worried.' I'm starting to cry as I talk, I tried not to but I can't help it, I love him so much.

'Hey, hey, what's the matter pet? I'm out now it'll be all right. It's okay darling where are you?'

'I'm at me auntie's in Berwick. There's something I need to tell you.' I can hardly get the words out.

'What's that then darling, there's nowt you can't tell me.'

I can't hold it back any longer, 'I'm pregnant.'

There's a stunned silence at the end of the phone, it just hangs there for what seems like hours and then, 'FOR FUCKS SAKE, WHAT'S FUCKING GOING ON HERE?'

I just burst into floods of tears now, I'm uncontrollable. I was so sure of how he felt and I convinced myself he'd be over-joyed at having a child with me but I was wrong. I love him and he's rejecting me, I went through all of that stuff with Vince and now Carlos is turning me away. I ached for him when he was in prison, I was physically in pain because I couldn't be with him and now he's cold on me and our baby. I can't speak and then through my tears I hear a voice saying 'Sharon, Sharon are you still there?'

'Yes,' I whine at him, then sobbing, 'you d-d-don't love me any more d-d-do y-you?'

He's talking slowly like you would to a child, 'of course I do you dafty, I love you and I'm made up that we're having a sprog. I'll definitely prove it when I see you but it might be a couple of days though, I think I've got some stuff to sort out.'

I instantly feel much, much better. 'What stuff Carlos?'

'Well I've just walked round the corner and seen what's left of my fucking gym.'

Terry

The law have just released Dave's body and the slag that did it has put his hands up so there's no need for them to hold onto it any more, he's been delivered here to Spanish's house and is in the front room. I look over at Spanish and he's fucking gut-ted, I am an' all, the poor old geezer did not deserve to go like that, no one does. There's a knock at the door and we look at each other, Spanish has picked his bat up.

'No need for that mate,' I say. We're all getting a little bit tense as tonight's the night apparently but even as I say it I'm bunching my fist as I get near the door. Bracing myself I swing it open, there's a big lad with a tan in front of me, can only be one man surely.

'Spanish, it's Carlos.'

I turn back to say hello and let him in but he's already pushing past and into the living room, he looks fucking furious but at the sight of Dave in the coffin his face changes and he leans back against the wall tears streaming down his face. Spanish, his dad, puts his arms around him and for the first time since I met the Reeves family I feel unwelcome, like an intruder into a private party.

Then the moment passes and Carlos is looking at me asking, 'Who are you then?'

I smile at him and extend my hand nervously, 'Terry Briggs, an old friend of your dad's.'

I needn't have worried; he grabs my hand enthusiastically and shakes it to within an inch of its life, 'I've heard a lot about you Tel,' he says, 'and I'm looking forward to having a pint with you and getting to know you properly mate, but first things first. Where is everybody and what the fuck is going on?'

I look at Spanish, raising my eyebrows, and he says simply, 'Take a seat son this could take a while.'

Billy

I've got the bag out in the garage and I'm practicing some moves, it's been a while since I had a proper fight and it can't do any harm to shake off the ring rust a bit. I've got my MP3 player on, music turned up loud and I'm slamming the fucking bag. The adrenalin's flowing and I'm picturing Merry's head on there. All I can hear is the music, my vision has narrowed and all I can see is his face on that bag.

He put my brother in prison, exposed him to fuck knows what. SMACK.

He's had me mam's windows put in and frightened the fuck out of her, she's a pensioner you sick cunt. SMACK.

He burnt Carlos's gym down. SMACK.

Killed owld Dave. SMACK.

What'll he do to my kids if I let him win? SMACK SMACK SMACK SMACK.

The bag's on the floor and I'm stamping the fucking life out of it, stabbing it with a screwdriver I've picked up, there's packing and filling all over the floor.

I'm ready.

Carlos

I've got Barry and we're heading up to Billy's at high speed, no fucking way is he taking on Merry on his own. Tried his mobile again but it's still off, where the fuck is he? Barry doesn't know when or where just that it's tonight and that Big Tony is involved, he knows something about a village up the road where Merry's got a grave dug for wor kid. That's not fucking happening, no fucking way, I will tear that man's head off with my bare hands if Billy even gets scratched, I swear to God. It's lucky Barry's driving as the tears fill my eyes 'til I can't see, yesterday the thought of doing thirty years was killing me but now I'll happily do it if it means I've killed Merry to save Billy.

Barry's noticed I'm crying and he's trying to gee me up, punching my arm, 'Howay man Carlos,' he says, 'Billy's told you before big lads divvent cry. We'll find him shortly and we'll deal with this prick together.'

I have to smile, he's right. Billy never cries, hasn't since we were about ten years old, not at me gran's funeral, nothing. Just says he can't. He's always taking the piss out of me for it, says I've got the Latin temperament.

We've screeched up to his and it's the same as everywhere else, all locked up and no one about. I'm banging on the door but there's no answer, no telly, no music, nowt. He loves his music, if he was in there'd be some playing somewhere.

'FUCK. Where is he?'

Barry looks up at me and says, 'I know where Tony lives,' so we're off again.

Merry

I promised I'd take young Dennis back to the gym with me today but I haven't got the time really. I've organised the van and parked it up in position, it'll be there all day so no one will suddenly see a white transit pull up just before we kick off, don't want to spook Billy now do I? Fat Kev's primed and ready, it's fucking hard keeping him on the leash, desperate for it he is; he's got a proper grudge against Billy going back years. I need to pick Tony up soon as well, make sure he hasn't got time to have any last minute chats with anyone. I need to keep pretending that we're onside me and him. People think you just have to be a hard case to be a gangster; they don't understand the brains that go into it. I'll need to let Dennis down gently an' all.

'Den we can go to the gym tomorrow mate, I'm a bit busy today, got to take care of some snakes who've been stitching me up.'

'Can I watch dad?' He's bouncing on the settee, excited about that. He's been telling all his crew at school that he's Vince Merry's boy and I take him training. Teenagers love shit like that.

'Not this time son but when you've been training with me for a while and we've built you up I'll be bringing you into the firm properly, nee probs like.'

Oh he likes that, proper beaming smile on him now. Right then that's him sorted, I'll go and get Tony.

Big Tony

It's getting dark now, nearly time. Merry's picked me up and we're heading back to his lass's house for one last run through of the plan. His plan that is. There's a bit of drizzle in the air, it's been on and off all day. I look at him driving this fuck off big motor, much bigger than he needs, and wonder how he ever got past me up the ladder anyway. I've been knocking people out in this town for twenty years now and this cunt just appeared from nowhere. By the time I'd realised he was a threat I was working for the red faced prick. Look up at the sky again, yeah it's raining properly now, not pissing down just raining, nice cold wind as well. A bad night to lose your job Merry.

Carlos

Tony's not fucking here either, his lass just said that Merry picked him up five minutes ago. Fucking hell, they're in it together and Billy thinks Tony's with him, we've got to find him. I'm getting frantic now and Barry's looking rattled as well.

'Fuck this Barry I'm ringing me old man. We'll work in pairs and comb the streets looking for him and if we haven't found him in an hour then we're all heading off to the village to look for the graveyard. Right?'

'Spot on Carlos,' he agrees.

Right then no time to waste, get the owld fella rung and get started.

Fat Kev

I'm in position head down in the back of the van. I've texted Vince so he knows. Checked the gun four times in the last ten minutes, fully loaded and ready to go. I hold it up aiming at an imaginary target on the back door of the van, it's taken twenty years Billy but I'm finally getting you back, beg Billy Beg, I might spare you. BOOM.

Ha ha

Merry

Kev's in position and we're nearly there now. Tony didn't flicker when I pulled my big knife out and waved it around in the kitchen. He's a cool fucker I'll give him that, either that or he really doesn't care if Billy gets it or not. Doesn't matter now, they're both dying anyway. The knife's just for the straightener, we're still having that, Billy can die knowing I'm harder than him as well; I don't do all this training for nothing. Fat boy's got the real weapon though.

This is it we're here. We park round the corner out of the way and trot quickly into the alley under the bridge, it's nice and dark in here, only one way in and one way out. Nice.

We settle ourselves back in the darkness and wait. There's a streetlight at the open end of the alley, it's sickly yellow light hurts my eyes and I have to look away. There's some toot left in my pocket so I heap it up onto the back of my hand.

Snniiiiffff.

It takes a second but I can feel it coursing through my veins, filling me with power, I'm ready for anything and anybody. Mostly though, I'm ready, waiting and looking forward to Billy Reeves turning up and signing his own death warrant.

Fat Kev

I saw Billy park his motor up and wander into the alley; he stopped for a minute then just disappeared into the dark. Vince said give it ten minutes then come to the front and listen. He wants to give Billy a hiding first, show him who's boss like, then let him know he's gonna die as well. I was going to wear a bally but there's no point as there's going to be no witnesses, I'm wearing the black leather gloves though, do this properly like a gangster would. Check the watch. Seven minutes to go.

Carlos

Cannot find him anywhere and time's getting on, I quickly bell me dad, nowt either. Fuck, fuck, fuck, fuck. Where are they? Has it happened yet? What if he's lying in a ditch somewhere and he needs me? If Billy's dead I will hunt that bastard down for the rest of my life I swear. Right, fuck it we're going to the cemetery and waiting for Merry to show. Buzz the owld fella back and tell him. Hold on Bill, just hold on.

Big Tony

Billy's squaring up to us both now, time to make my move, it's now or never. I walk towards Billy saying, 'Right you two cunts

243

get on with it, I don't work for you any more Vince.'

As I get to Billy he steps aside and lets me pass and I continue to the mouth of the alley. Vince hasn't said anything so I turn back to look at him expecting him to be in shock but he's laughing at me.

'Do you really think I didn't have a clue what you were up to Tony?' He says, 'I'm Vince Merry and I run this fucking town, once I've sorted out Mr. Reeves here you can be next.'

'Well I'm not going anywhere Vince, I'll be right here. I can't see you getting past Billy but if you do it'll be my pleasure to rip your fucking head off you junkie prick.'

He just laughs again and says, 'Let the big boys get on with it now Tony, I'll see you in a minute.'

Cocky cunt, I half hope he beats Billy so I can smash him to bits.

Billy

There's only two rules in fighting, I've used them pretty much all my life and they've always served me well, be first and be hard. I don't see any reason to change my style now so while Merry's attention is diverted I whack him twice in the face with my dustered right fist. I'm on his left side away from the knife and he can't swivel to stick me with it. He's backing off trying to get messages to his legs from his brain to stay up but they're telling him to fuck off and he's slumping back against the wall at the end of the alley.

Actually there's a third rule, once you're winning destroy the fucker, make it so he never wants to fight you again. I'm on the bastard as he crumples down the wall and I'm panelling his face with both fists and booting his ribs like you would a dog that had bit your kids. He's in pain and I've won, I never thought it would be this easy though, a couple more clouts and he's history. I should have done this fucking years ago.

I'm just about to move in for the last time when a BOOM echoes round the alley and a scream swiftly follows it, I look round and Fat Kev's standing over Tony who's down on one knee, Kev's got a manic look on his face and a smoking gun in

his hand. He's looking my way and slowly raising the gun.
Shit.

<u>Merry</u>

That fat bastard took his time; I was in trouble there. I never had Billy down as a sneaky bastard, I always thought he was an honourable man. I'm disappointed in him actually. Kev's pointing the gun at Billy's head when I shout at him to stop.

'Why Vince?' He whines, he sounds like a little kid who's been told he can't have any sweets.

'Because,' I snarl, getting to my feet a bit shaky like, 'Billy has just caused me some pain and there's no way he's having a quick death now.' As I'm talking I notice Billy's still transfixed by the gun and he's ignoring me, so I stab the cunt twice in the side. 'Not so fucking hard now are you Billy boy?'

He's on the floor now, blood pissing out of him and he looks broken, there's no fire in the eyes any more, he knows he can't win and he's given up. It's like on the nature programmes when a lion's eating a fucking zebra or something and the bastard just can't do anything about it so he doesn't even try. Maybe it's time to pile on the agony, maybe I should give him the message about his beloved brother. I've thought of something else as well just so he dies in fear for the rest of his family.

'Never mind Billy, at least you'll die knowing your family's okay eh?' I whisper to him as I'm bent over the fucker, 'or will you?' I sneak a look at the front of the alley, Tony's trying to get up and Kev's pistol-whipping the Judas bastard, 'Keep an eye on him Kev,' I shout in encouragement, 'I'm just giving Billy here something to remember me by.'

Turning to look back at Billy he's moved a little bit and sat up saying, 'There's fuck all you can do they're all protected.'

I just laugh at him and say, 'Your brother's already dead you prick, he had an altercation in the prison showers with a psycho named Bates.'

He's looking at me in disbelief.

'Utter bollocks,' he says.

I just laugh at him again, 'It's all true William and do you know what? Eventually Ron Carter won't be able to protect your family anymore and when he can't I'll be waiting. I'm giving your little boys to Clarty, he'll enjoy that won't he?'

His eyes are blazing now, this is more like it, 'And your wife, well, since Carlos nicked my bird I'm gonna need a shag from somewhere and she looks well dirty, she'd probably enjoy it the slag.'

He's not angry looking anymore, sort of calm, it would be a scary look if I wasn't sitting astride him with a big blade in my hand. Time to make him angry again, 'And your mam Billy, what about your mam? She's going to go the same way as owld Dave I think, still at least she'll be warm eh, not many pensioners can say that round here can they? Ha ha ha.'

That's got the cunt, the anger blazes into the eyes again and the nostrils flare. He's trying to say something but can't so I bend in closer to him.

'AAAaaaaaaagggrrrhhh,' he's bit my fucking right ear off. I roll off in pain and jump to my feet but he's up and pounding into me, I can feel ribs cracking and I'm lashing out with the knife then BOOM. He's down on one leg, Kev's getting handy with that fucking gun. I take the knife and stick him again, in the other side this time, he's down on the floor groaning now. My ear, or what's left of it, really fucking hurts and I'm going to do him now, I'm going to stab him to death slowly but Kev stops me.

'Not here Vince we need to get them up to the cemetery. No witnesses, no bodies, no life sentence.'

He's right so I console myself with booting his battered prostrate body into the wall.

'Put Tony into the van first.'

Carlos

We've met up with me dad and both cars are heading off north of the toon, we're going through Byker and heading to the central motorway in town when I notice Merry's motor outside Kwiksave.

'Stop the fucking car Barry.'

He hoys the anchors on and Terry does likewise behind us and we're out and round Merry's motor, locked up and no sign of anyone about.

'He must be round here somewhere, spread out.'

We're looking fucking everywhere, in every side street and alley, when I see Emma, the old barmaid from The Blue Bell walking up the road. She races over asking, 'Are you looking for your Billy?'

'Aye,' I say, 'have you seen him?'

'He went into that alley at the bottom of the road a while back and another bloke got out of a white transit van and followed him in. The van's gone now though.'

I'm racing back to the car by now, shouting for the rest of them. 'Cheers Mrs Redgrave, don't tell the bizzies you saw me will you?'

And we're off. I'm coming wor kid. I'm coming.

Billy

Bouncing around in the back of this transit van, blindfolded and overpowered by the smell of petrol and oil, all I feel is pain from the stab wounds and all I can taste is my own blood dripping down the back of my throat from my broken nose. I can't see anything but I can feel Tony next to me and he's crying that he doesn't want to die. I've got no idea where we are, I only know that when the van stops it will be the final destination.

The fight in the alley, vicious, brutal and painful for all concerned ended in a way I didn't imagine when I was planning for it hours earlier. Lying beaten, broken and bleeding on the floor I listened as Merry outlined his plans for my family and told me Carlos was already dead. I hadn't planned to flare up, I didn't want to give him an excuse to slot me there and then but I couldn't hold back. The rage I have struggled to contain all my life engulfed me, I could see only the man who claimed to have killed my little brother and I acted.

I could have easily killed him with my bare hands, I felt no pain from his blows and I couldn't feel him stabbing me, the adrenalin took care of that, it was only the bullet in the leg that slowed me down and finished me. I've never been shot before and it's not like you imagine. On the telly a bullet is like a sharp needle, instantly piercing the skin and bone that stands in its way but in real life, in a cold, dark alley on a Friday night in Newcastle, it's like a mini hammer tearing and smashing its way in, and it hurts. It fucking hurts a lot. I wouldn't cry though or beg, I bow down to no man least of all this prick.

Tony has been relatively silent for a while now just whimpering now and then, but in the alley, when Fat Kev shot his other leg 'just for a laugh,' when he'd put him in the van the screaming seemed to fill my head and even now it rattles round my skull; that great big man crying like a baby on the floor next to me. Merry then turned to me and I thought, for a second, my time had come. I thanked the lord for sparing Lisa and the lads and I braced for death but he just sneered at me as he said, 'You should have learned long ago not to fuck with me Billy Reeves. Now it's too late.'

The final irony was when they started the engine and the radio kicked in, he had on that same crap station that has dogged me for weeks and it was playing that song about not fearing the reaper.

You've got to admire God's sense of humour.

Then it feels like the van has suddenly speeded up and we're thrown around in the back, Tony screaming every time his legs make contact with anything. I wonder what's happening?

Carlos

We're doing a ton ten up to this Cragstone place on the A1 when I spot it, a white transit turning off onto a country lane. I've got Barry straight after it and Terry and Span follow behind us, no way can that fucker outrun us; he speeds up anyway though and tries.

'Ram the cunt off the road Baz,' I shout and he pulls alongside. There's a passenger and a driver that I can't make out and they look scared, Barry's inching the motor over to their lane and they slew off into a field coming to a halt about ten feet away.

I'm out of the car before it stops, beating Spanish and Terry by about half a foot. They're dragging the driver and his mate out who are shouting, 'What's the matter, what's the matter?' I ignore all this and burst the back doors open shouting 'Billy.'

Fuck all just some spirit levels, bricks and mortar. The two brickies are shitting it and I don't blame them, one sign of Billy in that van and they died. No questions. I give them a hundred quid and shout sorry as we race back to the cars. That cost us ten minutes. Fuck.

Billy

We slowly and quietly come to a stop and I'm dragged out of the van headfirst. There are no sounds; no traffic, no hum of conversation and the air smells and tastes fresher, the ground feels softer, this must be the country. I'm thrown to the ground, body screaming silently in pain; death would be a relief but I won't wince and I will not give him the satisfaction of begging.

I'm made to kneel and the blindfold is whipped off; I'm looking straight into my own grave as I hear the click of a hammer cocking behind me.

Merry's speaking now as Tony is thrown next to me, 'I had a word with the gravediggers Tony, had an extra deep one made, two for the price of one. Ha ha.'

Then Fat Kev's voice, 'Is it time?'

And I know it is, I know what's coming next and I brace myself for the shot.

BOOM

Carlos

We're fucking around on the outskirts of the village by the church when we hear the shots. It's a hundred foot away over a fence. We're sprinting over there with bits of wood but it's too late, there's two dark shapes pushing two other dark figures into the ground. It's too late and my heart is being ripped out even as I run. Fifty feet away and we're too late. I'm crying again as I run towards them, ripped off piece of fence in my hand, if it's the last thing I do I will avenge my brother. My eyes are narrowing as the shape sees me approaching at speed, the others well behind me. I am filled with hate and I will kill this cunt where he stands, I will kill him and his family and his friends and their families.

And then.

I hear Ron say, 'It's alright lads, it's alright,' and I see them both. And then I've got Billy, he's on his knees and he's crying like a baby, blood seeping out of him. He's saying to me, 'He said you were dead,' but I've got him and he's all right. It's all right, Merry's dead and Billy's safe.

Billy

I'm feeling the pain now and I'm dizzy with the loss of blood but I have to make sure Carlos is all right. I didn't believe that he was dead and Ron told me he'd sorted it but I had to be sure. Now he's here and we know that we're both still alive I can go to hospital. I don't have to be in charge anymore. Ron's organising everyone, I can just tell my brother I love him for the first time in my life and slip into unconsciousness.

Then Carlos is in my face telling me I can't go to sleep, to just stay awake and I'm back in the van again and he's with me. Ron's in the back telling us the score, Merry shot us and drove off, the bizzies are after him and he's fucked off. He keeps repeating it and then we're back in Byker.

Carlos and Ron are putting Tony and me on the path near

Kwiksave and saying the ambulance'll be here in a minute. Ron's taking the van and Carlos is staying with us and ringing the bizzies and I'm drifting off.

I can see me and him as kids having to fight that big prick the first time; we beat him then as well.

Then I see my kids; they'll never have to deal with this shit because I'm always going to do it for them, always.

Then I can see Lisa and she's crying but it's okay babe cos I'm all right. I can't hear anything any more though which is a bit worrying and then I see my grandma and granddad and I'm shitting my pants.

There's blue lights everywhere and people in my face but I can't hear them, it's like I'm tripping.

Then.

Nothing.

Epilogue

One Month Later

Val

I've always loved it down here on the coast, it used to be really nice when I brought the boys here when they were young and now I'm going to live right on the sea front and see out my days here. I'm looking out of my big old window onto King Edwards Bay, to my left is Cullercoats and Whitley Bay, to my right the lovely, old, ruined castle on the cliff and directly in front is the North Sea crashing on to Tynemouth's Longsands beach. I'm thinking to myself how lucky I am that it all turned out okay in the end, how that in death, Maxwell looked after both his son and me in a way he never bothered to in life. Michael and his cockney mate Terry are decorating for me and I'm in the house I always dreamed of, I've got a lovely back garden as well as spare rooms for guests and my soon to be growing number of grandchildren. I'm definitely having our Marj over to stay at weekends as well; the local men won't know what's hit them.

Billy will be out of hospital soon and he'll be okay. He's a tough lad, had to be, but I think this has actually, in a strange sort of way, maybe done him some good, he can open up a bit more now and express himself. He's been telling us all he loves us in that hospital bed, the last time he said that was when he came home blotto after Newcastle won the first division about fifteen years ago, thinking about it though he was pissed for a week and told everyone he loved them then.

I can see people walking dogs along the beach, joggers and families just out for a brisk stroll. I think how lucky I am and now that it's all over and my boys are okay, yes I think it was all worth it.

Carlos

So then this is it, it's official, time to move into adulthood. No more fucking everything that moves, strictly a one-woman man now. The doctor's just given Sharon the scan and she's gushing ower it, lasses eh what are they like? Then she hands it to me and starts pointing out all of his little features, he is a he by the way and I start filling up meself and the two of us are crying together. The doctor's just laughing and then I'm laughing as well. I notice something on the scan that concerns me and I have to ask the doctor, 'Is that his nose doc?'

The doctor just laughs at me again, 'No Mr. Reeves, that's his right arm.'

'That's a relief,' I say looking at Sharon again, 'I thought you'd been shagging our Billy there,' and we're both laughing together as she clouts me.

I'm looking forward to being a grown up me.

Big Tony

Shocker's in to see me with a couple of my main lads. They're well surprised that I survived what happened but they all know who's in charge now and Shocker's spread the word around that anyone who has a problem working for me had better relinquish their door licence - no one has yet. The club and pub managers have all been informed that they are now contracting their door staff from Tony Costello Corporate Events Ltd. and that Merry Security doesn't exist anymore, again, no problems there. As long as the price doesn't go up they'll pay whoever's in charge, death's an occupational hazard in our line of work. The dealers, well they'll work for whoever's paying them so that's sorted. I just need to get me legs healed up and to start training again, once the money starts rolling in then someone'll want a slice and I'll need to be ready.

Speaking to Ron Carter earlier, might be a few opportunities for a link up down south. He's going to put me in touch with a lad who wants to establish a couple of northern supply routes for his gear, sounds like the type of thing I could well get involved in.

A couple of the boys were asking if Merry got it goodstyle, to be honest I don't know cos I was blindfolded and had me eyes shut anyway but they're not to know that. I don't even know who pulled the trigger; I just know that when I got the blindfold off and they carried me back to the van there was about six people milling about, it's a bit hazy really. Anyway, I just told them the cunt's dead and that's all they need to know, I haven't seen anyone yet who's too unhappy about that either. Officially he's on the run and wanted for murder but everyone in Newcastle thinks that either Billy Reeves or Big Tony done him in. The bizzies asked a few questions but their hearts weren't in it and they made it plain they didn't really care so we're in the clear.

So time to move on, there's business to be done.

Clarty

'It is the recommendation of this court that you serve no less than fifteen years of this sentence. Take him down.'

That's it, the bastard doesn't even flicker as he takes my life away. I'm screaming 'Nnnoooo' at him but no-one's listening.

As the filth are taking me down the stairs I'm crying then I see that Davy fucker that got five years for the warehouse job. He's laughing at me and shouting, 'Let out on appeal you horrible cunt. The judge was bent in more ways than one. Ha ha fuck you and your dead cousin.' Then he's off back to life on the outside as I'm thrown into a holding cell.

'Better get used to this son,' the copper says, 'you're going nowhere for a long time.'

Duncan

So that's it then, back down to the Met. Job done.

I've officially handed over my report to the boss and he's dealing with it as I suspected he would. Chief Inspector Milo is now the pensionless civilian Mr. Milo. He's under strict instructions to keep his mouth shut on pain of a long time inside and if he publishes his memoirs he'll be nicked quicker than a motorist eating an apple at traffic lights. As for Judge Maxwell, well Merry did him obviously and rumour has it that Billy Reeves topped him but I'm not that bothered, at the end of the day he's no loss to society. Better get a wriggle on if I'm going to make that train, civilisation here I come.

<u>Billy</u>

I've got loads of cards and flowers, didn't know I had so many friends. Got a good one from Peter and the Radgepacket lads, a photo of the bouncer from their '*Gigolo Doorman*' single and on the back they wrote 'Thanks for getting rid of Big Bad Norman - get well soon charva, Peter and the boys.'

I've had others from owld codgers from the bakery, landlords down Shields Road and Wallsend High Street and even one from the staff at The Cavern Café, their takings must be down.

When I came round from the operations the first people I saw were Lisa and the lads and I just hugged them all. I was crying and everything, they couldn't believe it. The lads have never seen me cry before but I couldn't stop myself and I didn't want to anyway, I think it brought us a bit closer together in a funny way. Lisa didn't even bollock me for getting shot.

I promised the boys no more work. We're selling the bakery and the booze runs have finished, for me anyway, we're going to do loads of stuff together now. Money's not an issue any more and there's no point in having a dad if he's never fucking there, that's what I think now anyway.

Here they are now actually, got Ron in tow as well. I'm getting out in a couple of days and then we're off to Florida for three weeks, family holiday like. I can walk okay and the stab wounds are all healed up now so we're laughing. I'll look like a fucking pincushion on the beach like but hey, better than being dead eh? It was funny when Carlos came to see me the first time. He was giving me shit about getting fitter and how I'd let myself go a bit when I stopped him and said, 'The doctors reckon it was only my spare tyre that saved my life. They said if I hadn't had that then the knife would have pierced my vital organs. So fuck off and get us a bacon sandwich.'

Then I looked at him all straight faced and said, 'You'd tell us if I ever got a big arse though wouldn't you?' And we started pissing ourselves laughing.

Looking forward to Florida like, them yanks eat fucking massive dinners don't they?

<u>Spanish</u>

Terry's well chuffed, our Carl's rebuilding the gym and wants him to run it and do a bit of coaching. He can't believe it; his ex-wife and son disowned him twenty years ago and have never been in touch since so he's got nothing to go back down there for. He's sorting his own place out round the corner from me and things are looking good. Val's happy as well, Billy got her this lovely big house right on the sea front, it's what she's always wanted. And me, well my two sons, and they are both my sons, came through these last few weeks with their health intact. They're closer than ever and I'm glad of that. They can always be relied on to do the right thing, both of them, and that makes me happy as well.

I look over and Val's just looking at her favourite picture of the boys, she took it the day Carl started big school and the two of them are out the front of the house in their new uniforms. She's asked Terry to hang it for her, right in the middle of all the other ones, pride of place on the living room wall like and he's asking her if she's got a hammer anywhere. She rummages around the packing cases full of gear that's not away yet and digs out this silver mallet thing that looks like it's been covered in red paint at some point. Looks like a judge's gavel actually...fucking hell, it is a judge's gavel...penny's just dropped!

As she gives him it and he starts to bash the hook into the wall I catch her eye and she smiles, knowing that I know.

'All turned out well in the end then,' she says.

Fuck it she's right.

It did.

Industrial Strength Fiction

Visit us today at
www.bykerbooks.co.uk

On the site you can browse our books, read exclusive interviews with authors, check out the latest news from Britain's radgest underground press and read quality, FREE, short fiction from some of the country's up and coming authors.

NEWS *Get the lowdown on all of our latest books and authors.*

COMPS *Chances to win exclusive signed copies of top tomes.*

STORIES *Read quality British fiction on the site...for nowt!*

BOOKS *Browse our ever expanding catalogue of publications and ask yourself just how you ever managed without us.*

Come and have a look if you think you're hard enough!

www.bykerbooks.co.uk

Byker Books

Danny King

More Burglar Diaries

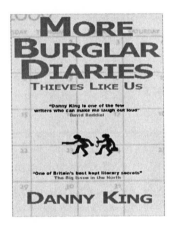

'One of Britain's best kept literary secrets'
The Big Issue in the North

Bex and Ollie are a couple of small-time burglars. They scratch a living robbing shops, burgling factories and emptying offices around the back-water town of Tatley.

Bex is the brains, Ollie drives the van.

Neither are particularly ambitious, preferring instead to think small and live comfortably, rather than aim high and risk time. The lads don't have it all their own way though; 'Weasel' of CID is only one faltering step behind them, the local criminal competition will do anything to stitch them up and the loves of their lives are wondering what the hell they've done to deserve them.

Things are about to finally catch up with Bex and Ollie.

www.bykerbooks.co.uk

Industrial Strength Fiction

Andy Rivers

I'm Rivelino - A Life of Two Halves

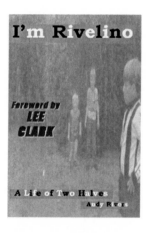

'funny, fanatical and thoroughly enjoyable'
Lovereading.co.uk

'When you consider them in a football sense you think of 'little Rotherham playing Newcastle? Oh the romance of the cup.' Well all I could see was fifteen stone, pie eating nutters covered in tattoos and no matter how much aftershave they'd slapped on there'd be no fucking romance going on there I can tell you...!'

Thanks to a family member taking him to his first match in the early seventies whilst he was at an impressionable age Andy Rivers discovered Newcastle United. Given the despair this has caused him over the last thirty years it's fair to assume that this action would be considered child abuse today. His story, peppered with terrace wit and rough charm, will be identified with by supporters everywhere.

www.bykerbooks.co.uk

Coming Soon...

Dumb Luck

Micky's having a shit day. On the one hand he's out of jail and on his way home but on the other his head still throbs from the whippin' he got on the inside. And something dark and nasty nags at him, something he wishes he could remember but at the same time feels sure he'd like to forget. And that's before someone goes and kills his Dad and pins it on him. Rams a bottle through his neck.

Nasty. Real nasty.

Still, Micky's no dumbarse. He's sure he can solve his Dad's murder before the week is out. He just needs a few beers to get his head straight. Lie low at his mates bedsit for a bit maybe...

Get ready for a race against time as Micky and his pigthick sidekick Rezza immerse themselves in the crap and dregs of London's bungling criminal underworld. Trying to prove his innocence and jolt his short-term memory before it's too late. Take a deep breath and prepare yourself for the thrill ride of a lifetime - just bring a sickbag, a bullet-proof vest and some codeine with you!

Just in case...

See next page for exclusive first look!

Dumb Luck

Chapter 1 - Mean Streets

Time's moved on and I'm on my way out. Three months of my life gone. But not forgotten. The shitstains of a thousand horrorshows are meshed and mashed and wiped all over my damaged psyche. On the outside I may be smiling but on the inside I'm crying. I keep this to myself. Stoic - that's me - stoic. Determined to survive and determined I'm gonna make something of my life. I'm gonna turn it all around and show those ignorant bastards what I'm made of.

Some part knows this is the kind of fighting talk you need to stand a chance back on the outside. I was only in for three months. But three months is more than enough for this kid. Still, the world's my lobster as my dear old Da' always says between pints of whisky. So long as I don't get in with a bad crowd again and stop spray-painting my cool-as graffiti all over our capital's train carriages I'll be alright. I guess.

I've got myself enrolled on a course - the government's gonna sponsor me - very nice of them. Smithy told me about this one. It seems too good to be true. But I checked it all out with the careers advisor and he pushed all the paperwork through for me. Nice one. Some sort of apprentice graphic artist at a big magazine publisher. They say I got talent. I also got a real big ability to screw things up royally. Honest, if something looks too good to be true - I usually cock it up. It's a gift. If there's a wrong place and a wrong time - I'll be there. Ever since I was a kid, the breaks never fell my way.

'Don't fuck this up now Michael - you've been given a chance - now take it,' the warden advised as he gave me my leaving pep talk.

'No sir, I won't - I won't fuck it up,' and even while I said it, all I could think was, 'Shit, I'm gonna fuck it up - I always do!' But I smiled at him and he seemed happy enough with my response. Another lost soul redeemed for the good of society.

So one door shuts behind me and the whole world opens up before me. My blank canvas is back. I'm itching to get down to something - not sure what though. Maybe go out and find me a girl. I had a few girlfriends before I went in, but not half as many as I made up. If I told you I shagged twelve girls then divide by two and subtract four - and then you're a bit closer to the truth. And with the women it's the exact reverse - whatever they tell you when they're acting all coy and innocent - well just times whatever figure they tell you by two and add four. No shit - it works - I reckon - though no-one's ever really gonna tell you, not really - everyone needs some private secret shit.

So I'm walking down the street now feeling a bit jittery about everything and overawed by the whole being outside thing when I decide to go home and get it over and done with. I notice there are more silver cars on the streets than when I went inside. Wonder why? I quite like it though - makes everything sparkle in the gay, bright, afternoon sun. I like thinking of the sun being so gay and bright - on the inside it was the kinda word to scare the shit out of you - 'you gay or what?' Bang! Black. All black. But out here I like to reclaim the word - cos I can. I stop all of a sudden in the middle of the pavement. My head throbs - throbs and threatens to burst with the pain. A wave of searing, stabbing intensity smashes through my brain and then it's gone. It's taken two months to get this far - so the pain only comes in small flashes every few days now - but the memories - some of them are still a bit hazy - 'specially my new ones. Maybe it's for the best - that's what the warden told me - advised me - if I wanted to get out...

* Released on 18/10/10 *

Available from selected book stores and all good online retailers.

Lightning Source UK Ltd.
Milton Keynes UK
UKOW03f1005280514

232443UK00001B/9/P